Bunty Avieson [illegible]
worked for twe[illegible]
papers and maga[illegible]
was editor of *Wo*[illegible] editorial director of *New Idea*, winning three Magazine Publishers Association awards. She is also a Williamson Fellow (1999).

In 2000 Bunty took up fiction writing full time. Her first novel *Apartment 255* was a bestseller in Australia and Germany. This is her second novel.

She divides her time between Sydney and India.

buntyavieson@bigpond.com

Also by Bunty Avieson

Apartment 255

The AFFAIR

BUNTY AVIESON

Pan Macmillan Australia

First published 2002 in Macmillan by Pan Macmillan Australia Pty Limited
This Pan edition published 2003 by Pan Macmillan Australia Pty Limited
St Martins Tower, 31 Market Street, Sydney

National Library of Australia
Cataloguing-in-Publication data:

Avieson, Bunty.

The affair.

ISBN 0 330 36410 3.

1. Marriage – Fiction. 2. Family – Fiction. I. Title.

A823.4

Typeset in 13/16 pt Bembo by Post Pre-press Group
Printed in Australia by McPherson's Printing Group

With much love to Mal Watson and
our beautiful daughter, Kathryn Rose

ACKNOWLEDGMENTS

Heartfelt thanks to my wonderful agent Selwa Anthony; my enthusiastic publisher Cate Paterson; three friends who were full of good advice, Anna Davison, Linda Smith and Mellisa Gillies; London journalists Diane Blackwell and Geoff Garvey; those fascinating men from Lloyd's of London, Nick Doak and Mark Whitfield, who were so generous with their time and knowledge; Amelia Chow, Melitis Kwong, Jin Yeo, Luc Dierckx and Wayne Tisdale for their hospitality and many kindnesses in Canada; Sydney yachties Louisa Geddes and Andrew Copley for their sailing expertise; Will and Fiona Ryan of Ryan Wines for their explanations of the wine industry (and many a fabulous chardonnay); my sister Christine Ronaldson for her medical advice; and to my Italian friend, Mauro de March, your name is an inspiration!

CHAPTER 1

7 February 2001

Nina was hit by a wall of heat as she emerged through the swinging glass doors into the bright sunshine. The doctor's rooms were five blocks away, at the medical end of the city, and she knew she would be wet with perspiration by the time she reached them. After eleven years in Australia she was still rendered limp by the relentless humidity of Sydney in summer. She found it difficult to breathe. The air tasted stale and sparse, as if there wasn't enough to go around. She missed the cool, parched dryness of rural Canada where every breath burst into her lungs, plentiful and fresh.

She checked her watch even though she knew the time. It was only a few minutes since last she had looked. Still, she was anxious. She didn't want James to be waiting alone at the doctor's.

Nina hurried, darting between the morning shoppers, and made good time, arriving a few minutes early at Kingston Medical Centre. James was already there, waiting for her in the foyer as arranged. He was a tall, well-built man, with strong, even features and closely cropped black hair, which was just beginning to grey above his ears. In his dark blue Zegna suit he looked like any of the other well-heeled professionals milling about. Only his manner set him apart. He was pacing the floor, running his hands through his hair and watching the revolving glass doors intently.

He greeted Nina with a relieved hug. They held each other closely for a moment, oblivious to the people around them. They had not spoken since that morning: they had left for work at 8 o'clock and dropped their son Luke at school on the way, as they did every weekday morning, before going on to their respective offices in the city. But this wasn't a normal day and each of them had spent the time apart in a kind of agitated anticipation, watching the clock tick away the minutes to this meeting. They took comfort from their embrace, feeling united in their private torment.

They separated and Nina took James's hand, squeezing it.

'Are you okay?' asked James.

Nina nodded.

'And you?'

James shrugged.

'Let's do it then,' he said, his voice grim.

Together they waited for the lift to descend,

watching the numbers light up as it counted down the floors.

Nina felt the anxiety like a leaden rock in the pit of her stomach. It was a mixture of dread and hope. She didn't want to take this lift up to the top floor and hear the doctor's pronouncement but she knew that until she did, their life would never return to normal. They had existed in a state of limbo since the moment a few weeks ago when James's mother had telephoned them and said the word 'haemochromatosis'. It was the first time Nina had ever heard of it. As if losing him wasn't enough, an autopsy on James's father showed that a massive toxic build-up of iron in his blood, causing his major organs to fail, had killed him. It was a genetic condition, hereditary. A rogue gene. Deadly if left untreated. It was what had robbed that huge bull of a man of, first, his energy, then, his dignity and, finally, his life.

It was one of the most common hereditary diseases and one of the least diagnosed, according to the book that Nina and James had read, standing side by side in the State Library, anxious not to leave Luke at home alone for too long.

Having just buried the family patriarch they now faced the news that this defect could just as easily be lurking inside James and Luke. There was no cure. The only antidote: regular and vigorous blood leeching. The very thought of it woke Nina in the night. It seemed like something out of a horror movie. But what scared her more than the treatment was the damage that might already have begun. Both James and Luke could be well on their way to chronic fatigue, arthritis, heart disease, cirrhosis, cancer, diabetes, thyroid disease, impotence, sterility. Excess iron could injure every part of the body, including the brain.

Luke's youth didn't protect him. Juvenile haemochromatosis was aggressive and potentially fatal.

It was unthinkable. James, a former Australian Olympic ski champion, was as strong and fit as he had ever been. And Luke? Nine-year-old Luke lived every day for football, and nights, too, sleeping in his favourite number seventeen jersey. He was so like his sport-loving father. He had inherited Nina's slight frame but it was James's fierce competitive nature and tireless energy that gave him the advantage on the football field. James felt it was a cruel irony that he may also have inherited this killer gene.

Nina felt a bottomless chasm threatening to open in front of her. She had spent the past week going though the usual motions of her life, talking to clients, cooking dinner, helping Luke with his homework. But all the time she was aware that at any moment the ground could open up before her and she would be lost, free-falling through the abyss. So she had lived in a state of constant vigilance, ready in case that chasm did suddenly snap open before her. Nina had had little experience with sickness. She was healthy and no-one close to her had ever died or suffered from anything serious. The idea that the two people she loved most in the world could die was a revelation as well as a shock.

The lift arrived and they shuffled into it with the pack. Kingston Medical Centre was a busy building. The lower floors contained various medical services, radiology, X-rays and the like. Ten years ago Nina and James had glimpsed their first view of Luke on the fifth floor, in the ultrasound department. He was just a swirling blob on a screen. The technician had happily explained which part of the blob was his head and which was his body. Nina had posted the photograph of that little blob to her parents in Canada. The first photo of their first grandchild. They had placed it proudly on their refrigerator, under the Opera House magnet Nina had sent them. Nina had tried to explain, over a scratchy telephone line to her mother, what the technician had told them.

Her mother had been in awe.

'You can tell from that picture that it's a boy?' she had asked, her voice a mixture of disbelief and wonder.

Nina watched a young couple get out at the fifth floor. They would have been in their twenties. They looked half terrified. Just like Nina and James, all those years ago.

Luke hadn't been planned. In fact he had been growing quietly inside her for three months before she became aware he was there. It had been a surprise to them both. The realisation that they would be responsible for a new little life had dawned slowly over the next six months.

When Luke was two they had decided to try for a little brother or sister, but it had never happened. They told themselves it didn't matter. Luke was their little miracle and together they were a family. They didn't need anybody else. The three of them were a complete and self-sufficient unit.

As the lift climbed past the fifth floor Nina wondered if James was remembering that time, but she didn't trust herself to speak. She was holding herself together with every ounce of willpower she could muster.

She dared not think about the possibility of life without James. Her whole world revolved around him. And she knew how worried James was about the thought of their beloved boy, good-natured, cheeky little Luke, carrying a time bomb in his genetic code. It threatened James's very core.

Nina had nearly walked away many years ago, before Luke had appeared in their lives, and when her loneliness in this foreign country had been so acute that she did not think she could bear another day. She had betrayed James then and on the few rare occasions that the memory rose unbidden in her mind, she felt great shame.

The lift emptied as it rose and stopped through the building until just Nina and James remained for the final few floors. The doors opened onto a wood-panelled reception area. Up here the rooms were rented by medical specialists, top surgeons and doctors, whose outrageous fees were reflected in the rarefied atmosphere – cool and quiet behind the double-glazed windows, a complete contrast to the hot, frantic city streets below. Blinds on the windows and occasional lamps kept the lighting dim and restrained.

James and Luke had been referred by their family doctor to the clinic on the seventh floor where, a few days ago, they had had their blood tests done, administered by a kindly nurse. To discuss their results they would see a specialist, a haematologist named Dr Jones.

Nina approached the receptionist, a respectable-looking middle-aged woman with neatly coiffured grey hair, sitting alone behind a large desk. There was no-one else around but Nina felt oddly conspicuous and ill at ease in the sombre surroundings.

'We are here to see Dr Jones,' she whispered.

'Please take a seat,' whispered back the receptionist.

Nina perched next to James on an uncomfortable upholstered bench. He passed her a magazine, *Town and Country*, British edition, and opened one himself, leafing through the pages without stopping, making a rhythmic flicking sound that played on Nina's already stretched nerves.

'Mr and Mrs Wilde?'

Nina jumped.

The receptionist had moved silently across the thick burgundy carpet to stand in front of them. She motioned them to a closed, heavy-looking multi-panelled door.

'Dr Jones will see you now,' she murmured. Her voice was so quiet and reverential that for a moment Nina wondered if she should curtsy.

Nina and James were ushered into a large, cool, light-filled room. The contrast from the shadowy reception area was so great they were momentarily blinded. The doctor's office faced east, giving him a breathtaking view across the domed roof of the Conservatorium of Music to the Botanical Gardens; then Sydney Harbour, busy with the morning's traffic; and to the Heads beyond. It was 10 am and just as they entered the room the clouds moved apart, revealing the full force of the morning sun, which flared through the floor-to-ceiling glass windows, dazzling Nina and James and creating a bright halo around the man behind the desk. From where the doctor sat he could swivel his high-backed olive-green leather chair around and gaze out the window, watching the boats on the harbour and the weather coming in from the east. Or he could turn his back on the view and face across the desk, to his patients, as he was doing now.

The warmth of the sun didn't penetrate the thick double-glazed windows, and Dr Jones's office seemed unnaturally cold. Nina, in her light summer shift, felt a chill. It was more like a gentleman's study than Nina had expected of a specialist's rooms. Instead of posters and medical paraphernalia, the walls were lined with opulent, jarrah wood panelling. A beautifully polished nineteenth-century silver microscope sat in a glass case in one corner. Another wall was lined with leather-bound books.

Nina felt out of her depth. James sensed her

unease and took charge. It was how he coped best, worrying about Nina so he didn't have to notice his own beating heart, pumping the adrenalin around his body. He was alert and wary, mentally reining in his energy, like a boxer, bouncing on his toes, ready for that first punch. The cost of his self-control was evident in a small tic beneath his left eye where a nerve had gone into spasm. It tensed and relaxed with each beat of his heart. He was completely oblivious to it.

James led Nina to one of the large leather Chesterfield armchairs facing the huge mahogany desk. Seated, she looked small and vulnerable, half-hidden from him by the wings of the chair.

Nina felt her eyes water from the sunshine as she looked at Dr Jones's silhouette behind his desk. She steeled herself for whatever he might say, trying to be ready in case, with a few words, he tore apart her world.

The doctor seemed such a long way away, across a wide expanse of wood and leather. He didn't appear to be a big man, dwarfed by his own desk and chair. He had a high forehead with receding hair but, against the harsh sunlight, Nina couldn't see his features clearly.

'I have the results of the tests performed on you, Mr Wilde, and the boy, Luke,' Dr Jones said.

He was so stiff and his speech so formal that it took Nina a moment to catch up. She had given no thought to what the doctor might be like. He had been a vague, white-coated figure that loomed somewhere in the enemy camp of the medical world. He had a soothing voice, a doctorly voice, meant to put a patient at ease. But the way he was expressing himself caught Nina off guard and she flinched involuntarily. Her hand moved suddenly to her face, as if to ward off a shock.

'Nina . . .?' asked James softly, bending his head towards her.

Dr Jones paused, studying what he could see of Nina's downturned face, trying to read what she was thinking. He willed her to look up but she stared fixedly at her lap.

The two men looked at Nina and the only sound in the room was the steady hum of the air-conditioning as the frigid air was pumped into the room from discreet vents in the ceiling. It was a low mechanical rumbling sound that helped muffle any vestige of noise from the world outside, enclosing the doctor and his patients inside his vast, private chamber.

Dr Jones had been watching Nina closely since she walked into his office and he noted the sharp reaction when he spoke. Every day he sat just where he was now, often delivering bad news to patients. He got better at it, more efficient some would say, but it never became routine. Nevertheless, any way you looked at it, this case was different. And the doctor, usually so in control, found himself unsure how to proceed.

The couple looked worried and anxious, which is what he would expect under the circumstances. Nina's hands had moved to chest level where they gripped each other tightly. The husband had a tic below his left eye. Dr Jones couldn't know if that was always there, or whether it was evidence of the stress he was under. But there was no mistaking the couple's shared anguish. It was obvious in the tiniest of gestures – James gently stroking the underside of Nina's arm, the tender skin near the elbow. His touch was instinctive and protective. It was so subtle, it would almost certainly have gone unnoticed by an observer, except that Dr Jones had been watching for it, or something like it. It told him exactly what he wanted to know. Often couples sat in front of him, side by side, yet a world apart. The sort of news he was often forced to deliver could break the strongest bond.

Dr Jones wondered, as he had wondered a lot in the past few days since the Wilde medical file had landed in his in-tray, just how strong was the bond between Nina and James.

Two folders lay on the desk before him: WILDE, James and WILDE, Luke. Dr Jones felt the cold hard plastic beneath his clasped hands. The blood tests had been done. And the genetic tests. Dr Jones knew, without any shadow of a doubt, that the two people were not related. Luke Wilde was not James Wilde's biological son.

CHAPTER 2

Ten years before, Friday, 18 January 1991

Nina huddled against the wall, trying to avoid the heavy drops of sudden summer rain that bounced off the awning and splashed onto the footpath, sending little wisps of steam into the air. Her light summer dress was already soaked. She wasn't cold, just uncomfortably sodden. She could picture her umbrella lying on the back seat of the car. Not much use to her now.

Rain dripped from the ends of her short dark hair onto her neck; water ran down her back in little rivulets.

It had been a hot and humid Friday afternoon when a sudden, unexpected storm had erupted across the city, bringing down the temperature and causing chaos. These were the worst possible conditions for finding a taxi. But Nina was the only person at this taxi rank so she hoped she wouldn't be there long.

She set the plastic shopping bags on the ground and settled in for an unpleasant wait. A low rumble of thunder rolled across the sky from the south, followed quickly by a flash of lightning. The full force of the storm wasn't far away and Nina hoped she would be home before it hit.

A man splashed across the road towards her. He looked slightly comical, his trouser legs tucked into his socks to avoid the puddles. He held a newspaper over his head as he sprinted through the traffic and leapt onto the footpath, taking shelter beside her against the wall.

'Are you waiting for a taxi?' he asked.

Nina nodded, sending fresh droplets of rain into her eyes. She wiped them away with a wet hand.

The man laughed. 'You look like you've been swimming,' he said.

'I feel like I have been,' replied Nina, smiling back.

The man tried to shake the water off his newspaper. It was a soggy mess. As he attempted to smooth the pages, shreds tore off making little balls of newsprint. He gave up and tossed it into the bin, laughing at himself as the paper balls stuck to his hands.

They continued their wait in silence, huddled together out of the rain, their shoulders almost touching. It was a forced intimacy that felt a little awkward. Instinctively they looked in opposite directions, angling their bodies as far away from each other as they could without losing the protection of the awning.

The stranger looked up the street at the retreating cars. He noted with idle interest the different makes and models. Nina looked at her feet, going through what she had in the shopping bags. A whole fresh Atlantic salmon. Mixed salad greens. New potatoes. A very expensive bottle of balsamic vinegar.

Friday night was her special night with James, her husband of just eight months. They rarely made plans to go out; they preferred to cook together at home, ignoring the rest of the world. It was their end-of-week ritual. Usually they finished off a bottle of wine while they cooked, then they opened another to drink during dinner.

James, who came from a family of vignerons in the Hunter Valley, would bring home the wine, usually something a little bit interesting for them to try, while Nina was in charge of the food. It had been another busy week for James with lots of new clients to see in the evenings and Nina had found herself alone each night in their apartment, not knowing what to do with herself.

She was looking forward to having him all to herself tonight. She missed him. Just how much she missed him was evident from the amount of money she had splashed out on the salmon – and the imported Italian vinegar. It was outrageously overpriced and Nina knew it. She brushed aside the twinge of guilt. They didn't have much time together so when they did, it ought to be special.

Cars crawled past, splashing muddy water onto the footpath. Nina spotted a taxi a short distance away, its roof light glowing, indicating that it was available. The man beside her saw it too. He moved imperceptibly back, indicating she would have no argument from him. Nina noticed the gesture and appreciated it. She was in no mood to fight for a taxi.

As she bent to pick up the shopping bags she had a flash of memory: the woman in the starched white cap handing her those bags and smiling at her from behind the cash register in David Jones Food Hall. Nina saw herself handing over a $50 note. She had received just a handful of coins back. That was all that was in her purse now.

She took out her purse and opened it, sorting through the coins, knowing exactly what was there, but hoping anyway.

'Damn,' she said softly. She turned to the stranger beside her. 'You take the taxi. It looks like I'll be getting the bus.'

The stranger's face showed surprise, then concern. 'The bus stop is five blocks away, all the way at the other end of the road,' he said. 'You'll get drenched.'

Nina shrugged and gathered her shopping bags, ready to brave the rain. If she didn't stop to think about how unpleasant the walk would be, if she just got on with it, she knew it would be easier.

'Which way are you going?' asked the stranger.

'Elizabeth Bay,' replied Nina. She thought she could make out a dozen or so people waiting under the bus shelter. She hoped they would make room for her and it wouldn't be too long before the number 311 rumbled along.

'I can drop you off at Elizabeth Bay. I'm going that way anyway. I'm going on to Rushcutters Bay,' the stranger offered.

It was tempting but Nina shook her head, sending more droplets down the back of her dress. 'I'm afraid I don't have enough money.'

Nina winced as she said it. She hated that phrase. It seemed that she had been hearing it – and using it – as long as she could remember. It had been a constant refrain growing up in rural Canada with lots of bills and a frugal father.

Something in her tone caught the stranger's attention. He had been about to graciously accept the offered taxi and be on his way, happy to be out of the rain and confident that he had tried to do the right thing by this half-drowned, vulnerable-looking woman. But the catch in her voice held him. He wasn't sure what it meant, what it revealed, but something inside him responded. Suddenly he was aware he wanted to make everything all right for her, to see that elfin smile again.

'I'm going that way anyway,' he insisted gently.

Nina looked into a pair of sympathetic blue eyes and a cheerful open face. It was disarming. The man looked to be in his late twenties, he was dressed casually in an open-neck white shirt and tailored trousers. Nina wasn't tall and nor was he. He looked pretty wholesome and safe but Nina was naturally cautious. She had been in Australia a little over seven months and was still unsure of herself in many situations. At home in Canada she would probably have bounded into the taxi, no questions asked. But this was Australia and she still didn't feel confident enough to presume anything.

'No, but thank you,' she said, trying not to sound rude. She didn't want to appear ungrateful when he was being so kind.

The taxi inched forward in the traffic and Nina separated her shopping bags into two bundles, taking one in each hand.

The stranger tried one more time. 'You have far too many bags to struggle down the street. I'm going past Elizabeth Bay anyway. It's no skin off my nose.'

Nina smiled at the expression. So he wouldn't lose any skin off his nose. James sometimes said things like that. It was one of those odd Aussie sayings, like getting 'rugged up' against the cold.

The man felt an unexpected ripple of delight to see the sudden smile. It completely transformed this woman's sad little face. He interpreted it as acquiescence. 'Good,' he said. 'We can split the fare at Elizabeth Bay if you like. Between two of us it won't be much.'

Nina thought she may have enough to scrape together half. She hoped so.

The taxi stopped beside them. The stranger took Nina's bags and moved past her to the curb, grimacing at the rain as it poured onto his hair and face. As he reached to open the back door he stumbled on a section of broken cement, splashing dirty puddle water up his trousers and onto Nina's dress. It had been intended as a gallant gesture and he felt immediately foolish.

'Sorry. I'm such a klutz,' he said.

He looked so genuinely embarrassed that Nina felt immediately at ease. Smooth, sophisticated people left her feeling intimidated. But clumsy she understood. It made up her mind for her.

'Don't worry,' she said. 'It can't possibly make any difference now. I'm already so wet.'

The man smiled. 'Don't let on to the driver that we don't know each other or it will cost us more,' he said softly as Nina climbed into the back seat.

Nina didn't understand what he meant but another flash of lightning stopped any further hesitation. She slid across the back seat, grateful to be out of the rain. The stranger handed her bags to her and climbed in beside her. They both were soaking wet, dripping water onto the vinyl seat and making muddy puddles on the floor with their shoes.

The taxi was new and spotless, with plastic covering the inside of the doors. Nina was conscious of the driver's eyes in the rear vision mirror looking from one to the other, taking in their bedraggled state.

'Where to?' he asked.

'Elizabeth Bay,' said Nina.

'Rushcutters Bay,' said the stranger.

They spoke at the same time then laughed.

The driver's eyes narrowed suspiciously. 'Are you sharing?' he asked, his voice indicating his disapproval.

They answered at the same time.

'Yes,' said Nina.

'No,' said the stranger.

Nina was confused.

'Well, what's it to be then?' asked the driver.

Apart from the rear vision mirror, all that Nina could see of him was the back of his shoulders and head. He was large and beefy with a small shiny, pink bald patch and a broad Australian accent. His tone was hearty but his eyes weren't smiling. They were suspicious.

Nina opened her mouth to speak but the stranger cut in. 'I'm going to Rushcutters Bay and dropping my friend here at Elizabeth Bay on the way.'

The driver stayed parked at the curb.

'You know it is 75 per cent of the fare per person if you are cab sharing,' he said, adding ominously, 'that's the law.'

Nina knew nothing of Australian cab etiquette, let alone cab law. In Canada if you wanted to share a cab that was your business. She didn't understand what this driver was making a fuss about. She was happy for the stranger to take charge so she sat back in the seat, confident he would sort it out.

The driver continued to stay parked at the curb, waiting for an answer. The stranger ignored him. He didn't like his attitude. And he wasn't about to be intimidated by a taxi driver. He knew the law, too, at least enough to work around it when it suited him. He conveyed his total lack of regard for the driver by ignoring him and beaming at Nina.

His smile was broad and open; it seemed to embrace her like a long-lost friend.

'What an incredible coincidence bumping into each other in that meeting,' he boomed in a loud, jolly voice. He was looking at Nina but she understood his words were for the benefit of the driver.

The driver's disembodied eyes looked across from one to the other of them in the back seat, then with a heavy and pointed sigh, he pulled the taxi away from the curb. He was muttering to himself, words that Nina couldn't make out. But his manner made it clear he was not happy and not altogether believing.

'How long has it been since we saw each other?' continued the stranger. 'Two years? Your hair is different. What have you done?'

Nina smiled. She had worn her hair short, tucked behind her ears for most of her adult life. The stranger looked completely guileless, his expression innocent and enquiring, yet he seemed so mischievous that Nina couldn't help responding.

'I decided I was too young for mauve so I've gone back to my natural mouse colour,' she replied loudly, deciding to play along.

'Oh, that's a shame. I always thought that menopausal mauve suited you,' replied the stranger. 'It went so well with the pink hotpants you used to wear.'

Nina saw the driver's eyes shoot up and stare at her. She repressed her smile. The stranger noticed the driver's attention. It spurred him on.

'Are you still working in . . . in . . .' his voice trailed off.

'Interior design? Oh yes. I'm doing my bit to turn slums into palaces.' Nina felt wicked. Like a naughty child, playing up at the back of the classroom.

'That's right,' nodded the stranger. 'Interior design. You're an indoor artiste, an ambience engineer.'

Nina had never heard it called that before. She rolled it around in her mind for a moment. *Ambience engineer.* Mmmmm. It had a certain appeal. She tried to picture it on her business cards and laughed out loud.

The driver sniggered as he turned left into William Street, joining the main throng of traffic heading out of the city. He made it clear he didn't think much of the job title.

The stranger looked at the driver then at Nina. He was clearly enjoying himself, his manner playful and infectious. Nina found herself relaxing, sitting by this amusing stranger. She shifted in the seat, liking the squelching sound her shoes made as she slipped them off her feet.

'When are you going to do my place?' he continued. 'I still need help with my lounge room.' His tone suggested that they had had this conversation many times before.

'Help?' responded Nina loudly. 'You need more than help. If I told you once I told you a thousand times, floral pink walls with that baby blue carpet would never work. But, oh no, you wouldn't listen.'

Nina watched as the driver's eyes flashed across to the stranger.

'Well, what would you suggest in that room?' asked the stranger.

Nina put her head to one side, feigning thoughtfulness. She adopted her best interior decorator tone, speaking slowly and deliberately, as if the possibilities of this man's lounge room were the most important thing in the world to her. 'I think you need to reflect your own personality, your own interests . . .'

The stranger raised an eyebrow. His shoulders were turned towards Nina and he focussed all his attention on her. She could feel the intensity of his scrutiny. Oh yeah, this will be good, his manner seemed to say.

Nina continued. 'A living room should be somewhere you feel comfortable because it says "you".'

The man could tell she was thinking while she was talking. He watched her with interest, keen to hear what she would come up with. He was relishing every moment of this game. Nina's large expressive brown eyes darted about, looking past him, her mind working furiously. She locked back onto his gaze with a triumphant little smile.

'The medieval jousting you like to do on weekends. Why not bring those suits of armour and the racks out of the basement, I mean, your dungeon. The racks would be perfect as the core idea for your living area.'

The stranger fell back against the seat laughing,

his enjoyment contagious. Nina felt it pass through her body as a wave of pleasure.

Outside the rain fell steadily, producing a pleasant rat-a-tat sound on the roof. The windows had fogged up from their breath, making it difficult for them to make sense of the buildings and people outside, which passed by in a whirl of unrecognisable shapes. The streetlights came on, casting feeble halos that barely penetrated the silver curtain of rain. Inside the taxi the air was steamy and close.

The car behind sounded its horn and the taxi driver was forced to turn his attention to the road. Nina knew he had been listening to every word of their conversation. His body and eyes were facing the road but his focus was very much in the back seat with them. His presence heightened their intimacy as every word they spoke was loaded with double meaning. Nina and the stranger seemed to exist within their own private world, a world they were creating together.

'And are you still wearing red-and-blue tights and playing Spider-Man at children's parties for a living?' asked Nina.

She looked across at the stranger, her eyes wide and innocent, her mouth gently lifted at the corners in an enquiring half-smile.

The stranger squirmed in his seat. He looked Nina over, considering her carefully. 'Touché,' he said softly so that only she could hear. He leaned forward as he spoke, his breath warm against Nina's wet shoulder. She was conscious of his closeness.

His light cotton shirt was plastered against his chest. He wasn't a big man but he was compact and muscular. She was very aware of his physicality, his broad chest and the heat that emanated from him, adding to the steamy humidity inside the cab.

He leaned back and looked at her, the smile fading from his face as he shook his head sadly. 'I'm afraid my Spider-Man days are over. Papa died a few months ago and I had to take over the family business.'

His mood changed so abruptly and his voice suddenly was so sad that Nina wondered if this were true. She was taken aback momentarily. 'Oh, I'm so sorry.'

They sat in silence for a moment, Nina unsure what to say. The driver kept his gaze intently on the road ahead, his windscreen wipers working furiously. Nina started to regret that she had been so flippant about Spider-Man. She had been having so much fun, she had overdone it. She had been guilty of doing exactly that since she was a child. Her father had always been telling her 'Nina, you've gone too far,' and so she had learned to tone down her natural exuberance.

The stranger saw the frown on her face. He hadn't meant to upset her with his seriousness. What a sensitive little creature she was. He wanted the carefree, playful girl back. He slid his foot along the floor, out of view of the driver, and gently tapped hers. It's okay, it seemed to say. He smiled and Nina felt herself relax again.

'It was a terrible shock for all of us,' continued

the stranger. 'And now I have so much to do. I have to go back to Italy to sort out the family estate.'

He kept his head down, then looked up sadly, theatrically, through the rain-streaked window. The taxi slowed in the traffic. They were approaching a huge flashing Coca-Cola sign. It towered over the intersection at the heart of Kings Cross. Usually Nina liked to watch the sign change shape, morphing into a new image. But tonight she ignored it, totally absorbed in the surreal conversation she was sharing with this interesting man. Nina realised she was completely happy, sitting in the back of the slow-moving taxi. The time, all the stresses of the day, her past, her future, everything fell away.

'Italy, why Italy?' she asked.

The stranger looked at the passing shops for inspiration. The taxi drew level with an inner-city coffee house, a place he knew well. He often popped in there for a leisurely breakfast with the newspapers. Nina knew it well too. She sometimes dropped by for a quick coffee while she was shopping. The windows of the café were covered in posters and large striped umbrellas dripped over empty tables on the footpath.

'Oh, don't you remember?' asked the stranger.

Nina could tell by his tone he was feeling pretty pleased with himself. She smiled, looking forward to whatever was coming.

'I'm sure I told you. My family owns the Lavazza empire.'

Nina followed his eyes to a poster in the window

of the café. *Lavazza Qualita O'ro* it declared in gigantic type above a photo of a steaming cup of rich black coffee in an impossibly white cup with matching saucer.

'*That* Lavazza coffee?' she asked, pointing.

The stranger reacted as if he was noticing the poster for the first time.

'Oh God, they have our old poster up. Oh, that's so frustrating. Yes, *that* Lavazza coffee empire.'

Nina considered the stranger. She allowed her eyes to range over his face, taking in his fair hair and freckled complexion. She raised one eyebrow and pursed her lips. Then she slowly and deliberately looked over the rest of him, ending with a derisive snort at his trousers tucked into mismatching socks. Without a word, she had conveyed her message. *Italian indeed!*

The stranger enjoyed her appraisal. He found it acutely seductive to have this enigmatic beauty, with the pixie smile and the big sad eyes, looking him over.

Nina felt the tension building between them. It was intensely, delightfully thrilling. She felt that delicious ache in the pit of her stomach, a luscious throbbing in the secret depths of her body. She was a little surprised at her physical reaction and shifted in her seat, smoothing her dress down where it had ridden up around her thighs.

'I knew you had a family business back in Italy but I didn't know it was coffee. I guess I just assumed your family was in the fashion business, you having seven sisters and all.' Nina smiled sweetly as she mentioned his sisters and the stranger's eyes widened in mock horror.

'Seven?' he mouthed silently.

'How are they all?' continued Nina. 'As head of the family I guess you inherit responsibility for them all. That must be a handful.'

The stranger started waving both hands about in what Nina supposed was meant to be an Italian manner. '*Si*, *si*, they are a handful,' he said, shaking his head gravely. 'Fortunately, I also inherited the family castle, with a moat of course, the family fortune, so that I can provide them each with a respectable dowry, and the title, which is one of the oldest in Italy. I am the fourteenth Count Mauro de March.'

He spoke with all the aplomb and elan that centuries of Italian aristocratic breeding might have produced.

'Count Mauro de March,' repeated Nina, drawing out the *r*s. She wondered where he had plucked that name from. He was wondering the same thing. It had just popped into his head. It was a name he had heard at school. A joke. The rest of the memory eluded him.

'At your service, signorina.' He bowed forward in his seat. Nina was captivated.

'I think Count Mauro de March definitely needs to bring his suit of armour out of his dungeon and put it on display.'

'Yes,' laughed the count. 'I think that might be perfectly suitable.'

Nina noticed with a start where they were. If

she didn't speak up soon they would miss her turn off. She leaned forward to instruct the driver and then settled back into the seat. She smiled at the stranger. She didn't want the ride to end. She felt like she had known this man all her life. She wanted to thank him somehow for his kindness and for keeping her so entertained. She slid her foot along the floor and gently tapped his ankle with her bare toe.

He understood her silent communication and smiled back.

'How lovely it has been to catch up with you,' he said. 'After so long.'

'And with you too. Please remember me to your sisters – all of them.'

'I will. And don't forget to drink lots of coffee. They have expensive tastes you know. And with seven of them . . . *Mon Dieu*!'

Nina laughed. 'It will be only Lavazza in our household from now on, I promise.'

The taxi stopped at Nina's apartment block. The stranger leapt out of the car into the rain and, before Nina could gather her bags together, he was opening her door. She thanked him and stood for a moment by the car as the raindrops fell silently onto her head, spilling down her face. She made no attempt to brush them away. The stranger was just as unconcerned by the rain. They were both already so wet. He leaned forward, as if he had all the time in the world and, half-bowing, gently took her hand.

'It has been a surprise and a pleasure.'

He sounded so sweet and sincere Nina felt herself blush. 'Thank you, count,' she said.

They shook hands, almost formally. His fingers were warm but wet and slippery with the rain. They slid across hers, slowly, sensually, and Nina felt an involuntary tightening of the muscles somewhere in the pit of her stomach. She was reluctant to let go of the stranger's hand. It was so pleasurable to feel it wrapped around her own. He was frozen by the magic of the moment also, and they stood together, stupidly smiling at each other in the softly falling rain.

Nina had no idea how long they stayed like that. She was conscious only of his eyes, locked onto her own, and his smile, open and engaging, dragging her into him. She felt joy bubbling up inside her. This man made her want to laugh and laugh and laugh.

He felt the same. She knew it as surely as she knew her own name. And she was right. He was feeling all those things. And then he did something that was so out of character, so spontaneous, he wasn't aware himself that he was doing it until he was. Perhaps it was the rain. Perhaps it was the softness in Nina's smile, or the laughter in her eyes, or the way tendrils of wet hair clung to her throat. Perhaps it was because he was overcome by the joy and delight of their impromptu meeting. Perhaps it was all of those things for at that moment, he stepped out of himself.

He wasn't shy or awkward or clumsy. He leaned forward, took her in his arms tango-style and bent her gracefully over one arm.

It didn't occur to Nina to fight him. She was completely at one with him at that moment and it seemed to her the most natural thing in the world, to fall back laughing in the arms of this stranger. She felt the world sway. The blood rushed to her head and the deserted street spun about her. She felt the rain on her face, dropping into her mouth and she savoured its taste. She felt light and free, anchored only by the stranger's hands on her waist. It was exhilarating

This most perfect of moments was all too brief. One minute she was in his arms, the next he was setting her back on her feet and the world was quickly becoming steady again.

The taxi driver intruded on them, winding down his window to call them to attention. 'Okay, Fred and Ginger. Wrap it up. The rest of Sydney has plans for tonight,' he announced. Then he wound up his window, shutting out the rain.

The stranger gave a smile of regret as Nina picked up her bags. With a final wave she ran through the open gates into the driveway of her apartment block.

It was only as she stood at the front door searching in her bag for her key that she realised she hadn't contributed anything to the fare. She laughed aloud, feeling good all over. How fitting. He had been her knight, her Italian count, coming to the rescue. She looked forward to telling James all about it over dinner.

CHAPTER 3

Friday, 18 January 1991

James Wilde hung up the phone, frowning. Nina should have been home by now. He looked past the wall clock at the rain falling steadily on the window. Cases of wine were stacked against every wall of his office. He had one more order to process and fax through to the family estate in the Hunter Valley. He had hoped to have it done by now and be home, settling in with Nina for their regular Friday night together. Well, no matter. She wasn't home either. The rain must have held her up. The buses would be extra slow in this weather. James didn't like to think of her getting caught in the rain.

A head peered around his door. 'God, I need a drink.' It was Felix, the accountant, who worked in the office next door.

James didn't bother to look up from his paperwork, waving instead in the direction of the fridge.

As the vintner of the office suite, James's door – and fridge – were known to be always open. Three school friends, each pursuing different businesses, rented this suite of offices, sharing a receptionist/secretary, a boardroom and an impressive address on the edge of town. They called it the Burman Suite after the house they all had belonged to at school. Felix opened the fridge and selected a bottle of semillon, half-finished from the day's tastings.

'Is this one okay?' he asked, showing the label to James.

'Bit young. But what does that matter to you? It's alcohol.'

Felix poured himself a hefty glass. Then he poured another and set it in front of James, who accepted it with resignation. He really wanted to finish what he was doing and get away. But Felix hated to drink alone. It wasn't sociable, he said.

James held the glass aloft out of habit, nodded to his friend and sipped the wine. It definitely was a bit green. The grape was still fermenting when it was bottled. It wasn't like his brother Mark to make such a mistake. This batch would have to go out below cost, somewhere not too conspicuous, like a small, out-of-the-way suburban bottle shop or bar.

James turned his attention back to the order in front of him: four cases of Wildes' Premium Shiraz and an ongoing order for Wildes' current vintage Chardonnay. The order came from a trendy new restaurant, the Lotus Bar. James had worked hard to have Wilde Wines included on the wine list. He had spent many evenings dropping by the restaurant to chat to the sommelier about the different wines Wildes could supply. Finally the sommelier had chosen Wildes' Chardonnay as their house white. But to secure the deal James had to let them have four cases of the highly prized Wildes' Premium Shiraz. The stock was dwindling for the much sought after wine and James only allowed Wilde Wines' most important customers to purchase them. It would matter little to Frederick Wilde that their wines were on the menu of the hottest new restaurant in town. But for James it was important, part of the exclusive brand image he was trying to cultivate as marketing director of the winery.

It was twenty years since Frederick Wilde and his wife Patty had planted the first grafted vine on their 400 hectares near Broke in the Hunter Valley. Initially it had been a weekend farm where they retreated from Sydney with their two sons, Mark and James. Weekends were spent clearing the land and planning the vineyard's future. Frederick and Patty planted the first three rows of grapes down on their hands and knees in the dirt while Mark and James fished for yabbies in the dam nearby. A few months later they sold their four-bedroom North Shore home and moved the boys – with their collection of pet spiders – and the family dog to the Hunter Valley.

Their first harvest produced 972 juicy sweet grapes that made exactly one-and-a-half bottles of salad dressing. By the following year their modest plantings had grown enough that they needed friends and neighbours to help them at harvest time. They sold their entire yield to local vineyards to combine with other grapes from the region to make blended wines.

The third vintage was such a success that they bottled ten cases of shiraz under the label Frederick's First. The soil conditions were right, the viticulture was right, the chemistry was right: it was a superb wine. Everyone who tried it agreed. Frederick and Patty, young, proud and confident, borrowed money to submit six bottles to each of the world's most prestigious competitions. They couldn't afford to go themselves, but with enormous excitement they sent their wine. They were rewarded with a series of midnight phone calls telling them they had won, again and again.

Wilde Wines was in business.

The boys grew up with the smell of sulphur in their nostrils and the stain of wine grapes on their hands and feet. By the time he was twelve, James learned to appreciate whether a wine had been matured in French oak or American oak, just by its smell. By the age of fifteen, he could tell a chardonnay's age to within a year just by holding a glass of it to the light.

Frederick and Patty never had a holiday or took the boys away to the beach for the weekend. Where in the world could be better than this, Frederick would ask, his sweeping hand taking in the rambling old homestead, called Winden after the little German town where he was born; the lush, green vines; the old waterwheel at the top of the creek; and the ancient willow tree where they held weekend picnics and tastings. And James would have to agree. It was indeed a special little corner of the world.

Every evening Frederick and Patty would 'walk the land', fussing over new shoots and watching, through the years, as they grew strong and the trunks of the vines became thick and robust. As they walked over the property they would monitor the health of each individual vine and reminisce about the vines' histories. Most evenings their walk naturally ended up at the vine nearest the creek, their first, the one that had been grafted from a great old vine, the Jacob Leesing, a legend in the region. It had survived the dry rot of 1987, the storms of 1990 and now was elegantly gnarled but still producing, huge, luscious, sweet shiraz grapes.

Mark, the eldest son, had studied oenology at college and worked for a few years at different wineries in South Australia, learning from some of the best palates in the country. He spent two Australian winters in Germany, harvesting and learning everything he could. Now he was winemaker at Wildes'. He lived with his wife and young sons in the nearby town of Broke. Like his father, Mark had wine in his veins. He was happiest with his nose buried in a glass, ascertaining parentage and year of bottling.

James's interests were less sure and his relationship with his father more ambiguous. He loved the family business, particularly the rambling old vineyard. But he had been torn between pleasing his father and his love of sport. Almost from the day he could walk, James could kick a football, wave a cricket bat and stay upright on a pair of skis. He was naturally gifted with balance and hand-eye coordination. He could have pursued any sport he chose.

For a while it had been football, but then, on a school trip when he was twelve, he discovered skiing. The next nine years he devoted to becoming stronger and faster than anybody else on the Australian snowfields. At 21 he won a place on the Olympic ski team going to Sarajevo but failed to bring home a medal. By 22 knee surgery meant his racing career was over. James went to university, where he studied marketing, and spent months each Christmas as a ski instructor in Canada. For the past four years he had lived at Whistler, near Vancouver, running the ski school in winter and marketing outrageously expensive ski wear to North America's rich. Between seasons he spent his time at the company's headquarters in Toronto.

His father wondered when he would come home and settle down. He managed to somehow insert that question into every phone call and letter. It wasn't that Frederick didn't approve of James's lifestyle. It was just that he didn't understand it. Frederick Wilde was a simple man. He believed in solid dirt under his feet, his family by his side and a good, honest day's work. James's travelling to far-flung places to teach skiing to a bunch of snow bunnies made Frederick highly suspicious. James was left in no doubt about his father's views and it was a constant source of frustration for him.

Then, one thunderous Sunday early in June 1990, James shocked them all, walking into the family home with Nina, his new wife. He had given his parents no warning of his return, nor did they know anything about his recent marriage. The last postcard his mother had received had been three months before, telling of the busy ski season that Whistler was enjoying and wishing the Wilde family a bumper harvest.

For three years James had succeeded in his aim of cutting himself off from his family. In that time he had been successful in his job. He had sought and won the love of an intelligent, independent woman. And he had gradually found a way to accept his defeat at the Olympics. All his reasons for leaving home had slowly melted away.

He was 'over' skiing and wanted to join the family business, he announced to his startled parents. He had waited till they had praised the roast lamb, Patty's signature dish, admired each of the home-grown vegetables and then savoured two bottles of burgundy from his father's private cellar, before he made this declaration. It was family protocol to save important pronouncements until after the main course was finished.

'I think it's time I contributed,' he said, fiddling nervously with the fine stem of his Riedel burgundy glass. His mother, noting the look on her husband's face, immediately stood up, cleared the plates and shepherded Nina into the sitting room.

'They have a lot to talk about,' she said, in a tone that left no room for argument. Patty spent the next three hours getting to know her new daughter-in-law. It was a gruelling session that covered Nina's family background, her level of education, her aspirations and how she met James, through to what she had been told of the Wilde family history. Along the way Patty ascertained Nina's politics, moral code and intelligence.

By the time Patty showed the exhausted young woman to her room, they had developed a mutual respect. They were still a long way from being friends, but it was a good start. Patty was a strong and formidable woman who wasn't about to be won over in the first ten minutes of meeting somebody. But she was a good judge of character and Nina, she told Frederick later, was a smart girl with a sensible head on her shoulders. She wasn't some flibbertigibbet that James had saddled them with. Both Patty and Frederick let out a sigh of relief.

While Nina was enduring the seemingly friendly interrogation, James and his father got down to business. They talked through the night. For a while they sat at the kitchen table, one or the other occasionally getting up and moving around the room and staring out across the vines, visible in the light of the full moon. At various stages during the discussion his father left the room to fetch something important, some papers, a file, the photographic history of the vineyard that Patty had lovingly collated, and at a certain point, another bottle of his prized burgundy.

By 10 pm they had agreed the business had gone as far as it could using a wine sales agency. To grow further it would require skilful marketing. The Wilde Wines label needed to develop its own brand with mass-market appeal. Frederick entered the major wine competitions but that was about the extent of it. He was too busy with the day-to-day running of the vineyard. Besides, he hated leaving the estate. Patty joked that just driving out of the gates put him in a bad mood. As winemaker, Mark was fully occupied gently nurturing the grapes, overseeing the picking, the crushing and destemming, the fermentation, then finally bringing the young wines to maturity.

An hour later, at about 11 pm, Frederick and James had agreed on a new marketing strategy for Wilde Wines and the budget that it would take to do it. James would set up offices in Sydney and aggressively promote the wine to restaurants and bars. He would also look at possible export markets. That was the easy stuff out of the way.

Negotiations for James's salary took much longer. Frederick Wilde may have been most at home with his feet in the soil, or grumbling over the latest international wine magazine's ratings, but he was also a smart businessman. James had to prove himself. There was a big difference between selling skis and selling wine, Frederick Wilde said in a tone that James remembered well. Until James could show he was an asset to Wilde Wines, he was on probation, just like every other person who joined the payroll. And his modest salary reflected that. In twelve months Frederick would consider the value James had brought to the business and reassess his salary accordingly.

Frederick had a fair idea what Patty would say when he told her of the arrangement over breakfast the next morning so he threw into the deal the family's harbourside apartment in the city. Knowing he was unlikely to win, he tried to avoid arguments with his opinionated wife where possible. James and Nina could live rent-free in the Elizabeth Bay apartment.

The two men shook hands in confirmation of their agreement. It was nearly 1 o'clock in the morning but only then did Frederick bring out a much-prized bottle from the dwindling stock of Frederick's First, put his arm around his son's shoulders and tell him he was pleased to have him home. It may have been the effects of the evening's wine, appreciation of the magnificent aged shiraz or just the end of a long and tiring day, but there were genuine tears in the old man's eyes when he said it.

Those first six months had been the toughest. James spent his time setting up his office and visiting restaurants and hotels to introduce himself to the purchasing managers and sommeliers, as well as courting the writers of all the wine magazines. It meant visiting restaurants and bars in the evening, getting to know who was who in Sydney's ever-changing hospitality industry and keeping Wilde Wines prominent in the minds of those who mattered. He was acutely aware that he had little to show for the long hours and hard work he put in. But he stayed optimistic. He knew he could make a difference. He was confident that his ideas would work over the long term.

Setting up the Burman Suite with his old schoolmates had turned out to be an extraordinary stroke of luck, though James preferred to think of it as genius. As well as his best mate Felix, sharing the suite was David, who specialised in event management. He was building up a reputation as *the* man to organise a party, wedding, cocktail function or corporate launch. When he wasn't seeking out nude parachutists to land in the middle of an elite outdoor soiree on a harbour home lawn, he was kissing the tightly stretched cheeks of the city's society matrons. And at almost every function, whether it was groovy, hip and street-smart or reeking of old money, the guests sipped Wilde Wines in glasses etched with the WW logo. It didn't hurt David's business and it was enormously useful in helping James establish his.

Felix was helpful in other ways. His family were Sydney blue bloods and part of the squattocracy. He was a member of the Australia Club and London's Army and Navy Club and had entree to most of the hallowed boardrooms across Australia.

Felix was a money whiz. He bought his first

apartment while he was still in his final year at school. He taught his schoolmates more about financial management than their economics master, Mr Van Der Pol, ever could. At school Felix hadn't wasted his generous monthly allowance on cigarettes and car magazines. He had loaned it out to the other boys at a hefty interest rate. Then he had charged them to do their mathematics and economics assignments. The money he accumulated he invested in the stock market. By the time he left school, well before he received his inheritance, Felix was financially independent. After school he moved into his two-bedroom flat near Sydney University, where he was studying for his Bachelor of Economics, then Master of Economics. He rented out the second bedroom to his best mate James.

Felix called himself an accountant but he was much more than that. He ran the business affairs of a number of wealthy clients, ranging from a millionaire jockey to the Australian interests of an actress who spent most of her time overseas. They trusted him completely and in return for their trust he orchestrated some highly original deals, breathtaking in their audacity, which made them all a lot of money. Felix was, quite simply, the most financially savvy man James had ever met and was ever likely to meet. He was also a great drinking buddy.

James had been so deep in thought, he hadn't realised Felix was still in the room. Now James watched his friend as he shuffled about the room, weaving around the crates of wine, picking up artwork for posters and putting them back on top of the table.

'Don't you have a home to go to?' James asked.

Felix dropped the poster back on the table. 'Sorry, mate.' He slumped down in the chair in front of James's desk. 'Actually, I need to talk to you.'

James looked over the papers in his hand to his friend. He noticed the way Felix drank his wine, throwing it back as if it were water. 'What's up?'

Felix opened his mouth to speak, then closed it again. Now that James was looking at him, he wasn't sure where to start. And he was tired. It had been a shit of a day. One of the worst. He wished with every ounce of his remaining energy that he didn't have to have this conversation.

James watched Felix try to smooth back his hair with his fingers. Felix had a number-two buzz cut leaving very little hair to smooth. The gesture was entirely a nervous habit. Every few seconds he would stop and clasp his hands together in his lap, then they would fly apart and he would try to smooth his hair again.

James wondered if he was having trouble with David. They often got snappy with each other. Or maybe the trouble was with his girlfriend Miranda. She was a flighty thing, always in a tizz about something. Did he want to borrow money? No. Felix was the one you went to when you needed cash. Short term, long term, lots or a little. He was your man.

'What is it, Felix?' asked James.

Felix shook his head. 'I've just come from a meeting about Lloyd's . . . It's a disaster . . . Asbestos claims have brought it unstuck . . . The unthinkable has happened . . . James, I don't know how to tell you . . .'

The words spilled out of Felix's mouth. He was talking too fast and the thoughts were disconnected. It made little sense but James caught enough to place his papers slowly and carefully onto his desk and give his full attention to Felix.

'What about Lloyd's?'

Felix took a deep breath, trying to bring his own panic under control, and looked his friend squarely in the eye. 'James, it's a disaster. They owe billions. They are calling in the names.'

Calling in the names. James felt a chasm open beneath him. It was the day Felix had said would never come.

Leo melted happily back into the taxi seat as the small dark figure that was Nina let herself into the building's foyer. Did she look back? He rather fancied that she did. That last moment, just before she disappeared completely from view, she seemed to stop for the smallest amount of time and look back in this direction, at him. The rain was falling in sheets around the car rendering everything a blur, but Leo was convinced. She *had*. She had taken one last peek at him. In the same way and at the same time that he was leaning forward, peering through the rain trying to keep sight of her, she had wanted one last glimpse of him and had turned for the merest fraction of a second. It was almost imperceptible, but he *had* seen it, Leo told himself.

He sighed deeply, feeling the warmth spread right through his body. He felt elated, euphoric. It was as if something in him had woken up. He felt he was a different man from the one who had fled that boring meeting just . . . how long ago was that? He checked his watch. Three-quarters of an hour. Just 45 minutes. That was all it had been. And in that short space of time the world had completely and irretrievably been transformed.

The taxi driver chuckled loudly, eyeing Leo in his rear vision mirror. 'I didn't pick you as the Fred Astaire type.'

Leo smiled and shrugged.

'You make a good couple,' continued the driver. He clearly wanted to engage Leo in conversation but Leo wasn't about to be drawn.

He wrapped his joy tightly around himself, hugging it close. He wanted to savour the little ripples of delight that were running through him. He didn't want to share any of it. He made a sound that was half grunt and half laugh and turned back to the window.

Who was that woman? That delightful girl-woman with the brown eyes that looked bewildered one minute and brimmed with gentle laughter the next. And that lovely, lilting, soft Canadian accent. It was as if her voice bubbled. Leo laughed as a snippet of their conversation floated into his mind. Spider-Man. Huh!

Leo had experienced a few heart-stopping instances of clarity in his life. Rare and precious moments that pinned him to the spot with their sheer perfection. The feel of Nina's warm, wet skin when he held her in his arms with the rain falling softly and silently about them was one of them. He relived the feeling, trying to recapture its joyous intensity, but already that intensity was fading, leaving in its wake a faint but delicious yearning.

Leo paid the driver and splashed his way to his apartment block, no longer caring that the dirty water was turning his trouser cuffs brown.

Ah, what serendipity that he had found that taxi rank. It had been just a whim that propelled him out of the meeting at that moment, and down that particular street to that corner. He hadn't known there would be a taxi rank. It was a part of town he seldom visited.

And he had so nearly stayed for the rest of the meeting, just because he knew Felix wanted him to. But Leo had been unable to concentrate on what was going on inside the boardroom twenty floors above the city. He had paid little attention to what was being explained to the assembled group in such sombre tones. He had looked straight past the lawyer who was doing most of the talking, to the sky and the approaching storm. It was Friday night sailing and his boat was in top condition, ready for the evening's races. Tonight was the night he and his crew were going to win. While the lawyer droned on about asbestosis and cash calls and worst case scenarios, Leo had kept an anxious eye on the storm clouds. They wouldn't stop the race. Not unless the weather bureau predicted the wind would be over 25 knots and it didn't look like that to Leo. He watched the approach, over the lawyer's left shoulder, of the distinctive cigar-shaped cloud coming up the coast. The southerly buster would bring rain and a welcome drop in temperatures but not so much wind it would stop the races.

The boardroom was stuffy and airless. Leo could feel his energy starting to flag and his eyes were feeling dry and scratchy from the airconditioning. It would suit him to arrive early at the Cruising Yacht Club in Rushcutters Bay. He could talk through the evening's race with Nick, the crew member who always arrived first, ready to prepare the boat.

While the meeting went on around him, Leo rationalised that it was a waste of everyone's time for him to stay, given the scant amount of attention he was paying. He would find out from Felix later what it had all been about and what it meant to Leo's business affairs. That was why you had accountants – to attend boring meetings on your behalf, not to make you sit through them too.

It took just a few seconds for Leo to justify the thought in his own mind and the next thing he knew he was on his feet and halfway out the door, excusing himself as he went. Leo pretended he had just received an urgent message on his pager. Felix hardly noticed him leave. He was engrossed in what the lawyer was saying. Leo had seen that look before. All the women in the room could have taken off their clothes and Felix wouldn't have flickered an eyelid.

And so Leo had raced out into the rain, hoping to stop a passing taxi and get home as soon as possible. Then he had spotted that bedraggled figure huddled against the wall.

Leo wandered through his apartment smiling to himself, turning on lights and gathering together his sailing gear. Within minutes he was splashing through Rushcutters Bay Park towards the Cruising Yacht Club, where his boat and crew waited. Tonight was the night *Bessie* was going to beat its arch rival, *Pure Indulgence*. *Bessie* was a bit older and heavier. She would have the advantage in strong winds. All the conditions were right. Leo would wipe the smile off the face of that cocky building developer and his crew. He was feeling lucky.

The switchboard light on the front reception desk in the Burman Suite flashed again. It was James's line. The receptionist had flicked it over to nightswitch when she left four hours earlier. James couldn't hear it, and, from his current vantage point face down on his desk blotter, he was unlikely to see it.

James's eyes were open, staring unseeing at a doodle he had drawn on the blotter. It was lots of lines and sharp angles scribbled in heavy black biro. It filled his vision.

It had taken Felix over an hour to explain it

fully to James. Felix had just come from a meeting in the city where all the ghastly truth had been revealed. He had explained to James exactly how much of a mess James was in, they were all in, and then he had gone home to fret in different surroundings, leaving James alone with the echo of that phrase.

They are calling in the names.

The cleaning staff, a hard-working young Taiwanese couple who spoke no English, had been in and vacuumed the carpet, shifting the hose around James's feet and emptying his wastepaper bin from under his desk. They smiled and nodded as they moved purposefully about the office. They were used to him working late. The storm had long ago passed and after the couple had moved on to another floor, everything about him was quiet.

They are calling in the names.

James wished he had the energy to go home. All the life had seeped out of him. He forced himself to stand, leaning heavily against the table. He stood there for a minute, collecting himself. His head swam and he felt rising nausea. His mouth was dry. His hunger had curdled in the acidic pit of his stomach. He felt wretched. Exhausted. He left the order on his desk unfinished, picked up his briefcase and made his way through the deserted building to the carpark.

Nina stared at the fish. She had been sitting in the dining chair looking at it for the best part of an hour. At first she had admired it, how good it looked with its garnish of chervil and thinly sliced spanish onion. But after some minutes congratulating herself for her good purchase, she had started to feel guilty that she had spent so much. Then she had started to worry that it would spoil before James got home. *Where the hell was he? Why didn't he answer his telephone? Why wasn't he home?* Then she had started to hate the fish for sitting there staring back at her. A fly buzzed around and landed on it, poking into the succulent pink flesh. Nina made no attempt to brush it away. She glared at the glassy, milky eye for one more long moment.

Then she picked up the plate and the bottle of wine she had half finished, and walked out her front door and onto the walkway that connected the apartments. With the plate in one hand and the wine bottle in the other, she walked unsteadily past old Mr Hilton in number 656, Mrs Biggs in 657 and the newlyweds in 658. At the end of the row of apartments, she took the lift down as far as it would go, and let herself out into the garden and the fresh, post-storm night air.

Swaying slightly she carried the plate across the manicured lawns of the private garden to the harbour's edge and looked out over Rushcutters Bay. She stood watching the water lap against the brick wall just centimetres beneath her feet. Then she tossed the fish, plate and all, as high as she could in the air. The fish flew off the plate, disappearing with a small plop into the still water. The plate, with its tidbits of onion and garnish, skimmed the surface then slipped into the inky darkness below.

Long after it had sunk from view Nina gazed at the surface of the water. Then she sat down heavily on the lawn. It was damp from the evening's rain. She didn't care. She took a swig of wine.

The sound of music and merriment drifted across the water from a party at the Cruising Yacht Club. She raised the bottle towards them in a toast and took another swig. Above her in an upstairs apartment she heard a door close and muffled voices. That would be her neighbours. Huh! She didn't know any of them really. They were friendly enough, she supposed, but not what her family would call 'farm friendly'. Not like the neighbours where she grew up. The nearest one could be a couple of blocks away but you could knock on their door at any time of the day or night and know you would be welcome. She couldn't imagine knocking on anyone's door at this time of night and saying 'Hi, I'm lonely. Want a drink?' It seemed to Nina that the closer people lived physically, the further away they really were. It made her unbearably sad. She looked in the direction she thought Canada might be and sobbed.

CHAPTER 4

Saturday, 19 January 1991

Nina sat and watched James across the table as he read the Saturday morning newspaper. He knew she was watching him and she knew he knew. It heightened the tension that seemed to resonate between them. Nina wondered if he would read anything out to her. Usually on Saturday mornings they read the newspaper together, dividing the sections and reading out stories that took their fancy. Nina took news, lifestyle and employment while James liked sport, which he usually read first, business and the comics. The classified sections – cars and real estate – were dumped in the recycle bin as soon as they were picked up off the mat by the front door, where the paper boy left them at 6 am every morning.

The only sound in the apartment was James

turning the pages. He started on the business section this morning, Nina noted, scanning each page as if looking for something in particular. He held the newspaper high so that Nina couldn't see his face. It was a perfectly reasonable way to read the newspaper, but Nina saw it as an irritatingly effective way of screening her out. He had retreated somewhere she couldn't reach him. She felt dismissed, disregarded, unimportant. She seethed silently, turning back to the front page laid out on the table before her.

She tried to focus on the printed page as James's words from the night before reverberated in her head. *Sorry, love. Held up at work.* And that was it. He had announced this to her when he finally came home at 11 pm. Then he had gone into the bedroom. Nina had thought he was changing out of his suit and would rejoin her in the living room, where he would explain what life-threatening emergency could possibly have kept him from their Friday night together. He would be profusely apologetic. She had waited and waited, sitting on the couch, her feet folded beneath her. When finally it seemed as if too long had passed, she had gone into the bedroom. James was lying on the bed, his face to one side. He had managed to remove his shoes, tie and jacket before collapsing on top of the bed. The unmistakable smell of wine emanated from his open mouth.

Sorry, love. Held up at work.

Sorry? Love? Held up? Nina felt like kicking him, as he lay there gently snoring, oblivious to her hurt. She stood and stared at him for a long time, various thoughts flicking through her mind.

The honeymoon was over already. This was marriage and she had better get used to it. She had made a dreadful mistake and this is how it would always be. He didn't love her any more. He had never loved her. He was having an affair. They shouldn't have married so quickly. Her father was right. She didn't belong here. She had a home and people who loved her in Canada. Her husband had turned out to be a selfish pig and she didn't have to put up with it. How dare he!

Anger welled up inside, temporarily obliterating her loneliness. The anger felt good, releasing some of her tension. It made her feel stronger and more empowered than the heavy, dull ache of loneliness. She raged silently against his snoring mound.

The next morning James skirted around her, avoiding meeting her eyes. He poured himself a coffee, sat down at the table and apologised again for missing dinner, adding almost as an after-thought that he was sorry for not calling. His voice was distracted and he addressed his apology more to his coffee than to her. Then he had lifted up the business section of the newspaper and that was that. The end of any discussion as far as he was concerned. Nina thought how insufferably like his father he could be.

He hadn't even sounded apologetic. Nina searched for it in his face and in his voice, but couldn't find it. He seemed to be mouthing the words and sentiments that were expected of him, but he wasn't there. She didn't know where he was, but it wasn't in the sunlit living room of their apartment with her.

Nina was right. James wasn't sorry. That was a feeling beyond him at that point. He was consumed by the implications of Felix's words. *They're calling in the names.* The threat inherent in those five words had set off a chain reaction of possibilities in James's brain. He felt as if he were standing on the tip of a precipice. The world he had so carefully constructed around him was about to be blown apart.

The ramifications were so vast and horrific that James was having trouble taking them all in. Missing dinner, being late home, seemed so inconsequential in the face of it. He didn't mean to hurt Nina even though at some level he was aware that he was doing just that. But he didn't have the energy to pursue the thought. So he avoided it. And he avoided Nina.

James scanned the newspaper. Surely something so monumental would dominate the news. He found it on page three of the business section. *Aussie names owe millions.* It was a short account of the meeting that Felix had attended the previous afternoon. The reporter hadn't paid nearly as much attention as Felix had and seemed to have only half the story.

Nina watched her husband, her eyes narrow and accusing. She knew he was disengaging from her. She just didn't know why. It felt like a cold, hard, stinging slap. She felt utterly and wretchedly alone, sitting opposite her husband of eight months, watching him ignore her. She wondered how to communicate that to him. She sat with her hands neatly folded in her lap, perfectly in control. She wasn't going to become emotional. She wouldn't raise her voice. And above all she wouldn't cry. But she wanted to tell him how she felt, how she hurt. She needed to share it with him. He was her husband, her lover, her best friend. But for months now he had been busy at work, then exhausted at home. It had been ages since they had talked, really talked.

She twisted her hands in her lap as she thought through different ways to broach the subject, trying them out in her mind. And then, before she had a chance to voice her thoughts, he was gone, out the door. Back to the office, he said. Had some orders he had to finish. Was meeting Felix in there to go over some business. Sorry, love, he had said, avoiding looking her in the eye. I won't be late. Nina had been too shocked to respond as he announced, 'I'll leave you the car and I'll walk into town.' Nina found herself once again alone at home.

Well, not really home. Alone in James's parents' apartment, where they lived. She didn't think of it as home. There was a difference. Nina supposed she should feel grateful to be allowed to stay here rent-free. But she didn't. She resented it. This apartment, with its breathtaking views across Rushcutters Bay and its still-new modular furniture, straight out of an Ikea catalogue, never felt like home.

Home was her parents' neat two-storey house on the main street of Eyebrow, the country town in Saskatchewan where she spent her first eighteen years: the cosy weatherboard with its mismatched furniture and marks on the laundry doorjamb where she and her elder brother Larry had measured their childhood in inches hewn into the wood.

Nina wished she had brought more of her own things with her. Pieces of home, pieces of her past, reminders of the person she was: winner two years in a row of the Saskatoon Junior Trout Fishing competition, winner of the 1978 tapdance championship for the whole of Saskatchewan province. Why hadn't she brought that trophy with her? Things that screamed NINA LAMBERT, interesting individual, person in her own right.

She felt she had been absorbed into the Wilde family. She'd been left with no identity or existence of her own independent of them. Nina wandered around the small apartment. It was just 9.30 am. The day stretched endlessly in front of her.

She did the calculations in her head. It was 4.30 pm on Friday in Canada. Her mother would be bringing in the four dogs, giving them their dinner, then she would start peeling vegetables for the evening meal. Nina imagined the smells of dinner filling the house. If it was Friday night her father would be singing at the Raymond Hotel with his barbershop chorus. They were four men, old friends, dressed in pin-striped shirts like old-fashioned barbers, who sang harmonies together, unaccompanied. They had been singing together every Friday night for sixteen years. The locals loved them. Nina had loved them as a child, singing along, knowing all the tunes. When she hit her teenage years she had been embarrassed to watch them, ashamed to admit to her friends that, yes, Jake Lambert was her Pa. In her twenties, seeing them through adult eyes, they somehow touched her. Four old codgers, their voices starting to crackle and break, still crooning about their sweethearts. Nina remembered the look on her mother's face when she watched the show. Smiling serenely, tapping her foot, perfectly secure in her husband's devotion, taking it as her due. The older Nina got, the more poignant those Friday nights became.

Nina sighed as she looked out across the bustling bay, busy with weekend yachts and the Saturday morning traffic. She had thought that security and devotion were what marriage was all about. Were her expectations unreasonable? Had she got it so wrong? She had never felt less loved and secure. She felt she was on the outside looking in, not in the driver's seat of her own life any more. Years of feeling that way, lonely and trapped, stretched before her.

It seemed like just a minute ago that she and James had been so desperate for each other they couldn't live a moment apart. What had happened? Why had James withdrawn from her?

Being married was nothing like being lovers, wild, passionate and carefree. James no longer made her feel special. In fact she felt more insignificant than she had ever felt in her life. Perhaps it wouldn't have seemed so bad if she had been able to find a job in interior design, her great love. But she didn't have the contacts in Sydney to get started. Instead she worked as an office manager for a group of architects. She spent most of the day answering the phone and making coffee, being bored and hating it. It was just for the moment, she reminded herself a dozen times each day, until she found a job she really wanted. Lately she had been too dispirited even to look.

Nina had no friends, no career to throw her energies into and, she felt, a husband who was too busy to notice her. What had happened to their love, that intense, driving need that had all but consumed them, compelling them to be together every possible minute of the day? Where did James go? And when exactly did he leave?

Nina remembered her last day at Whistler ski resort in Canada's south-west coastal range. It was just over eight months ago. James had been like a madman, crazy with love for her. And she had felt the same. Those last few hours they spent together, trying to say goodbye, to gently disengage from each other, had been the most emotionally charged hours of her life.

It was just as the ski season had ended. Patches of rock and dirt were beginning to show through on the slopes of Whistler and Blackcomb. Nina's job as guest relations manager of the ritzy Chateau Whistler was seasonal and, with the ski season finishing, she was no longer needed. This was the day she was supposed to leave and move to Toronto to start a new life. She and James had both known it would happen. And yet, in spite of logic and necessity, her heart cried out for another way.

James had been having similar thoughts. Why did he have to be here at Whistler for the next week? So what if the bosses were flying in from Toronto to go through the books with him. They were up to date. It had been a smasher of a season, better than any previous year. They were happy with him. Didn't he deserve a week off? It was a rhetorical question. His sense of duty was too much part of his nature to allow him to consider putting his love interests ahead of work responsibilities. And yet he couldn't let this woman just walk out of his life. Not now that he had found her.

James had known many women. Being fit, good-looking, a former Olympic champion and working at Whistler meant he was surrounded by opportunities – young women looking for a little après-ski fun with the jovial Aussie. James had always been only too happy to oblige.

But Nina was different. For a start, she hadn't been interested in him. It took weeks of James showering her with charm before she agreed to go out with him. Their first 'date' had been to a burger bar, surrounded by unshaven locals in lumberjackets, in Squamish, a redneck logging town an hour south of Whistler. The kitchen in

Nina's little studio had caught fire and she needed to replace her toaster, kettle and some crockery. Whistler stocked such things but they were marked way up in price, so Nina had been planning to catch the bus to Squamish on her day off and shop there. When James heard this he had offered to drive her. It had taken some juggling for him to get away in the middle of the week during the height of the season, but he had managed. To make it seem less like a favour, he had fabricated an urgent job he had to attend to in Squamish.

A beautiful crisp winter morning and the snow-covered forest along the spectacular Sea to Sky Highway provided the perfect romantic backdrop. Away from Whistler with its pseudo-Swiss village appearance and emphasis on money and glamour, James and Nina were able to enjoy the real Canada, wild and untamed. As Whistler grew smaller and smaller behind them and the pristine beauty of the unspoiled countryside started to work its magic, Nina felt herself relax.

That drive turned out to be a revelation for them both. Nina had seen the women hanging around James and dismissed him as a pretty boy, a lightweight philanderer, too good-looking to be taken seriously. She had met the likes of him before. All he would be interested in was his next lay. Not her type. She was surprised to discover a deep-thinking, kind man with a strong character. He was playful, with a wonderful sense of the absurd, which had her laughing from the moment they set off. She was delighted to discover that he was, in fact, exactly her type, more so than anyone she had ever met.

James could see Nina's impression of him changing before his eyes. He had sensed that she somehow disapproved of him, though he had no idea why. She was so beautiful and serious and decent, it became very important to him that she like him. She was different from the bed-hopping snow bunnies he had grown used to spending his time with. James and Nina got to know each other over lunch at Squamish's legendary Mountain Burger Bar, which boasted no pretensions, just good honest prime beef and a clientele of rough and ready loggers who swore there was nowhere else in the world you could get a real burger, a man's burger.

It was the start of a conversation that they never seemed to finish. The day ended all too soon when James dropped her back at her little apartment on the other side of Whistler from his own. He stopped by Chateau Whistler the following day to lend her the rare early Van Morrison tape that she had been unaware existed; they caught up that night for a drink and she lent him the book by Italo Calvino she had told him about. Soon they were spending all their free time together, as easily and naturally as if it had always been that way. And all the time they talked and talked, endlessly fascinated with each other's thoughts and way of thinking. James had never met anyone he felt so comfortable with. Nina was sharp. She challenged him, kept him on his toes. And he responded to it. He liked himself when he was with Nina.

Being a former Olympic skier had given James much public kudos but even more private angst. While it seemed to impress the majority of people he met, and James happily accepted whatever benefits went with that, in his own mind he had failed, big time. He hadn't brought home a gold medal. He had spent years of single-minded dedication and focus only to fall short. He didn't find what he regarded as his failure easy to accept. It was an uncomfortable paradox for him that the more lauded he was, the more he felt like a fraud. But with Nina it was different. He saw himself through her eyes and he liked the man he saw. He could respect him.

It was inevitable they would become lovers. The tight-knit community of Whistler assumed it had happened weeks before it actually did. But Nina preferred to take it very slowly. Unlike the rest of the hormone-driven young staff working a season at the international ski resort, she didn't see sex as sport. It had to be special or she wasn't interested. James had not been celibate for so long in years. And he was surprised to find he didn't mind at all. He just wanted to be with her.

When finally it happened it was explosive for them both. The desire had been building for so long that once unleashed it erupted in an uncontrollable fury. At that first instant of naked skin against naked skin they both became delirious, pushing and yielding, trying to absorb the very essence of each other.

It was erotic, carnal, primal and thrilling. Afterwards they lay side by side, in awe, looking into each other's eyes, feeling compelled to touch and stay entwined. Their gentle caresses enflamed their passion again and soon they were reaching hungrily for each other, desire building and exhausting itself, then building again, in one long continuous wave that lasted all night.

The next day Nina should have been exhausted. She wasn't. She was exhilarated, full of energy and gaiety that rubbed off on everyone she came into contact with. James was the same. He marvelled at everything he saw. Suddenly the world was a most glorious, radiant place.

Their passion stayed at fever pitch for the next three months. They just couldn't get enough of each other. A snatched five-minute cup of coffee was excruciating. It only fuelled their desire but they thought it was worth it just to be together for those fleeting moments.

And while it was never spoken of, it was always understood that at the end of the season Nina would go. She would move to Toronto with her newly acquired qualifications in interior design and start her career. The money she managed to save from her winter role would keep her going till she found a job.

But her plans hadn't taken into account falling in love.

Nina and James's farewell had been the hardest. It had been heart-wrenching, funny and frustrating. Once Nina had given back her apartment key and her suitcases were at the bus station, they had an hour left.

The outdoor bars were almost empty, a far cry from just a few weeks ago when the tables had been filled with holidaymakers, laughing and chatting and stomping about in their heavy ski boots after a day on the slopes. Lit braziers kept the chill at bay, turning the outdoor areas into cosy beer gardens. The braziers weren't lit now and the sun had set but, wanting privacy, James and Nina chose a seat outside in the forecourt of a trendy bar-café.

They stared at each other, hands entwined, saying silly things. They both knew how the other felt. Words wouldn't make it any easier. And yet they were engrossed in each other. James stroked Nina's hand, turning it over in his own, tenderly tracing the lines on her palm. Nina watched him. She admired again the thick black hair that felt so springy to her touch, the tiny lines around his eyes from time spent in harsh sunlight on the slopes.

When the waitress brought their order she stopped for a chat. James and Nina didn't feel like sharing each other and responded politely enough, hoping she would soon leave them alone.

'I leave on tonight's bus,' Nina blurted out finally.

'Oh, you probably want to be alone?' she smiled apologetically. 'Sorry.'

No sooner had she gone than a young professional couple from Vancouver spotted James and made their way to him. It was like the world was conspiring to interrupt this most poignant of moments.

'Maaaate,' said the man, mimicking the Australian accent.

Luc and his Singapore-born wife Jin were two of James's personal clients who paid a fortune for the privilege of spending an afternoon heli-skiing with the Olympic champion. James introduced Nina as Luc leaned against the low fence separating the two couples. He was obviously settling in for a chat. For a few minutes Nina followed the conversation about some dotcom millionaire she had never heard of, all the while looking at her watch and feeling helpless as her last minutes with James ticked away. Then she excused herself and disappeared into the café. She visited the washroom and rushed outside to James.

'Sorry, Luc,' she said cutting across him. 'It's an urgent call. It's Mr Shima. He needs to talk to James now.'

James was momentarily confused. Shima was the name of Nina's dog who lived at home with her parents. His lips twitched but he leapt to his feet. 'Oh, right then. I'd better go. Sorry, Luc.'

James squeezed Nina's hand as they bolted inside the café. 'Mr Shima, huh?' he said, eyes twinkling.

Ignoring the telephone they paid their bill just as they were spotted by Amelia, the lively boss of the ski school, sitting at a table by the wall.

'Over here,' she called.

'Can't stop,' Nina called back, dragging James out the door. 'Late already.'

Then giggling and feeling like naughty children in hiding they had walked slowly, arm-in-arm, to the bus station, not wanting to arrive. Along the way they ducked into doorways and behind lamp-posts, trying to evade clients, locals and guests.

James watched as the driver put the suitcases inside the hold of the Greyhound bus. Other people milled about, waiting to board or seeing someone off.

'Sorry, folks, we'll be another ten minutes,' said the driver.

Nina felt the lump rising in her throat. This was so hard. James's hand was familiar and reassuring, holding her own. She wondered how she would ever be able to let it go. She knew she would have to very soon. When she did she wanted to be somewhere private, not in this public, sanitised street. She wanted to fling her arms about his neck and draw his face down to hers that one last time.

A voice boomed behind them. It was Wayne, a mountain of a man and another of James's clients. He was friendly and affable. Nina and James had enjoyed dinner with him a few times. He grinned at them both.

'You're off tonight then?' he asked Nina.

'Yes,' she replied in a small voice.

'Well, just as well I caught you.' With that he enveloped her in a smothering bear hug. He smelt of woody aftershave and pine needles. Nina hugged him back.

Then Wayne launched into a new business proposition he had for James while Nina felt the panic rise inside her. She looked at James, willing him to do something, but he looked back helplessly. He couldn't get a word in.

Nina was tired of being polite. She excused herself and disappeared up a side alley. When she had gone far enough down it that she was sure only James could see her, she undid her parka, lifted her jumper and pranced about. At first James's expression was incredulous, then he had trouble holding back his laughter. Next thing Nina knew, he was in front of her, lifting her off the ground and covering the top of her head with kisses. They embraced, holding onto each other with a desperate intensity.

'Bus to Vancouver, now leaving,' boomed the voice of the driver. 'All aboard.'

Nina felt the tears beginning to well. She couldn't speak. James led her to the bus. He squeezed her hand and she bounded up the stairs. Quickly. Without looking back.

James stood at the curb, waiting for her to reappear. She sat halfway down the bus, peering at him through the darkened glass windows. She gave a forlorn little wave. James stood mutely, unable to wave back. The last few passengers climbed aboard and James felt the loneliness roll over him.

She couldn't go.

He bounded up the steps, just as the doors were closing and bought a ticket from the bemused driver and took his seat by a grinning Nina.

'What are you doing?'

'I'm seeing you safely to your destination,' he answered gallantly.

By the time the Greyhound pulled into the Vancouver bus station two and three-quarter hours later, James had proposed and Nina had accepted.

It wasn't something James had planned or Nina had expected. Sitting in the darkened bus, Nina's serious little pixie face illuminated by the occasional passing headlights and the few other passengers well out of earshot, the words came tumbling out of James's mouth. He was trying to articulate the enormity of his feelings. Nina had become integral to his sense of wellbeing, he told her, and he needed to know that he would wake up next to her tomorrow, the week after and every day for the rest of his life.

It was like a waterfall. Once the words were out they had a momentum of their own. There was no way to take them back. Not that James wanted to. As he heard himself say them, it felt right. This was what he wanted.

Nina was astounded. He spoke with such conviction and fervour that it seemed his love for her was solid and almost tangible, quivering in the air, enveloping her. She felt humbled and honoured.

They spent the night at a Vancouver hotel and the next morning James returned alone to Whistler shocked, elated and with a vague plan for the future that started with packing up his life and heading back to Australia.

The ski world was no place for them to start married life, he reasoned. Nina deserved so much more than that. Suddenly he felt very responsible. The future was about more than just the next winter season. It was about building a life together, one day starting a family. The very thought of it brought out all the traditional ideals of his own upbringing that he had managed to submerge most of the time. Sitting beside Nina on the bus, holding her hand, he had started to tell her about the waterwheel on Wilde Wines estate.

They married in Vancouver within two weeks and landed in Australia a week after that. It was all so breathlessly exciting. Before they left Canada Nina took him home to the quaint town of Eyebrow on the edge of the Saskatchewan prairies to meet her bewildered parents. Jake Lambert was not pleased. He told her it was a mistake, she was too young, and a host of other things Nina chose to ignore.

Her father couldn't understand why they had to go to a country he knew nothing about on the other side of the world. Nina had tried to explain. The words fell out of her mouth, tumbling over each other in her excitement. She was in love with this man and would follow him to the ends of the earth, she told her unimpressed father. James had a future in his family's wine business in Australia and she could just as easily start her new career there as in Toronto. It would be an adventure and she hoped her father would be excited for her. She stopped in midstream, suddenly aware of how she must sound. Nina hated to appear foolish or out of control in front of Jake Lambert.

Seeing the crestfallen look on her face, her father had softened slightly. 'You will always have a home with us, always. Don't ever forget that.'

Her mother asked if she was in love.

Nina replied, 'The rest of my life isn't long enough to spend with him.'

Dorothea Lambert rolled her eyes and said, 'That's unfortunate.'

Then she had pressed ten $100 Canadian notes into her hand and told her to keep them somewhere safe.

'Never let on you have it, no matter how dire things become. It's your money,' her mother whispered.

Nina didn't ask where her mother had got the money, how she had managed to save it. She was too shocked. Jake Lambert had always been careful with his money. As a security guard at the Royal Bank he worked hard to put Nina and her brother Larry through school and university. He disliked spending money and most evenings retreated to his shed with the latest do-it-yourself magazine to build furniture for their home. On weekends he gave his time as a volunteer firefighter and park ranger. Dorothea was kept busy with the house and the children and in her spare time was a devoted member of the Quilters' Guild.

Nina had always believed her parents' marriage was unshakeable and her father in control of the family finances. In an instant her mother had blown away both assumptions.

'Don't look so horrified, honey. I stayed, didn't I? And all the time I could have gone. I guess in a funny kind of way that's how I could stay, through the really tough times, knowing I had that money. It was my insurance. I think there can be nothing worse than feeling trapped. No matter how bad things were I always knew at the back of my mind that I could go and take you kids with me and we would be okay. Of course, I never did. Your father can be a bear with a sore head at the best of times but I kind of got used to him.' Dorothea spoke with a smile of such complicity that Nina wasn't sure how to respond. She felt she was getting a glimpse into a private adult world where her parents were different people. It both confused and touched her. She didn't trust herself to speak. There was a huge and painful lump in her throat.

'No matter how good things are between you and James now, promise me that this stays just between you and me. It's our little secret. Your father never knew and there is no reason why James should ever know. But if ever things get so bad you want to come home, you will know you can.'

Then it was time to go. She and James were flying to Australia the next day from Vancouver. She wondered if his parents would be as accepting as hers had been at the news of their sudden marriage. She was so very proud and grateful to her mother for trying valiantly to appear happy for her daughter, even though it meant losing her to a foreign country at the other end of the earth. Dorothea Lambert was used to loss and hardship and she was a stoic woman. She hugged her daughter to her, tears in her eyes and a loving smile lighting up her weatherbeaten face.

Nina remembered it all. The intensity, the mad impetuousness. She stared out the window. She wasn't seeing the harbour with the Saturday morning boats leaving for the races. She was seeing a fit and wiry, neat grey-haired woman with big soft eyes and a heavily lined face, standing by the gate waving her goodbye. And she was remembering that mad, passionate ardent lover. Where had he gone?

CHAPTER 5

Saturday, 19 January 1991

Felix was already in his office when James arrived just before ten.

'You look how I feel,' said Felix.

James tried to smile. It didn't work. He sat down heavily in the chair opposite Felix. James was still numb. The sharp shock of last night's revelations had passed, leaving a creeping acceptance. It was like a wave of dread had encompassed his whole being, swallowing him up so that he felt he was looking at the world from the end of a long tunnel.

'How did this happen?' he asked.

Felix sighed. What could he say? It shouldn't have happened. It was never supposed to happen. He was having trouble coming to terms with it himself. Lloyd's of London, the world insurance giant that insured everything from ships to rock stars' lips, was facing a staggering five billion dollar debt.

The name Lloyd's was synonymous with prestige and privilege. Those lucky enough to be invited to become an investor and join the exclusive club-like organisation had the potential to make handsome profits. It was like a 300-year-old gentlemen's money-making club.

Felix, who came from a long line of sheep farmers and was welcome in most of the elite clubs of Sydney, Melbourne, Perth and London, had been invited eight years ago to become an investor in Lloyd's, known in such hallowed circles as a 'Lloyd's name'. He had, in turn, brought in a few of his special wealthier clients and, four years ago, his best mate James.

Felix believed he had been doing James and the other clients a favour. Not only did they gain access to one of the most prestigious old-money organisations in the world, he was guaranteeing them some easy money with no risk. After all, it was Lloyd's. And for the first two years, as they each received healthy cheques, it had seemed a wise decision. Indeed it had felt like money for nothing.

But now the ground had suddenly been wrenched from under Felix. Lloyd's, the financial icon, was facing a disaster of biblical proportions, and it was up to the 'names' to bail them out. Felix, knowledgeable and canny as he was about money, with years of experience of the unpredictability of world markets, was battling his own sense of shock and outrage. Instead of sending each of the Australian 'names' their regular hefty cheques, Lloyd's had sent out letters demanding money. And lots of it.

He stared across his desk at his friend. James looked crumpled and tired. He was hoping Felix would make sense of it for him. There was no anger in his eyes, no blame or bitterness. He looked – Felix struggled to identify his expression – panic-struck? No, it was an emotion stronger than that. Felix realised with a start that his friend looked frightened. A tic had appeared below his left eye. Felix had seen that before. It only happened when James was under extreme stress.

Felix ran his fingers through his hair, and, feeling the sharp ends of his buzz cut, remembered he had had it all cut off. To give his hands something to do he shuffled the papers on his desk. He felt his own throat tighten. What had he done? Felix coughed, trying to relax his throat muscles. He wanted to erase the panic from his friend's face but he wasn't sure he could.

'No-one could have predicted this. Over the past few years the world has been hit by a string of extraordinary natural disasters the like of which we have never seen before.'

James looked at him uncomprehendingly. Felix continued.

'The Piper Alpha oil rig explosion in 1988, the Exxon Valdez oil spill in July 1989. There were massive European windstorms that caused millions of dollars of damage in 1987. Crop failures in Florida. Hurricane Hugo. More catastrophes have occurred in recent years than have ever been recorded.'

'You sound like a news bulletin,' said James, his voice sharp. He was floundering. He was in over his head and he knew it. 'What's Hurricane Hugo?'

Felix looked at the papers in his hand. 'A storm that hit South Carolina in 1989, causing billions of dollars of damage.'

James looked incredulous. 'You have got to be joking. A storm? I have to pay for a storm in America?'

Felix read from his papers. 'It was a category 5 storm, category 4 when it hit America.'

James shook his head. Felix continued.

'It killed 82 people. The eye of the storm was 30 miles wide. They found dead deer over twenty feet high in trees.'

'They're pretty tall deer.'

Felix smiled thinly at James's humour.

'The deer were normal size,' said Felix patiently. His tone made it clear this was not the time for any of his friend's jokes. 'They were found twenty feet up the trees.'

'Sorry, bad joke.' James sighed. 'Okay, okay. A very bad storm. And I feel sorry for the deer. But I don't get what that has to do with me.'

Felix took a deep breath and tried to focus his mind. He needed to simplify this. James obviously had little idea how Lloyd's worked. Felix wondered how much had sunk in that evening in 1987 when he had taken James to the cocktail party for prospective names. Possibly not much.

He remembered his friend's awe at the luxurious surroundings and the well-known people in the room. But Felix didn't remember him asking too many questions. Felix felt guilty. He was the finance expert. He should have made sure James understood exactly what he was getting into.

'Lloyd's insure against the likelihood of something happening. They figure out the risk and calculate a premium accordingly. The odds against half of the state of South Carolina being blown away would have been horrendous. Just as the likelihood of the Exxon Valdez tanker running aground on a reef and spilling nearly eleven million gallons of oil must have been considered pretty low.

'But for reasons known only to Him, God unleashed His fury and they happened and the Piper Alpha oil rig fire happened as well as a host of other disasters in a short space of time and that left Lloyd's with a whopping great bill for billions.'

James shivered. Exxon Valdez. That definitely rang a bell. It conjured up pitiful poster images of animals covered in black slime. He remembered protesting about it afterwards in Sydney's Botanical Gardens on a warm sunny afternoon.

'How could I ever forget the Exxon Valdez oil spill? It happened in 1989, when I was in Canada. Everyone there was outraged. Nina spent hours one night explaining to me why they all were so upset. Canada is very environment conscious and at Whistler, well, the world is divided into rednecks and greenies. Thousands of otters and rare sea birds died. Just three weeks after we arrived in Australia,

Nina had us marching with thousands of others through the streets of Sydney to demonstrate our outrage at Exxon. They tried to pass it off as a freak accident but the truth was it was just one of a long line of oil spills.'

Felix raised an eyebrow.

'Well, they *were* held accountable,' he said. 'They *were* made to clean up their mess. At a cost. Sorry to tell you, buddy boy, but that cost was borne by Lloyd's insurers. By you.'

The irony wasn't lost on James. He gave a rueful smile. God had a wicked sense of humour. 'How much am I up for, Felix? Give it to me straight.'

Felix shook his head. 'It's too soon to say. Lloyd's are still working out how much they need to pay out for these disasters. Then there's the asbestosis – that's going to be a corker. This is all just the tip of the iceberg. When they have worked out their sums, they will charge the relevant syndicate.'

The syndicate. James remembered when he had heard about the syndicates. They were groups of individual investors who were placed together to underwrite specific policies. The idea of being in a syndicate with the likes of former prime minister Malcolm Fraser and British royalty such as Prince Michael of Kent had completely overawed him. He didn't have to have any money. To join a syndicate with such people he just had to show on paper that he had assets worth $250,000 and he was in.

He had swanned around that Sydney penthouse

suite with a glass of champagne in his hand feeling like he was king of the universe. There were so many names he recognised, Baillieu and Myer, assorted CEOs of Australia's best known companies, faces he recognised from the social pages, the business pages, even the sports pages. Only 616 Australians had been invited to join the exclusive 'club' and James was one of them. It was a badge of honour, like having 'old money' stamped on his passport.

James remembered his pride and excitement, standing there alongside the moneyed elite. He hadn't needed any convincing. He was ready to sign on the dotted line. And then, just when he thought it couldn't get any better, came the icing on the cake: he would have to fly to London to be vetted by a committee, a mere formality he was assured, and to sign the papers.

To the young man who felt that he had failed his country and never measured up to his family, it was a heady mix. How proud his father would be. James pictured his father slapping him on the back jovially and saying something like 'Well done, son.' The image gave him a warm glow.

He broached the subject with Frederick at the first opportunity. James was working on cellar door sales and tastings right next to his father's office at the vineyard but it had taken nearly a week to find his father alone, away from other workers, his brother, his mother, the telephone and the relentless stream of daily problems. Finally, he had his father's undivided attention.

James had been all keyed up and excited, the words bubbling out of his mouth. Frederick had gone on reading his wine magazine, grunting about the latest wine ratings, barely bothering to look up. Frederick mistrusted investing in anything he couldn't plant his feet on. He didn't see it as the golden opportunity that James did nor was he the least bit impressed by the celebrity of the other investors. He wasn't interested in being in a syndicate with judges and prime ministers and royals. What for? He didn't know them. And they could go broke just as easily as anyone else, he had told James. James felt deflated and dismissed.

He had looked at his father in near despair. Frederick would never understand. He didn't think big enough. For two days after the Lloyd's discussion, James had quietly fumed. He resented what he saw as the small-minded way his father ran the business and it started to irritate him how easily his brother and his father worked together. They were like peas in a pod. Apart from being so physically similar, they seemed to know exactly what the other was thinking. Being around them in the vineyard was like hearing only half a conversation as they didn't seem to need words to communicate. James found it hard to keep up. Dinner times were spent with the two of them talking business, Patty agreeing and James keeping his rebellious thoughts to himself.

James carried around two images of himself. On the one hand he saw himself as a hard-working, contributing member of a successful wine family, a former Olympian and a globalist who had seen some of the world and exuded a certain level of sophistication. When his confidence was high and he was happy, that was the person he believed he was. He felt like that around Nina. At other times, when his confidence was low or he was intimidated by people or surroundings, he saw himself as lightweight, a mere adjunct to the family business, a failed Olympian who hadn't brought home a gold medal and the son of nothing more than a small-time, hokey farmer.

James's memories of the summer of 1987 were painful. He didn't like the way that he had behaved and he couldn't think about that time with any sort of clarity. There was an overlay of tumultuous emotion that obscured any sense of reason.

Felix had been surprised to see him standing on the doorstep of his city apartment with his suitcase but had welcomed him anyway. James had told Felix he couldn't join Lloyd's because his father was too much of a dullard and country bumpkin. James remembered every self-superior word he had uttered.

'I need to get as far away from that place as I can,' he had said.

Felix had been happy for James to stay at his apartment but he was leaving for London in a few days. On the spot James decided to go with him. By the time their plane left, James had decided that it was fate and he was meant to go to the sort of places that Lloyd's could take him. He shouldn't allow his father to hold him back.

Tucked into his backpack when he boarded the plane was a letter of credit from his bank in Phillip St, Sydney, secured against his third share of the family business, which he had inherited when he turned 21. That single sheet of paper showed that James had assets of $250,000. It had been so simple. Now all he needed to do was to give that to a bank in England to secure a letter of credit from them and he would be in – a Lloyd's name by the end of the month.

James was quite sure his actions wouldn't have an impact on his father or the business. He didn't waste any energy worrying that he was going directly against his father's wishes. He told himself that his father lacked the foresight and vision that James possessed.

Pride certainly did come before a fall. He had been so puffed up. Now came the fall. It was going to be colossal, commensurate with the appalling degree of pride he had exhibited. Sitting in Felix's office remembering his feelings that night, the gloating and the arrogance, James was filled with self-loathing.

Nina bundled the shopping bags into the boot of the car. A heavy pall of despondency had settled over her as she moved about the supermarket aisles. Toilet cleaner. A replacement for the mop head. Bleach for James's shirts. Nothing glamorous about any of it. She had resented every item, seething against James as she picked them off her list, one by one. She piled it all into the boot, feeling the heavy thud of depression in her chest.

She slammed the boot hard. What was she going to do for the day? She had hoped the weekly shopping would take longer.

She started to manoeuvre the little car into the traffic. Joining the throngs on the road was like being swallowed by a big, moving crocodile. Nina tightened her hands on the wheel, steeled herself and, when she spotted a gap, threw herself in with the rest. Then she could relax, confident she had little else to do. The traffic would take her past Rushcutters Bay to the turn-off for home.

It was turning into a glorious day with the merest hint of a fresh easterly breeze. Nina wound down her window and inhaled the salty air. On the radio an old Mungo Jerry song was playing. It made Nina smile. She had grown up on the edge of the windswept prairies, surrounded by snow for a large part of the year, listening to this music. For the first time in her life the song made sense.

In the summertime, when the weather is fine, you can jump right up and touch the sky . . .

At the foot of the hill Rushcutters Bay was laid out before her, its boats heading out for a day on the harbour from the busy marina of the Cruising Yacht Club. It was the same pretty bay she looked onto from the apartment windows, but seen from an entirely different angle. Instead of little toy boats, parked in orderly rows along the marina, many of the yachts were massive, she realised. And beautiful. They came in all shapes and sizes. Some were small and streamlined, obviously built for speed. Others were the size of a four-storey building. Millions of dollars in fibreglass and brass, floating peacefully in the sun. One had a helicopter perched on its deck.

The park was awash with colour as people frolicked under the massive fig trees. All across the grass they were doing their thing – reading newspapers, playing football, holding hands, watching babies take their first few tentative steps to the picnic rug or dozing mindlessly as flies buzzed around them.

In spite of herself, Nina felt her mood lift. What a beautiful day. A day you would never see again, as her father would say. He used to say that at least once every weekend, pushing her and Larry out onto the back porch with their coats and telling them to make the most of it, regardless of the weather. So here she was with this beautiful day to enjoy. How could she feel miserable? What a waste. What an insult to God.

Suddenly Nina knew exactly what she wanted to do. She wanted to get in amongst it. She wanted to lie on her stomach on the grass reading the newspaper. She wanted to toss off her shoes and wriggle her toes. She wanted to laugh with the small boy unsteady on his feet and smile knowingly with his parents. She wanted the football to land near her newspaper so she could throw it back to those strapping young men in the short shorts.

A car pulled out of its parking spot and Nina swiftly took its place before any other car had a breath of a chance. When she reached the edge of the lawn, she took off her sandals and enjoyed the feel of the spiky cool grass beneath her feet. She walked slowly across the park, skirting around a cricket match and picking her way through groups of people, some alone, some clumped together. In the centre of Rushcutters Park was a kiosk with a few plastic tables and chairs.

Most people bought their toasted foccacia and coffee at the kiosk and took them to their chosen pocket of grass. A gentle slope provided many vantage points to watch the boats coming and going on the harbour. Nina gave her order to the young woman behind the counter and looked around the park, wondering where she would sit. The woman handed across her foccacia and coffee and a paper serviette. She smiled at Nina, a simple, friendly smile. 'Enjoy,' she said before she took the next order, but the spontaneous friendliness was enough. It made Nina feel good. She picked up a discarded newspaper from a plastic table, tucked it under her arm and headed for one of the magnificent fig trees that made the park such a popular spot. Half-a-dozen people were already taking shade under the tree's sprawling canopy.

Nina nestled herself between two massive roots that protruded through the dirt and settled back against the trunk. She appreciated its rough solidity through the thin fabric of her shirt. A cool breeze came off the water. The leaves above her shimmied and twirled, making a gentle, dappled light. There was so much to watch and enjoy as life buzzed around her. The loneliness, her anger at James, all of it was forgotten as the last of the tension in her body dissolved.

Leo had spotted Nina just as she was crossing the grass. She was a graceful figure, lithe and dainty, moving with sensual elegance. She wasn't tall or imposing but she had a presence. It was in the way she carried herself. With her long legs and her short skirt she attracted the attention of most male eyes. Only the men that were more interested in each other didn't look up and follow her progress as she threaded her way through the different groups of people to the kiosk.

Leo was chatting with Nick, his sailing partner, at the edge of the grass. They had met for breakfast to relive the previous night's satisfying victory and then spent a few hours checking the boat and making minor repairs. They were just winding up. Nick was about to get into his car and Leo would walk across the park to his apartment.

Nick spotted Nina first. Just 24, good-looking and full of testosterone, Nick had two interests in life – sailing and women. The merest hint of the female form in his peripheral vision acted as a trigger.

'Whoa, check her out,' he declared, interrupting Leo in mid-conversation.

Leo glanced in the direction Nick was looking and saw what had caught his friend's eye: Nina making her way from the kiosk, shoes held casually in one hand, juggling a paper bag and coffee cup in the other. Leo recognised her immediately. The girl from the taxi the previous evening. She seemed to bounce ever so lightly on the balls of her feet, gliding across the grass.

Nick gave a low whistle. 'I'd give her one, and then one more.'

Leo felt his hackles rise. 'Hey, lay off. I know her.' Leo was as surprised as Nick at the words that came out of his mouth and the sharp tone he heard himself using.

Nick shrugged. Two young women in shorts were unloading hampers of food from the boot of their car. In an instant he was over helping them, leaving Leo alone to watch Nina settle herself against a tree.

Nina licked the last of the melted butter from her fingers, then screwed up the paper bag and relaxed into the tree trunk. All about her people laughed and played and enjoyed the day. She looked at all the high-rise apartments circling the park. She fancied they were like giant filing cabinets that had spilled their contents out onto the grass. She let her thoughts wander, disconnected images passed through her mind and were gone, leaving no trace. The sun warmed her bare legs. A butterfly fluttered for a moment in front of her face. She tried to follow its path but even that was too much effort. She let her eyes blur and enjoyed instead the movement of colour in front of her vision.

It was into that lazy, hazy, mellow world Nina

was enjoying that Leo stepped. There he was, suddenly standing in front of her, smiling in his cheerful, open way, his eyes laughing as if at some private joke. His head was tilted to one side, his baseball cap askew. He wore oversized baggy shorts and a jaunty air. He looked cheeky, like he had just done something very naughty but wasn't going to tell.

'Hello again,' he said.

Nina's immediate reaction was to laugh. 'Hello again,' echoed Nina.

'What are you doing under my favourite tree?' asked Leo.

'Your favourite tree?'

Leo nodded solemnly. 'This tree and I have had a long and fruitful relationship. We are known around these parts as something of a couple.'

Nina felt herself responding. This man is mad, she thought. Quite, quite mad. 'I'm so sorry. I had no idea. I didn't mean to come between the two of you.'

'May I?' Leo gestured with his coffee to a spot beside her.

'But of course,' replied Nina. 'Is it all right with you if I stay?'

Leo appeared to think for a moment, then nodded. Nina moved across to make room for him. It was entirely unnecessary. They were in a park with acres of grass. The nearest person was at least four metres away. But somehow it felt appropriate. Leo waited till she had resettled herself then took the spot she had vacated.

'I often come by after a morning on the boat and sit right here watching the world go by for a bit before heading home. I like this exact tree because it offers the best view of both the marina and the races. Well, you need binoculars to see the races from here.' He looked so naughty that, even though what he said sounded innocent enough, Nina wasn't sure whether he was teasing or not.

'You have a boat at the marina?'

Leo nodded.

'Which one is it?'

He looked across at the mass of boats.

'It's about fifth from the end along there,' he said, pointing. 'The timber sloop with one mast.'

Nina tried to follow his directions.

'She's the wooden one surrounded by a row of fibreglass ones. *Bessie*. A real beauty.'

Coming from inland Canada, Nina knew next to nothing about yachts. The closest she had come to being on one was catching the ferry across the harbour to Manly shortly after she arrived in Sydney. It had been a fun, if slightly nerve-racking experience, feeling the timber sway and vibrate beneath her feet.

Her mouth formed a perfectly shaped O.

Leo laughed. 'Obviously you're not a yachtie.'

Nina shook her head. 'And I'm guessing you're not an Italian count, heir to half of Italy.'

Leo feigned shock. 'You didn't believe that?'

'Not for a minute.'

Leo gasped.

'Okay, maybe for a minute . . . or two,' she said.

'Your Italian accent was quite good, and the hand-waving, very Latin. But I believe the phrase *Mon Dieu* is French.'

'Did I say *Mon Dieu*?'

Nina nodded. 'Uh huh.'

Leo threw his hands in the air. He was so harmless and appealing in his baggy shorts and baseball cap.

Here we go again, thought Nina to herself. 'But I shall always think of you as the fourteenth Count Mauro de March, heir to an Italian coffee empire.'

She felt spontaneous joy bubble up inside her. Leo gazed at her big, round brown eyes flashing with humour and intelligence. They stared at each other for one long moment. Neither spoke. Something gentle and sweet passed between them. It was like there was a subtle shift in the air vibrating around them. They were acutely aware of each other.

And so it began. Under the shade of a sprawling fig tree with a pair of noisy currawong birds quarrelling in its branches and ants crawling unnoticed over their bare feet, Nina and Leo fell in love. Years later, whenever Nina allowed herself to remember that time, she thought of it as slipping rather than falling. It had been so easy and natural, like meeting up with an old friend after too long apart and picking up where they left off. It seemed there was an aura of synchronicity and inevitability about it.

Time ceased to be relevant, but for the next two hours they chatted, laughed, watched and listened.

They were completely intrigued by each other. At times Nina sat leaning against the tree trunk, her legs stuck out in front of her, with Leo cross-legged, his hand on his chin and his face earnest. At other times Nina knelt while Leo lay stretched out beside her, waving his hands about to emphasise a point.

Their conversation was open and wide-ranging. They didn't dwell on the personal, yet they shared some of their most intimate feelings. Nina referred only once to James, though not as her husband, then moved on, revealing nothing of her unhappiness, but sharing her self-consciousness and sense of alienation living in this foreign country. It touched a chord deep within Leo. He understood. He talked of his own school days when he was humiliated constantly by the sports-loving boys. He was the class geek, happy in the science lab, miserable on the football field. He sounded bitter. Leo revealed that he chose sailing because it was a sport he could excel at and it went some way towards healing the scars of his youthful humiliation. He had never admitted that to anyone before and he looked at Nina shyly as he spoke. He talked of his studies and his parents who had died within six months of each other when he was just eighteen, leaving him wealthy and in shock.

They talked of themselves and of the world as they saw it. Important things, trivial things, things that they were excited to discover, things that made them both feel angry or made them both laugh.

Leo told Nina about how, when he was eight,

he used to catch flies then keep them in little prisons he made out of corks, hollowing out a cave in the middle and using his mother's sewing pins to create prison bars. He would proudly present them to his nextdoor neighbour, ten-year-old Kimmie Butler. Together they would tie a single hair around the fly's head and let it out, flying the flies as if they were on a leash.

Nina described Chooky, the chicken she had hatched as part of a school project. Chooky refused to believe it was a chicken. It would not stay in the chicken coop but insisted on living indoors with the family. For the first year of its life it had the run of the house, sleeping on Nina's bed and watching TV from the arm of her father's chair. Then one day it had mysteriously disappeared. Only recently Nina's mother had admitted that Chooky had ended up in the family's Sunday night casserole.

There was nothing untoward in their time together, nothing for Nina to feel guilty about. They were just like two old friends catching up. Yet Nina did not even know his real name. Nor did he know hers. But Nina did know, as she walked back across the grass to her car, that she would see him again. She didn't know when or how it might happen, and it didn't matter. It was as if her world had just expanded and he fitted in somewhere within its new parameters. She didn't explore the feeling, or question it, she just enjoyed it. She had made a new friend. Everything was as it should be. While just that morning the world had seemed a dark and unfriendly place, now everything felt okay again.

There was no thunderbolt from the sky or heartstopping moment to warn her about what she had begun. So there was no moment when she could choose to reject what was unfolding. But by the end of the afternoon, this man had planted himself firmly in her life. It was only looking back, months later, when she was agonising over what she had done and how it had happened, that she realised what had started that day. That gloriously sunny Saturday would be seared onto her psyche forever. Bittersweet and poignant. The beginning of a tender, beautiful and illicit love.

CHAPTER 6

Dr Jones's rooms, 7 February 2001

James continued to stroke the underside of Nina's elbow, gently and unobtrusively trying to impart his strength to her.

'You have our test results, doctor?' he asked.

The doctor addressed himself to James.

'Yes, I have here the results of the genetic tests. The gene for haemochromatosis is carried on chromosome 6 and neither you nor Luke Wilde carry the defective gene that would indicate a predisposition to haemochromatosis.'

James and Nina sighed together with relief.

'Thank God,' she said.

James felt Nina's relief almost before he registered his own. The doctor's words were as direct as they could be. Neither James nor Luke had this deadly, crippling disease. They weren't going to waste away in agony as Frederick had. And James hadn't passed on any genetic weakness to his precious son. Luke was as fit and healthy as he looked. The realisation washed over James like a cool, refreshing shower.

Nina sought out James's hand and squeezed it. She smiled at him.

'He's okay,' said James. 'Luke got the good genes.'

Nina nodded. 'And so did you, my darling.'

They stared at each other for a long moment.

Nina felt a twinge of guilt for putting James through such anxiety. She knew he had been more worried about Luke than he had been about himself. She had caught him looking at the boy with an intense expression of love and fear. It had stopped her dead in her tracks. His anxiety mirrored her own.

Nevertheless, since that startling conversation with Patty a week ago, Nina had known that Luke would be okay. She only had her husband to worry about. But Nina had kept that information to herself, tossing and turning in the night, agonising over what might be the best thing to do.

It was a cruel paradox that if she told James what she now knew to be the truth, he would no longer worry about young Luke – and yet he would be devastated in the process. It was the classic good-news, bad-news scenario. The good news is Luke can't possibly have the genetic weakness. Why not? Ah, that's the bad news. Because he's not your son.

Nina remembered her own shock and pain on being told that very news. And the horror of the revelation was all the more marked because it was James's mother who told her.

Patty had come to town a week ago to sort out some legal matters after Frederick's death. She met Nina and James for lunch and James had left the two women to enjoy dessert and coffee together. As soon as he was gone Nina burst into tears. She was sick with worry that James and Luke might have inherited Frederick's errant gene and the emotional effort of staying positive and cheerful for James's sake had begun to wear her down.

Patty listened and said nothing as Nina poured out her fears, clutching her napkin and sobbing into it, aware she was making a scene in front of the other diners in the otherwise serene hotel dining room. When Nina had finished and her breathing had returned almost to normal, she became aware that Patty wasn't really paying attention: she was looking across to the other side of the dining room. Nina felt immediately contrite.

'Oh Patty, I'm so sorry. How thoughtless of me. You have just lost Frederick and here I am going on about James and Luke. Of course you are as worried about them as I am.'

Patty shrugged. 'Maybe.'

Nina looked at her mother-in-law. Patty's lips were pursed and her eyes were thoughtful. She wouldn't meet Nina's gaze. Nina had known something was wrong, she just didn't know what. And then Patty had dropped her bombshell.

'I'm not so worried about Luke,' she said, watching her own hands as they folded her napkin and placed it neatly by her plate.

Patty lifted her gaze and looked into Nina's eyes. She spoke quietly, with no evident emotion. 'You see, James is sterile,' she announced abruptly. 'He had mumps when he was a boy.'

It took Nina only a few seconds to understand what her mother-in-law was telling her.

'He was about fifteen and his testicles swelled up hard like cricket balls. It was very painful for him, as you might imagine. The doctors said it was the worst case they had seen. It is very rare for mumps to cause sterility, but there you go. James was incredibly unlucky.'

Nina took in little of what Patty was saying. She had just one thought. James was sterile. Luke could not be his son. And Patty had known this all along. She felt the room swim about her. *Of course Luke was James's son. Of course he was.* Her heart cried out for Patty's revelation not to be true. But a little nagging voice, somewhere at the back of Nina's brain, told her otherwise. It was a voice she had silenced long ago.

The possibility had occurred to Nina but only in the early days, when she first discovered she was pregnant. She had worked out her dates and realised there was a chance it was not James's child. But from the moment he was born, Luke was every bit James's son, and Nina had put all such thoughts aside. James believed he was Luke's father. Nina wanted him to be. And anyway, there was every chance he was, she had reasoned. Then she had quite deliberately put a wall around the idea that Luke could be anyone but James's biological son. She never allowed it to surface again.

Her memories of the summer of 1991 were so raw and painful that Nina chose not to think about it. Occasionally they would surface in her dreams and she would wake with an indefinable feeling of longing and desire. Her body would be aflame and she found it hard to concentrate. But she would shake off the feeling and go about her daily life as a wife and a mother.

From the moment Luke was born Nina had been overwhelmed by her love for this scrunched-up little bundle. She was in awe of the ferociousness of her feelings. Their intensity scared her. And she could see her own helpless love mirrored in her husband's eyes. Like Nina, he had fallen completely, devotedly, in love with baby Luke. They had taken turns getting up to him in the night. James had happily danced with him around the lounge room to the *Play School* video. And as Luke grew older, James was the proud father cheering his boy from the sidelines each Saturday, cricket through summer and rugby in winter. He was Luke's father in every sense of the word. Nina felt her blood rising in angry defence. But sitting here opposite her mother-in-law, she stopped herself. The time for self-delusion had passed.

'You have known this all the time,' she whispered.

'Yes,' said Patty matter-of-factly. 'We've always known it. Frederick and I.'

Nina felt the noise of the dining room recede. She remembered discovering she was pregnant and James's surprise then joy. They hadn't planned to start their family so soon. What a special time it had been for them. She had wanted it to be the sign of a new beginning. Those little voices that she had managed to avoid for so long were loud and triumphant in the back of her head now. The guilt and shame of her past had just come screaming up to greet her. The thought of James finding out tore at her soul. She felt a sickening thud in her chest. She could lose him to this illness or she could lose his love and respect. Or both.

Patty's eyes narrowed and she looked at her daughter-in-law with disbelief. 'Don't tell me you didn't know,' said Patty.

'That Luke wasn't James's son?' replied Nina. She shook her head dumbly. Tears poured down her face. Her own napkin was already soaked. Patty handed across hers. Nina struggled to compose herself.

'Why have you never said anything?' asked Nina.

'I wanted to at first but Frederick wouldn't let me,' said Patty. 'He said it wasn't our business. It was between you and James.'

Nina stared at the older woman. There was no trace of malice or judgement or even anger in her demeanour. She could have been telling Nina she would like more cheesecake.

'I've seen the pleasure that child has given my son, and I know the joy he's brought me. As far as

I'm concerned he *is* my grandson, every delicious inch of him.'

Patty's face softened and she smiled at Nina. Nina marvelled at her generosity of spirit. In the past ten years there had never been a hint from Frederick or Patty. They had accepted Luke as if he were their blood. Patty had given Luke as much attention and affection as she had given her other grandchildren. She had always treated Nina warmly, made her welcome in her home. Over the years they had fashioned a relationship of mutual affection and respect. It was quite independent of James's own, sometimes fraught, relationship with his parents.

And all the time she and Frederick had known of Nina's betrayal. Then Nina thought of James and Luke together, side by side on the couch watching some televised sports match. They were close, as a father and son should be. James had encouraged Luke in sport from the moment he could walk. He spent hours throwing a ball for him to catch. When Luke caught it he would say 'What do you expect? He's my son.' When he dropped it, he would tease Nina, saying that it must be her family's lack of sporting abilities coming through. James clearly thought Luke was carrying his genes.

'I don't understand. James believes Luke is his son.'

Patty nodded.

'Yes, I think he does. A few times I have heard him comment about Luke inheriting his talents. So I gathered you hadn't told him.'

'I didn't know,' protested Nina quietly.

'I realise that now,' agreed Patty.

'What I don't understand is, doesn't James know he is sterile?'

'Oh,' said Patty. She looked chastened, guilty almost. 'Well, no. He doesn't know.' She sighed. 'It wasn't something you would tell a boy in puberty. We didn't want him to develop any kind of hang-ups or inferiority complexes. He wasn't interested in girls then so it didn't seem relevant. And when he got a bit older he gave no indication of wanting to settle down. I suppose I also thought that, with medical advances, the problem might be solvable by the time he wanted to start a family.'

Patty's manner changed abruptly. She spoke unnaturally fast, nodding and looking intently at Nina, as if to justify her actions.

Is she trying to convince me or herself, wondered Nina.

'I always intended to tell him but somehow the time was never right. Then he became very angry with us in his twenties. I don't really know why. He just reached that age where everything we did was wrong. Our politics, our way of living, our way of thinking. He grew away from us. I suppose a lot of it was to do with not winning at the Olympics. He became a very angry young man. He and Frederick didn't get along. We hoped he would settle down and work with us on the winery. Then he suddenly took off overseas.

'We were as surprised as anyone when he arrived home with you, his bride. You were both so young, we didn't think you would want to start a family for many years. Frederick and I talked about telling James. We knew we had to and we were just trying to choose the right time. But then you announced you were three months pregnant. I hoped against hope that it was some kind of miracle. But I knew as soon as I saw baby Luke, he wasn't a Wilde.'

Nina heard herself cry out. She had never, ever allowed herself to think that. She had told herself that Luke had inherited his fairer colouring from her side of the family. Larry was sandy-haired. When she looked at Luke, head buried over some comic, or transfixed by the television screen, she had been sure she had seen traces of James. It was in the way he held his head or the way he furrowed his brow in concentration.

She had seen what she wanted to see. The realisation of her own delusion was painful. She had duped everybody, even herself. And all the time Patty and Frederick had known her shameful secret.

While Nina was still absorbing the ramifications of Patty's disclosure, the older woman put her hand on Nina's arm. Her touch was firm and, as she spoke, her fingers tightened around Nina's arm. She increased the pressure until it was almost painful.

'Of course, you can't ever tell James,' she said in a low controlled voice. 'He must never know. You have deluded him this long, it would hurt him too much to find out. You cannot hurt my son in that way. I won't allow it.'

Nina looked into her mother-in-law's face and felt the full force of her iron will. Patty sounded sharp, almost vicious, and her gaze seemed to bore into Nina, pinning her to the spot.

Nina felt a sudden flash of understanding about the family dynamics that had shaped her husband. James's father wouldn't tolerate failure and, she suddenly realised, his mother would not accept a defect in her offspring, her precious son. She would rather live in denial than admit to anything amiss.

Nina felt a rush of loathing for the woman opposite her. What about James? How dare he not be told about something so important. No wonder he stayed away those years, she thought. This family was so controlling, so invasive. And here was the result. What a mess.

But who was she to blame them? Wasn't her betrayal much worse?

For the next few days she had agonised over what she should do. Not to tell James was a further betrayal. But what would telling him achieve? Maybe Patty was right. It might assuage her guilt but it would only hurt James. And it had all happened so long ago.

Nina tried not to revisit the memories of that time. She had done the unthinkable and loved two men. And she had betrayed them both. Yet Nina didn't regret falling for Leo. It had been such a powerful experience she felt it was somehow inevitable that they should meet and fall in love. But a nagging feeling persisted, that she had ended it badly. It was much easier not to think about it, and it had no bearing on their lives today.

She had turned it around and around in her mind, tried out various ways of bringing it up. Every imagined scene ended with James angry, hurt and humiliated. Nina made her decision. She would do everything in her power to keep him from ever finding out.

And so she had gone through the charade of having Luke tested. Her worry was genuine. She hadn't had to fake that. Nina was terrified that James carried the defective gene. But she had kept her enormous relief over Luke to herself, even as she had watched her husband tear himself apart in agony.

Dr Jones watched her smile at her husband. She turned back to the doctor, her expression relieved and happy. Lying bitch, thought the doctor. To be fair, she may not know. There's only one way to find out. He felt a surge of self-righteousness and power.

'*Your* son doesn't have *any* bad Wilde genes,' he said, looking directly at Nina and enunciating the words slowly and clearly. There was a nasty tone in his voice that cut straight through her. The doctor, sitting in his high-backed leather chair, lord of all he surveyed, felt enormous satisfaction as he watched the smile freeze on Nina's face.

CHAPTER 7

Saturday, 19 January 1991

The Bondi Hotel was in full swing. Saturday night at the huge beachside pub was a regular event for many of the bright young things of Sydney. Local surfers in long shorts left their boards on the front verandah while they enjoyed that one quick beer for the road, which would inevitably turn into six or seven. Other patrons, more painstakingly dressed, had driven in from suburbs as far away as Marrickville and Caringbah to shout to each other above the pandemonium. In one bar the three-piece Saturday night band played cover versions of popular songs from the seventies and eighties.

The main bar, full to its 650-person capacity, was frantic, the energy level constantly at fever pitch. By the end of the evening the bar staff would limp out the back door, drenched in sweat, hoarse from yelling and physically exhausted. In the pokie room a couple of purple-haired local pensioners, immaculate in stockings and floral frocks with neat beaded handbags over their arms, sipped their shandies, sitting alongside a group of young men out on a buck's night.

The quietest room was arguably the vast attic bar upstairs where a jukebox played and people gathered around 24 constantly busy pool tables. Patrons poured in here from the dining room and the other bars to watch a bit of pool, or play a quick game before heading somewhere else. Or they settled in for a serious night of competition.

This was where Nina and James and a group of friends had spent the past few hours. They weren't fall-down drunk yet, but both had passed the point of being legally allowed to take control of a car. Nina was feeling vivacious and flirty. The vodka tonics she was merrily downing enhanced her mood. She felt especially sexy tonight, vibrant and full of energy. She sat perched on a bar stool, laughing with the girlfriend of one of James's friends.

James was a few drinks ahead of her, throwing back the beers with an almost manic intensity. He drained the last of the jug into his glass while his mates were still a drink behind.

Felix joined him at the bar where he was ordering another round. 'How are you doing?' he asked, leaning against James's shoulder.

'I'm pretty well,' said James.

His speech was beginning to thicken, a few of

the words running into each other. Felix wasn't much clearer. 'I'm pissed but I want to get pissederer,' he declared.

The two men laughed at the word, repeating it and trying to make it sound correct.

'More pissed,' said James finally.

Felix grinned. 'Okay, Mr English master. I want to get more pissed.'

The barman presented them with two fresh jugs of beer.

'And two tequila shots,' added James.

Felix nodded. 'Good man.'

The barman placed two short glasses in front of them, filling them exactly to the brim.

James and Felix clasped their hands behind their backs and bent down to the counter, looking sideways at each other.

'Up your kilt,' they muttered in unison.

In one fluid motion they took a whole shot glass each in their mouths, threw their heads back, downing the contents, and then spat their empty glasses to land upright on the bar. The barman swept them into the dishwasher tray, wiping away the small rings they left behind and moving on to the next customer. It would get a lot messier than this by the end of the night.

James and Felix each carried a jug back to where their group were playing pool. It was their once-a-month friendly tournament, the girls versus the boys. Felix's girlfriend Miranda had teamed with Nina to play against James and Felix. The stakes were high. Whoever lost made dinner for the other two the following weekend. Already the score was two games to nil, in the boys' favour.

'Your turn, loverboy,' said Nina, handing James a pool cue.

James put down his beer and sauntered up to the table, rolling the cue down his back. He stroked it and caressed it, all the time looking at Nina. He looked more like a B-grade porn star than the pool shark he was trying to be. Nina laughed and sneered.

All around them the pool tables were busy, games being played on each one, and more people waiting for their turn. Cigarette smoke and perfume hung heavily in the air. INXS belted out their current hit – *You want to make her, Suicide blonde, Love devastation, Suicide blonde* – from the jukebox while a couple of girls in cropped tops and tight jeans gyrated nearby.

'It's yours, James. Do your stuff,' Felix called over the din.

James surveyed the table. It could be the winning shot. He and Felix had just the black ball left to sink.

'Baby, hope you have those cookbooks ready,' yelled James to Nina, relishing the moment. 'I'm feeling like duckling à l'orange. What do you say, Felix? Feel like some duckling à l'orange next week?' It was the most exotic sounding dish he could think of.

Felix chuckled. 'I sure do, mate.'

It was the perfect antidote to the pressure James and Felix had been living with for the past 24 hours. They both needed to let off some steam. The alcohol they had been steadily consuming all evening was just beginning to numb some of their anxiety. It also helped to direct their adrenalin towards the game of pool.

But Nina wasn't about to accept defeat lightly. It wasn't in her nature. That, plus her sassy mood and James's cockiness made a volatile combination. She would always rise to a challenge. She winked at Miranda then slid off the bar stool and sauntered to the other end of the pool table, keeping her eyes focussed firmly on James. She was wearing a leather mini that showed off her long, shapely legs and a fitted open-necked shirt.

She slowly and suggestively undid another button on her shirt, revealing more than a hint of cleavage and a lacey red bra. James chalked the end of his pool cue, without taking his eyes of her. Pouting and purring Nina leaned slowly over the table, making sure James had an unobstructed view straight down her shirt. When she was quite sure she had every ounce of his attention, she licked her lips. Michael Hutchence finished his song and while the jukebox lined up the next record, there was a brief lull.

It was during that lull that Nina announced loudly, 'If you get that ball in, I won't do that thing you like.' She said it with all the swagger and bravado of Mae West in a saloon bar, which, in fact, was pretty much how she was feeling. Her words carried across the table to James, past him to the next table and across all the tables in all directions.

It brought every game and conversation to a sudden and complete standstill.

Other players stopped what they were doing to see what would happen. People laughed and sniggered. James looked at Nina, his head on one side, his lips curling with amusement. Nina, emboldened by the alcohol and her already high spirits, licked her lips again and smiled suggestively. The crowd egged her on, yelling ribald comments.

'Go, girl. You've got him by the balls,' called out one woman.

'You poor bastard,' added her date with sympathy.

The mood around the tables was buoyant and charged with expectation as everyone waited to see what James would do. It was clear from their comments that the women had universally sided with Nina and the men were unmistakably with James. No-one, it seemed, remained neutral.

James looked from Felix to his sexy wife pouting at him from the other end of the table and gave an exaggerated shrug to the crowd. Leaning over the table he took careful aim, then slowly and deliberately missed the ball.

The women cheered.

James threw his hands in the air. 'I had no choice,' he wailed.

'No choice, mate,' agreed a man standing nearby.

'Dirty tricks. That's why you don't mix pool with women,' said another.

The crowd peeled off and returned to their own games. Someone fed more money into the jukebox and a whiny country and western singer crooned, *I lost my heart, then I lost yoooou . . .*

Nina sashayed around the table and wrapped her arms around James's neck. She gave him a long, lingering kiss.

'You're wicked,' said James.

'I could be even more wicked,' she replied.

The rest of the group decided they had played enough pool and started to disperse. Nina, hands still around James's neck, made it clear she was keen to go home. But James didn't feel he was drunk enough. As long as he could think, he was aware of a nagging nastiness, somewhere in the back of his mind. He had to keep moving to keep it at bay. Felix understood. He felt the same.

The two men decided they were bored with the pool game and that they must all try another bar up the road. There, Nina and Miranda watched as James and Felix downed successive tequila shots, mumbling incomprehensibly to each other. They were like men possessed.

It was over an hour before Nina got James into a taxi to go home. By then she was beginning to sober up while he was very, very drunk. He tried to engage the driver in a discussion about the Exxon Valdez oil spill. The driver wasn't at all interested but James was far too drunk to notice. He wanted to make a point, but his thinking was confused and he kept changing direction. The company should be made to pay. The company had paid. But had it been the company that finally paid?

Nina could make no sense of it. She hated it when James got like this. She tuned out, turning her head away and watching through her window as the suburbs rolled past. Woollahra. Edgecliff. Rushcutters Bay. The marina. The boats. The park. Beautiful old fig trees. She could see their silhouettes in the dark. Tall, majestic, solid. Their leaves rippling and swaying a little in the evening breeze. She looked at them with longing. And then finally the car entered their cul-de-sac in Elizabeth Bay.

Nina half carried James down the driveway as he sang loudly and tunelessly, *I lost my heart, then I lost yoooou . . .* She didn't bother trying to silence him. She didn't care if he woke all their neighbours.

The next morning dawned bright. The sun burst rudely through the bedroom window at 5.50 am, slamming straight into them both. James buried his head further under the pillow and was again lost to oblivion. Nina lay very still, trying to ignore the painful throbbing inside her head. She was closest to the window so she forced herself to get up and close the curtains. Why hadn't she done it the night before? Urrgh. She eased herself back into bed and was asleep again in seconds.

It was just after 10 o'clock when next she woke. She lay looking at the digital figures on her bedside clock wondering whether today was Monday and they were very, very late or it was the weekend and she could go back to sleep. Flashes of the night before came back to her. The vodka, the pool game, James blabbering in the taxi. That meant it was Sunday. Shit, shit, shit. They were expecting James's brother Mark, his wife Amanda, and their two young boys for lunch.

She rolled over and looked at James. His face was red and creased from the pillow. His mouth was open and the stale, bitter smell of alcohol and the previous night's dinner made her flinch.

She stroked his face. 'James, wake up.'

James opened one eye, groaned and buried his face further in the pillow.

He was still lying face down when she returned from the shower ten minutes later. Nina was feeling less sympathetic than usual. She was still annoyed with James and spending the day with his family wasn't her first choice for a Sunday. Invariably they would talk about the family business and invariably James would get uptight. Nina would feel compelled to try to keep the peace.

Mark and James weren't close. They were too competitive for that. And Nina found Amanda to be hard work. Lunch would be an effort for everybody. But Mark's family were staying in Sydney for the weekend to attend a wedding, so it was natural that they would catch up with Nina and James for lunch. The fact that nobody would enjoy it was beside the point. That was what the Wilde family did.

Nina put her hand on James's shoulder and shook him awake. 'You *have* to get up. They will be here soon,' she said loudly and firmly.

James wondered vaguely what Nina was talking

about. The world came to him through a thick, dense fog. If he opened his eyes everything appeared overbright and sounded overloud. He really didn't want to join in. He wanted to stay in that deadened space, numb to it all.

Nina shook him again, harder. 'Get up.'

The curt tone penetrated the fog and James opened his eyes to glare at its source. 'All right, all right,' he grumbled. It was a bad start to the day. Already they were out of step.

Mark Wilde was a younger, leaner version of his father. Where James took after Patty's side of the family with his black hair, solid build and more refined features, Mark was unmistakably Frederick Wilde's son. He had inherited the Wilde nose, aquiline and strong, and the lanky body and prematurely grey hair. The many seasons spent outdoors amongst the vines showed on his face, which had weathered like his father's, with deep lines etched into his forehead giving him a slightly worried expression. At 32, he looked almost ten years older. Craggy but distinguished.

He had loved Amanda from the moment he met her. Just 26 at the time, handsome, shy and polite, he was also heir to one of the most promising vineyards in the area. Amanda worked during the week for the local federal MP and on weekends she helped Patty and James with tastings at the vineyard. She was just 21, dainty, blonde and self-assured. She could outpick the best of the professional pickers, knew the bottom of a beer schooner as well as a wine glass and, at the age of seventeen, had been Miss Singleton 1981. Mark had a lot of competition. Every man in the Hunter Valley, and a few valleys beyond, knew Amanda Craig.

Mark was never quite sure how he did it, but the day he heard her saying she 'probably wouldn't say no' if he 'popped the question', was one of the happiest days of his life. Although, he had to admit, the arrivals of Lachlan and Harrison, came close. He had a job that absorbed him and a family he adored. All in all Mark was a pretty contented man.

Of all the Wildes, Mark was the one Nina warmed to the most. Although he was only a few years older than her, he reminded Nina of her own father – straight and honest. When family dinners threatened to turn into something more akin to a business board meeting, which happened whenever the Wildes got together, it was often Mark who would stop the conversation to patiently explain something to Nina. Frederick and Patty had few other interests and would happily talk wine every minute of the day. James was so busy trying to prove himself to his father that he didn't seem to notice if they had lost Nina along the way. But Mark did and Nina appreciated his kindness.

Someone who didn't appear to appreciate Mark's thoughtfulness to Nina was Amanda. It seemed to Nina that whenever Mark, or even her own husband, paid attention to her during a family discussion, Amanda would bristle. If Nina dared voice an opinion about wine, Amanda would cut in and talk over her. Nina thought she got the message. What would a Canadian know about Australian wine?

At first Nina had been hurt. She didn't understand the other woman's coolness and wondered what she had done, if she had offended Amanda in some way. At other times, Amanda would sidle up to Nina, link arms and give her the impression she wanted to be her very closest friend. She would ask about Nina's life in Canada, how she liked Australia. She would place her face just inches from Nina's, looking her over, which always made Nina squirm inside. Nina didn't believe Amanda was really interested and would answer her questions warily, waiting for Amanda's attention to wander, which it inevitably did. As a result Nina never trusted Amanda and was unable to relax in her presence.

Most of all, Nina didn't like the way Amanda behaved with James. She was overfamiliar, placing a hand on his arm when she spoke to him or laughing too loudly at something he said. She always seemed false. Sometimes Nina caught Amanda staring at James, turning away when she became aware of Nina's gaze. And just as Amanda seemed to resent Nina's participation in family business discussions, Nina sometimes was left with the impression that Amanda resented her very presence. But then, in an instant, like the flick of a light switch, she would be all smiles and enthusiasm. It was confusing.

Amanda was in complete social mode when they arrived, hugging Nina warmly to her like a long-lost friend. Nina and James, who had barely been speaking before the family arrived, presented a united front, smiling a cheery welcome that they did not feel.

Laden with hampers, rugs and toys, they all wandered down to Rushcutters Bay Park. James and Mark strode ahead, choosing a huge plane tree to settle under. Nina looked about anxiously. She would have preferred to be further away from the Cruising Yacht Club but she couldn't think of a single logical reason that she could present to James as to why this spot wasn't absolutely perfect. They were already touchy enough with each other. The air between them was frigid. Nina hoped Amanda wouldn't notice. Looking all around the park, she laid out the rug. Amanda was watching her with eyes like slits.

'What's wrong with you? Why are you so jumpy?'

Nina immediately felt guilty, caught out. But that was so stupid, she told herself. She had done nothing to feel guilty about. 'Sorry, Amanda, I'm just a bit hungover this morning. What were you saying?'

Amanda was not so easily deterred. Her eyes ranged over Nina's face in a way that Nina was coming to know well. Amanda stared intently at the fidgeting woman in front of her, then looked across at James.

Nina hunted around desperately for something

to say that would divert her attention. She really wasn't in the mood for her sister-in-law today. 'Oh, look at Lachlan. He won't fall in, will he?'

It did the trick. Amanda's head spun around to locate her eldest son. He was leaning over the sandstone seawall, his stubby little legs kicking in the air, watching a dog swimming in the shallow water. He looked perfectly balanced and relaxed but Nina knew Amanda wouldn't see it that way. Amanda sprinted across the grass calling out sharply to her son, scattering the flock of birds in her path and disturbing every other picnicking group. But she didn't care. In fact, thought Nina, it was unlikely she even noticed.

At least it gave Nina some peaceful moments to herself. She laid out the salads and meat plates she had prepared. Snatches of conversation drifted to her from Mark and James. James sounded defensive.

He was always like that with Mark. Nina couldn't understand why. She didn't think it was rational. Mark, it seemed to her, was a gentle soul, used to the slow country life. He deferred to James on anything to do with the city and business. Mark knew just about everything there was to know about wines but you had to spend a lot of time at Wilde Wines to know that. Mark was self-deprecating and humble. 'You've seen the world, little brother. I'm just a country hick. You know more about business than I'll ever know,' he would say admiringly.

James should have taken such comments as his due but he didn't. In any discussion with Mark about the family business or wine, James would become tense and defensive. Nina couldn't make sense of it.

The children provided a welcome distraction through lunch, talking constantly, spilling their food and making it possible for the adults not to address each other directly. Nevertheless, Nina felt strained and on edge.

A young woman carrying a cage in one hand and a large basket in the other took up a position near them. Nina watched in fascination as she settled herself. She spread out a rug, unravelled a long electrical cord she had fashioned into a lead, poked it into the cage, and attached it to whatever was inside, then carefully lifted the lid. Nina expected to see a cat jump out. But instead there was just a mound of motionless brown fur. The woman, oblivious to the curious gaze of Nina and other onlookers who also had started to watch her unusual antics, continued with what appeared to be her weekend ritual, unpacking the newspapers, stripping down to her bikini and lying down to soak up the sun. The mound of fur stayed still and the young woman paid it no attention while she turned the pages of her newspaper.

The boys started to bicker and Amanda rebuked them sharply. Her voice was shrill. Nina didn't think she could bear it one minute longer and before she realised what she was doing, she had leapt to her feet.

'Come on, boys, let's go and see the nice furry animal,' she said with a smile.

Amanda looked surprised, then grateful.

Nina took a boy's hand in each of hers and walked them across the grass. The mound turned out to be a very shy rabbit.

'I live in a high-rise apartment so I bring him down here to run around on the grass, but he is so timid he just stays curled up in there,' explained the young woman with a sigh. 'I have to run around with him to get him to do any exercise.' She was English and happy to talk.

The boys took it in turns to pat the rabbit. Nina marvelled at how quiet and respectful they were. But the bunny still looked terrified, huddling in the corner of the cage.

'It's the doggy smells, I think,' said the young woman. 'He can smell them all around him and that's why he won't come out.'

They chatted about the rabbit until Nina was aware they had outstayed their welcome and should really let the woman get back to her newspaper. When they returned to the others, Mark was asking if James remembered a friend from school, William Nichols. His father owned a sheep farm in the Riverina. He had boarded with Mark. They were in the same year. It took some prompting but finally James could picture him.

'Red-haired guy?' asked James. 'With really skinny legs. A swimmer?'

'That's him,' said Mark. 'Always won the swimming races.'

James nodded.

'Well, it looks like he has lost the lot,' said Mark.

'You know his father died and he took over the farm?'

James nodded.

'Well, he put it up as security with Lloyd's, the insurance company in London . . .'

James sat very still, staring at his brother.

'. . . and was in a syndicate that has been called on for the payout. Apparently he is up for a fortune. It looks like he will lose the farm.'

James felt the sweat break out above his upper lip. He didn't want to brush it away. He suddenly felt self-conscious and didn't want to draw attention to himself in any way. His ears thudded as the blood pounded through his veins. He could see Mark staring at him, expecting him to say something but he was frozen, unable to respond. He didn't trust himself to speak. He just stared, the tic beneath his left eye beating wildly.

The change in mood was palpable. Mark wondered what he had said this time. His brother was so prickly. It didn't seem to matter what Mark said, it was the wrong thing. Had he forgotten some old feud between James and William Nichols? Had James dated his sister or beaten him at footy? Mark felt momentarily exhausted by the effort of finding safe topics to talk about with his brother.

Nina was also looking at James, noting how ill he looked. She wasn't surprised. She had wondered when those tequila shots would catch up with him. The spicy Italian sausage he had just eaten probably hadn't helped.

Amanda had not been paying attention to the

conversation, noting instead Nina's bare unpedicured feet. She was critical of James's wife. She shared some of her observations with Mark but was careful not to go too far. He seldom had a bad word to say about anybody and didn't like it when Amanda did. Indeed, he would have been surprised if he knew just how intensely Amanda disliked their new sister-in-law. Suddenly aware of the silence, she stared blankly at James, wondering if she had missed something important.

James felt all their eyes on him. To him they were accusing, knowledgeable. He felt them boring into him. His breathing became shallow and his chest tightened with the strain on his lungs.

Finally Nina broke the silence. 'Honey, are you going to be sick?' she asked.

She explained that at 3 am that morning he and Felix had been merrily downing vodka shots. Mark remembered his brother's drinking buddy Felix and laughed, relieved he wasn't the cause of James's sudden agitation. Amanda smiled politely and turned her attention back to Nina's feet. Really, they were too big. Unfeminine, she thought.

James looked gratefully at his wife. 'You're right. I don't feel so good. Perhaps we should go.'

Everyone immediately stood up, agreeing that it was time to leave.

When they were alone at home, James and Nina turned on the television news. They were both exhausted from the weekend and sat in companionable silence. James looked at the screen but paid it little attention. He was thinking about

William Nichols and wondering why his brother had mentioned him. James's own troubles with Lloyd's were just a little too close for comfort. Did he suspect something? James shuddered. He felt the chasm opening up in front of him.

His mind moved to safer ground. Nina. She had saved him again. She always did, whether she meant to or not. He thought about her inherent goodness and what a lucky man he was. He put an arm around his wife's shoulder, while continuing to stare at the television.

He didn't know how to articulate these feelings and would be uncomfortable trying. They didn't come in neatly defined snatches. Rather, he felt his love for Nina as a warm wave that washed over him and rendered him mute. He felt humble and grateful. He also felt terrified and shamed. Terrified at what was going to unravel and shamed because he had done it – to his family and to Nina. Trusting, loyal, loving Nina. How could he tell her? He couldn't stand the thought of that trust and admiration fading from her eyes. His mind switched back to the file of papers in his briefcase. He felt cold all over.

He wouldn't tell her. Perhaps there was a way out of this mess and she would never have to know. He was clutching at straws and somewhere in the deepest recesses of his mind, he knew it. But he wasn't ready to admit that to himself just yet.

After dinner he took his briefcase into the study, closed the door and carefully laid out the papers that Felix had given him. Somewhere amongst them there must be a way out.

Nina was surprised to hear the door close. For a moment, when James had put his arm around her shoulder, she hoped he might be coming back to her. For the first time in a number of days, she had started to relax, thinking that they might be falling back into step.

But just as Nina had relaxed and the resentment of the past few days had started to melt, James had removed himself and shut her out. He may as well have slammed the door in her face. That's how she felt. The loneliness and anxieties of the past few days welled up again inside her. She felt tears prick her eyelids. She wished she had someone she could talk to. A girlfriend. A parent. A neighbour. But there was no-one.

All those people who knew her best, and supported her, were back in Canada. Now she had just James. And the sad realisation was dawning that, in fact, she didn't have him. He was miles away from her. She wondered again if he was having an affair. If he had stopped loving her, if their marriage had been a mistake. The thoughts weighed down her heart and she felt very alone. She remembered her mother pressing the Canadian notes into her hand. They were in a sock in her bottom drawer. She had been troubled about putting them there without James's knowledge. Now they gave her comfort.

A familiar face rose suddenly in her mind's eye. It was grinning ear-to-ear with a lopsided cheeky smile that made her feel so good. Her tears stopped.

The vision comforted her. She did have a friend. Kind of. He was more of an acquaintance really but she felt intuitively that he would become a friend. A vague twinge of guilt returned but on closer inspection it seemed silly. Why should she feel guilty? Because he was a man? She shouldn't, she decided. It was just friendship she was contemplating. Good and simple. But what good did it do her? He wasn't here either. Nina wondered when she would see that funny mad man again. She didn't doubt that she would. Her confidence surprised her. Where did that come from?

The TV droned on. Behind the closed study door all was quiet. Nina flicked around the stations unable to settle on any particular show. She looked at her watch. It would be early morning in Eyebrow. Her father would already have been up for an hour or so. His day started before dawn and ended at dusk. Her mother would be in the kitchen making him a hearty breakfast. Nina decided to ring them. It was probably a bit early but she desperately wanted to hear her mother's voice.

CHAPTER 8

Sunday, 20 January 1991

James sat very still behind the closed door of his study. In front of him his briefcase lay open, the Lloyd's file staring up at him, ominous and accusing. He could hear the muffled sound of the Sunday night movie on the television. Last Sunday he and Nina had curled up together on the couch to watch it. His biggest problem then had been how to convince her to watch the Arnold Schwarzenegger movie. He had had no idea of the impending doom. Feelings of failure rose up, like bile from his gut. He had thought he was such a hot shot. Oh, hadn't he felt like Mr Big that afternoon at Lloyd's of London with Felix. He remembered holding his breath as the glass elevator had taken off, three-and-a-half metres a second, quietly and effortlessly propelling them upwards to the top of that awesome building, Number 1 Lime Street, London. At the top the impressed Aussie lad – just 25-years-old – had looked out over London, 27 kilometres in each direction, the city literally at his feet, believing he was a master of the universe. Here I am, James Wilde. Are you ready for me, world?

James and Felix and a group of ten other potential 'names', plus the three insurance agents responsible for bringing them there, had been taken on a leisurely tour of the vast steel-and-glass Lloyd's building. Their fellow recruits were from America, South Africa and New Zealand. Felix and James were the only Aussies and, as James noted to Felix, almost the only ones to have a full head of hair.

'We'd be the youngest by at least twenty years!' whispered James. That idea appealed to him. Just 25 and already he was doing business with the movers and shakers.

The group tour started in the middle of the vast ground floor, surrounded by hundreds of brokers and underwriters shuffling paperwork and talking together, doing deals and moving millions of pounds around amongst themselves. Some spare millions for a new Arab airline fleet, a share in a re-insurance premium for an American shipping line. Who wanted some action? The sheer enormity of the figures being bandied about boggled James's mind as he followed their guide, an attractive young broker, Miss Leanne Dunn, in a conservative blue skirt suit, through the open trade room.

She pointed out the Lutine Bell hanging beneath four huge ornate wooden pillars in the centre of the room. Centuries old, it was traditionally rung whenever a ship went down or was rescued. It could be seen from every corner of the ground floor by every Lloyd's employee, a reminder of their heritage as insurer of the world's greatest shipping lines. James revelled in the history and solidity of it all.

'Fifteen thousand people come through our doors every day to do business using the asset base of 22,000 names,' said Miss Dunn. 'We insure everything from an actress's legs to a shipping tanker.'

'Including the *Titanic*,' whispered Felix. 'Cost them a fortune.'

The American recruit was panting with excitement. He was in his fifties with a high forehead and so much hair, James decided it had to be a toupee.

Miss Dunn smiled at him. 'And we insure Bruce Springsteen's vocal chords. Any damage to them and we are his first port of call.'

The American looked even more impressed. James was worried the man's chest would burst if he puffed it out any further. The group moved up the escalators to the next floor, gliding up the bright yellow conveyor belt, with James keeping his eyes on the Lutine Bell till it disappeared from sight.

'Woody Allen once said that the worst thing in the world is to have dinner with an insurance salesman,' said Miss Dunn. 'This building makes insurance sexy.'

James had to agree it was the sexiest thing he had ever seen. Then it was into the lift, the glass-walled lift that took James's breath away. Up to the twelfth floor, all marble, where the chairman and deputy chairman presided. The chairman was clearly visible through the floor-to-glass walls, sitting at his huge desk, head down, attending to matters of monumental importance.

James got the unstated message. Nothing was out of bounds to a 'name'. When you became a name you became part of this awesome, powerful Lloyd's family. James felt like it was his birthday and he had just been given the whole of London for a present. He tried to be nonchalant, and not look too impressed. He realised he was failing when Felix elbowed him in the ribs, whispering, 'Shut your mouth, James, you're drooling.'

Miss Dunn pointed out a collection of Terence Cuneo paintings in the chairman's anteroom. James had never heard of Terence Cuneo but knew from the tone of awe used by Miss Dunn that he should be impressed. So he was. She explained that Cuneo's specialty was hiding a mouse in each of his paintings. She invited them all to find it, then stood back, a smug smile on her face.

James peered at the enormous picture. It filled most of the wall behind the security guard and showed the opening of the previous Lloyd's building, built in 1957. The Queen Mother and Princess Margaret were surrounded by hundreds of women in elaborate evening gowns and men in ceremonial dress. James studied the painting, sure he would be able to find the mouse, but eventually they all admitted defeat.

Miss Dunn was delighted. She pointed to a pot of flowers on a table in the foreground. James looked again. A tiny mouse was peeking out from the flowers.

'You will find a mouse hidden in each of these paintings,' said Miss Dunn in the clipped tones of an educated Englishwoman. 'It was Cuneo's little joke.'

Felix rolled his eyes as she moved on.

'Cuneo's conundrum. How twee,' he said so only James could hear.

Even though it was Felix's first visit to the new Lloyd's building, which had only opened the year before, he was taking all this wealth and prestige far more calmly than James. Miss Dunn, sensing James's mood, said quietly so that only he could hear, 'I have worked here for five years and I still get hairs on the back of my neck every day I come to work. It really is magnificent.'

When they reached the eleventh floor James nearly lost it, so overwhelmed was he by the unexpected grandeur of the Adam Great Room. Used by the Council of Lloyd's, it was also where they brought prospective 'names' to complete the necessary paperwork.

James gave up all pretence of cool. He was agog at the splendour and magnificence that faced him. Inside this ultra modern, industrial-edged building was the completely intact original 1763 dining room from Bowood House, one of England's most stately homes. James stared about him, his head swimming as Miss Dunn explained how the room had been bought at auction by Lloyd's and moved, piece by piece, including architraves and ornate mouldings, to be reinstalled inside their city headquarters. Priceless artworks lined the walls. Three enormous cut-glass Georgian chandeliers provided light over an eleven-metre boardroom table.

Even Felix had to admit he was impressed. *Finally*, thought James. A liveried waiter ushered the group into the room and invited them all to sit down at the highly polished boardroom table. Miss Dunn handed them over to Mr Nicholas Tuckfield, then withdrew to organise tea.

Mr Tuckfield was stiff and grey-haired with a dark blue suit, double cuffs and Lloyd's cufflinks. He sported a striped regimental tie. His skin was so pale it was almost translucent. He sat upright in his high-backed chair, melding into the fabric so that he could almost have been part of it. He looked like a headmaster at a posh boys' boarding school and James suddenly and irrationally worried that his shoes were muddy.

Mr Tuckfield introduced himself as a senior working name and the rota committee chairman. Next to him sat his clerk, another pasty-faced dark blue-suited gentleman with an array of papers in piles spread out before him.

James thought they could have been undertakers, so sombre was their manner. But he was too overawed by the magnificence of his surroundings to be capable of verbalising any smart comments to

Felix. Seated alongside James and Felix, stretching the length of the highly polished boardroom table, were the ten other new recruits and their agents.

Over the next hour Mr Tuckfield conducted the formal proceedings, explaining how the syndicate system of Lloyd's worked. There were 33,000 individual members, arranged into just over 400 syndicates that underwrote various policies.

There were 37 forms to sign. After explaining each form Mr Tuckfield asked in a grave tone whether the recruits understood that they were accepting unlimited liability. He looked each of them steadfastly in the eye as he spoke.

'Down to your last cufflink, gentlemen,' said Mr Tuckfield.

Surrounded by enormous oil paintings of ancient ships ploughing through rough oceans, James felt he was writing himself into history as he signed his name with a flourish at the bottom of each page.

Finally, his hand cramped from endorsing so many documents, James returned Miss Dunn's Montblanc fountain pen and sat back in the chair, grinning at Felix. It was done. He was a Lloyd's name.

Then they had taken Miss Dunn out for a drink. A drink had led to dinner and an animated discussion between Miss Dunn and Felix over the British financial system, the bond market and why the American stock market's excesses could bring down the world economy. James had left them there, having lost track of their conversation. He had stumbled down to the Tube and shared the platform with half a dozen other men in suits heading home after a few too many at the pub.

James remembered it all. Standing in the midst of the financiers, bankers and traders at the Bank Tube station, he had been unable to stop grinning. He had been so happy.

Sitting in Sydney, four years later, he again heard that clipped sonorous voice repeating the phrase, 'unlimited liability'. He had paid no attention to it then, blinded by his own puffed-up self-importance. Well, now he was going to pay. The unlimited liability that he had so readily dismissed as unimportant meant he owed Lloyd's every single thing he owned, down to his last cufflink.

James didn't own much. He lived in the Wilde Wines apartment, drove the Wilde Wines car. He didn't have art or investments. Though he did have a pair of diamond-encrusted solid gold Cartier cufflinks. They had been his present to himself the day after he had signed up as a name. He and Felix, feeling very important, decided they needed something to commemorate this momentous occasion. They were outrageously expensive but after the way Tuckfield had droned on about 'down to your last cufflink, gentlemen', they had thought it fitting. James didn't care about them. Lloyd's could have them.

But he did care about his third share in Wilde Wines. He had no idea how much it was worth but felt pretty sure it would be at least three or four times the $250,000 of his letter of credit. Unlimited liability meant they could take it all. Every cent he owned. They had no obligation to leave him with even the clothes he was standing up in. How would he ever tell his father? He may as well tell him he had gambled his family inheritance in a poker game. That's how it would appear to Frederick Wilde.

James came out of the study and placed his briefcase by the front door. He had many questions for Felix tomorrow. There were so many things he still didn't understand. The feeling of being in over his head had returned. He wondered who Nina was talking to on the telephone at this hour. Or, more correctly, who was talking to Nina. She stood with her profile to him, looking out across the bay, listening and smiling.

'All right, Mum. Give my love to Dad. I should go now. It's quite late here.'

James watched as she replaced the receiver, smiling to herself. 'Was that Canada?' he asked.

Nina jumped. She hadn't heard him come out of the study. 'Yes. I was just chatting to Mum.'

James's face darkened.

'She said one of the dogs has just had puppies –'

James cut in. 'How long did you talk for?'

Nina looked baffled. She didn't understand his tone or the question. 'What do you mean?'

'How long did you talk for?'

'I don't know. The usual. Half an hour. Maybe more.'

James heart sank. He didn't want to snap at

Nina. It wasn't her fault they were broke. He had always encouraged her to phone her family in Canada as often as she wanted. But that was then. Pre-crisis. It seemed a lifetime ago. He chose his words carefully.

'Please, can you go easy on the calls to Canada? They are expensive and we need to try and save a bit. Sorry, love.' He gave a wan smile.

Nina felt stung. There it was again. No money. She heard her father telling her again, 'No, Nina. We have no money.' How that had hurt. James had unwittingly touched that tender spot.

It also confused Nina. James had always been so generous. It was part of what made her feel safe. He used to take such delight in letting her have whatever she wanted. Now it was suddenly a problem for her to phone home. What was going on? Why was he doing this? Why was he being such a bully? She felt powerless and realised how little control she had over her life now. James had the purse strings and he could dictate what she did. How had her mother known it would become like this? At that moment Nina hated James.

When he came to bed Nina was turned away from him. Her bedside light was out. The message was clear. Usually it didn't matter what had gone on in their individual days or how busy they had been, at night they would always share a kiss and a cuddle before sleep.

James could have tapped his wife gently on the shoulder and poured out his problems. But it didn't occur to him. This was his problem and until he had figured out a way to fix it, it would stay that way. Nina also could have reacted differently, asking James to talk, to open up about whatever was worrying him. But fear and resentment had closed her heart.

So they lay there, rigid and separate, as far apart from each other as they could be without falling out of the bed.

Wednesday, 23 January, 1991

Nina looked at the little ball of fluff sitting on her foot. He was trembling and whimpering, his eyes huge and round as they gazed up at her. Nina's heart was lost in an instant. Around her puppies of all shapes, sizes, breeds and ages rolled over each other in a cacophony of noise and colour. Nina ceased to notice any of them, turning all her attention to the one gently chewing her toe. She leaned down and picked up the little white fur ball, cradling it gently in her hands. It was so tiny, she thought it would fit into the palm of one hand.

'Oh, you poor little thing,' she crooned.

The owner of the dogs' home watched from a distance. Good, she thought. That would be the little bichon frise gone at last. Not a popular choice. Most people who came to Ellie's Puppy Palace in suburban Oatley were looking for a family dog. Labradors were the most popular. Crossed with anything. Everyone, it seemed, had fond memories of a favourite lab-cross from their childhood and wanted one for their own children. That was fine by Ellie. Plenty of those were brought in. But it made it hard for her to find homes for the rest and that made Ellie sad. You didn't run a not-for-profit dogs' home without having a huge soft heart and love for all things canine.

Ellie labelled people according to dog breeds. She did it instantly and instinctively. And once she had made her call, she was immovable. This smartly dressed young woman with the large, sad eyes and short boyish hair reminded Ellie of a dachshund. Small, sleek, even-tempered and loyal. She liked dachshunds, so it was meant as a compliment to Nina.

Ellie waited for Nina to look around for her before she went over. She would give her as much time as she needed to make her choice. Nina cradled the little white bundle, stroking its thin body through the mass of fur. It stopped trembling, responding to the warmth and security of Nina's arms.

'Would you like to come home with me?' she whispered.

The little dog nestled further into the crook of her arm, licking traces of sweat off Nina's skin.

She smiled across at Ellie. 'I'll take this one,' she said.

Getting the puppy home hadn't been a problem. He had sat in the passenger seat watching Nina while she drove. Nina popped him easily into her handbag for the trip up in the lift. And once inside the apartment he had curled up happily on the couch where he watched her move around the room, his huge plaintive eyes melting her heart more with every moment.

By the time James came home the little puppy, which Nina was now calling Tiger, had relaxed enough to sniff around the apartment. Nina had shown him to the kitty-litter tray on the balcony, though he had been disinclined to use it. She was cleaning up the latest little puddle when she heard James's key in the front door.

She shut Tiger in the bathroom and greeted James.

'You look exhausted,' she said.

'I am,' said James.

He had spent the past hour at the pub nearest his office with Felix, going over strategies to deal with Lloyd's. None of them looked good. He sank heavily onto the couch.

'I've got a surprise,' said Nina. 'Stay there.'

She reappeared with a bundle of white fur tucked into the crook of her arm.

It took James a moment to register what Nina was holding. At first he thought it was inanimate, some sort of fluff-covered ball, but it moved its head and James could see a pair of huge brown eyes.

'What is it?' he asked.

'A puppy. A bichon frise,' replied Nina.

James stared at it blankly. 'A dog?'

Nina nodded, smiling. She sat down next to James so he could see Tiger properly.

James moved back. 'Why is he here?'

Nina looked James squarely in the eye. 'I bought him,' she replied.

James stared back at Nina. She wasn't minding him for someone. She had bought him. This wasn't making sense to James's tired brain. There was an edge to Nina's voice that made him wary. 'You bought a dog?' he said.

Nina nodded, keeping her eyes firmly on his. They were sending a message. She was tense and defiant. James supposed it was because she didn't discuss it with him before buying the dog. She was expecting him to object to her foolishness, he thought.

'His name is Tiger.'

Nina sat on the edge of the couch, leaning forward toward him, holding his gaze. She didn't offer the dog to James, holding Tiger possessively in her own arms, against her chest.

Nina hadn't really planned to buy a dog. She had been sitting at work feeling bored and miserable when she decided to give herself the afternoon off. She told her boss she had a toothache, then somehow found herself amongst a bunch of puppies at the lost dogs' home, and next thing she knew she was bringing one home.

That was what she was telling James.

There was a lump in her throat and she felt like she wanted to cry. The effort of keeping her real emotions from erupting was causing her stress.

The dog was a call for help, though she couldn't articulate that. It was a plea to her husband for his attention. Nina was lonely. That was the message.

She held the dog tightly to her while she waited for James to respond. A few options ran through James's mind. He didn't want a dog. Dogs belonged on farms, not in small inner-city apartments. He hated yappy dogs. Nina's manner seemed to be double-edged. James didn't want a fight. Was this some continuation of last night? He couldn't remember what that was all about, just the coldness of Nina's back when he came to bed.

James felt the muscles in his neck spasm. He was tired. He just wanted to sit down and relax, switch off his brain for a few hours, then fall into bed. He wasn't up to the mental gymnastics of a fight with Nina, with anybody.

'Okay, Nina,' he said. His tone was neither cold nor warm, just resigned. 'If you want a puppy I guess you've got yourself a puppy.' With that James stood up and made his way into his study.

Nina stared coldly at the door as it closed behind him. She stared at it for many minutes, her face a hard mask. Then the tears rolled slowly down her cheeks, falling onto Tiger's silky fur.

Australia Day
Saturday, 26 January 1991

James and Nina drove to the Hunter Valley with Tiger asleep on Nina's lap. James had agreed, under sufferance, to take the puppy along, tossing a box and a rug onto the back seat. But Nina had insisted on nursing him. He sat in her arms all the way, seemingly helpless and content, a constant irritant to James.

The dog had become almost physically attached to Nina. Wherever she was in the small apartment, so was Tiger, looking up at her adoringly. It seemed to Nina that he would have been happy to share his affection with James but he knew instinctively it wouldn't be welcome. James repelled him with every look and bodily gesture. That made Tiger nervous so when James was around the dog stayed closer to Nina, which irritated James even further.

The dog had become the physical manifestation of the unspoken tension that sat between James and Nina and, though they would not admit it, they each secretly welcomed the diversion. Neither wanted to address the gulf that was opening between them. They had too much going on elsewhere in their lives.

James was tense about spending the day in the company of his father. It was Australia Day and he had toyed with various excuses as to why he and Nina could not attend the traditional family lunch, but he couldn't bring himself to use any of them. It would disappoint his mother too much.

He knew how it would be. Frederick and Mark would talk business and he would contribute and play along as if nothing out of the ordinary had happened, as if the business's major concern was whether the cabernet grape in the east field had received too much sun. Not whether he had lost his share of Wilde Wines in an investment he had told nobody about. It was possible Frederick Wilde might simply kill him when he knew. James could not imagine telling him. He wasn't about to tell him today. Of that he was certain. It meant continuing to live what he felt was a lie – that everything was all right when it wasn't. It was a disaster. But he wouldn't say anything until he was sure he understood all the ramifications and that he had exhausted every possible way out before he would say a word to anyone. He thought that was the right thing to do. A wave of self-loathing washed over him and he clutched at the steering wheel. His grip stayed tight for the duration of the drive. For the rest of the day the muscles in his hands ached and he wondered why.

Nina was relieved that James seemed so preoccupied. It suited her. She stroked Tiger's fur and watched the countryside speed by. She didn't want to speak to him. She was angry and hurt. She was thinking of her life. It seemed sad and lonely and stretched ahead of her, years and years of living in this alien country without friends, trapped in a marriage with a man who didn't care. She stole a look at James's profile. He was frowning at the road. He seemed so far away from her. He had retreated somewhere she couldn't reach. Where had he gone? Why had he gone? She missed him.

She thought of her Italian count. Being around him made her feel so good. How did he do that? Just a hint of that lopsided grin and she was smiling. She couldn't help herself. She wondered what he was doing right at that moment. Pottering about on his boat? Wandering through Rushcutters Bay Park? Buying coffee?

Out of the corner of his eye James noticed Nina smiling to herself as she patted Tiger. He felt guilty. He had been so negative about the dog. Annoying little thing that it was. All fur and saliva and high-pitched yapping. But he obviously made Nina happy. She looked so far away and dreamy. And he had been so bad tempered. He smiled at her and she smiled back.

It was a lovely warm day and the family started with pre-lunch drinks on the verandah. The bougainvillea was in full bloom, a riot of hot pink entwined around the wooden railing. James, Nina and Amanda sat in huge wicker armchairs with faded floral cushions, looking out across the vines. They watched as Mark walked the two little boys around the rows, trying to tire them so they would be quiet through lunch. Patty was inside, putting the last-minute touches to the cold buffet and Frederick was still in his office, a converted shed attached to the tasting barn.

Nina tried to make polite conversation, turning to Amanda and asking if her week had been busy. Amanda looked at Nina thoughtfully, gave a patronising little smile, then turned to James.

'I understand you allowed the Lotus Bar to order four cases of the 1990 Premium Shiraz. Is that right?'

Nina groaned inwardly. Amanda was in bitch mode, not sisterly mode. How silly of her not to have picked it. Nina hoped, for a brief instant, that James might step in, come to her rescue. But of course he didn't. Instead he seemed to give the question his full consideration.

'Yes, I did. And as a direct result of that our chardonnay was mentioned in two very favourable restaurant reviews . . .'

Nina sighed. She didn't care. Let them talk business. She wouldn't know anything about their precious Premium Shiraz. Nor did she care. 'Come on, Tiger,' she said. 'Let's go and see if Patty would like some help.'

James looked up at Nina as she went past. His face looked stricken. Nina was surprised. It was the same helpless look he would give her when someone cornered him at a party and he wanted Nina to come and rescue him. No way, thought Nina to herself. You are on your own.

Patty asked Nina to prepare a salad. As she shredded the lettuce she watched James and Amanda through the window.

James's arms were crossed and he kept staring either at his shoes or out at the vines. He wouldn't allow Amanda eye contact. Amanda, on the other hand, was leaning forward in her chair, her long bare legs crossed at the thigh, the skirt falling teasingly high.

Nina chuckled to herself. 'Sorry, honey, it ain't going to work.' She amused herself imagining the conversation they were having.

'Hi, look at me, I'm Amanda. No man can resist me.'

‘I’m sorry Amanda, I don’t think so. Too much peroxide for my taste, I’m afraid.’

‘But James, how can you say such a thing? I’m gorgeous. Sex on legs.’

‘No, Amanda. You’re not. You’re a shallow, rude, mean person. And you have fat ankles.’

Nina giggled aloud. She felt a twinge for James. He was so obviously uncomfortable. She sliced through the lettuce, picking out stray snails. It was a huge iceberg, fresh from Patty’s vegie patch.

Nina realised with surprise that James was always uncomfortable around Amanda. She had never put it together before. And yet he would not say a bad word about her. When Nina tried to complain about her mercurial sister-in-law, James would just shrug and say ‘Oh, that’s Amanda.’ And the topic would be closed for discussion.

It was the same with any discussion of his family. Nina had tried to gently coax James to open up about his brother, but he would not be drawn. Everything about the Wilde family seemed complicated. Or that was how they made it. Nina thought of her own family – simple, mad and erratic. But she could cope with that. At least everything was out in the open. With the Wilde family Nina often felt that she was wading through thick treacle.

Amanda fitted in so much better than she did. Nina supposed it was because she was a local girl. She shared their history. And she understood the business, as she was always at great pains to point out to Nina. Until she had children Amanda had worked alongside the family on tastings and door sales. She knew her merlot from her malbec. She was the perfect addition to the Wilde family. It was Nina who was the outsider.

Nina watched as Amanda leaned even closer to James, placing her hand on his arm. Her face was intent and serious, as if she were explaining something very important. Nina was annoyed. That woman, she thought, thinks she is such an expert she has an opinion on everything. How dare she tell James how to do his job. And she couldn't sit in a chair and have a conversation like a normal person. She had to drape herself all over him. Nina studied Amanda's face. She was very beautiful. Much as she disliked her she had to concede that. Large almond-shaped blue eyes, full mouth, high cheekbones and blonde hair that fell about her face in perfect waves. She continued talking at James, her face just inches from his.

James's reaction was a surprise. Nina expected him to be polite, like he usually was. Instead he leapt out of his chair, his face stormy. He turned on Amanda, his body language aggressive and threatening. Although he was a few feet away from her, she cowered visibly, her face shocked. Nina wasn't sure what she was witnessing.

Patty returned to the kitchen and started speaking to her. Nina was frozen to the spot, unable to turn away from the scene on the verandah. Patty didn't seem to notice that Nina didn't reply and disappeared through the swinging doors, ferrying another tray of food to the dining room.

Amanda stopped cowering and with her hands on her hips, she blazed back at James. This looked to be a full-scale row. Nina wished she could hear what was being said. It made little sense. There was something quite nasty about this scene. These were deep feelings that were being expressed. The veneer of civility that hid their relationship had just peeled away and there was something rotten underneath.

As Nina watched, Frederick Wilde appeared at the doorway of his office and ambled slowly towards the couple on the verandah. At first they didn't notice him, continuing their argument. James spotted him first, said something to Amanda, and in an instant their body language changed. They turned to greet him. The argument ended abruptly. Nina couldn't see their faces but could tell from the broad smile of welcome on Frederick's that as far as he was concerned, nothing was amiss.

'If you bring that salad through I think we are ready,' said Patty, coming back through the swinging doors.

Nina went to the verandah to call everyone to the table. As soon as she appeared James moved to her side, putting his arm around her shoulders. He wasn't usually a demonstrative man and Nina wondered what had prompted the sudden rush of affection. Amanda ignored her, but it was hard to say if that was unusual behaviour or not.

Throughout lunch Nina watched them both. James was subdued, preoccupied and, it seemed, over-solicitous of his mother. He avoided Amanda completely. Most of her attention was taken up with her boys, cutting up their food and helping them to eat it.

Nina waited until the drive home to broach the subject with James. She knew instinctively that she hadn't been meant to see the altercation on the verandah. She was more than a little curious.

'What was that fight with Amanda about?'

James's head snapped around to look at her. He seemed defensive, caught out. She heard him take in his breath sharply. It made an audible hiss. 'What fight?'

Nina stared at him. 'What fight? The blazing row you had on the verandah before lunch.'

James's pupils contracted and he looked instantly shifty. It was not an expression Nina was used to seeing. He was about to lie to her. She knew it with absolute certainty.

'Oh, nothing. It was just about work . . .' His eyes slid off Nina's and returned to the road. '. . . Nothing to worry about. She doesn't agree with some of the things I've been doing. She thinks it was a mistake to let go four cases of the 1990 Premium Shiraz. She thinks we should keep that back for a few more years and . . .'

It sounded plausible but he was lying to her. She knew it. He had never done that before. She would stake her life on it. She felt the ground shifting beneath her, leaving her shaky and scared. What was going on? She petted Tiger and watched the countryside rush by.

★

Saturday, 2 February 1991

Nina busied herself with the newspaper. She didn't want to look like she was sitting here waiting for someone. She had had enough trouble finally admitting that to herself. She took Tiger for an early walk around Rushcutters Bay Park. When he was exhausted, she brought him home for a midday nap. Then she had gone shopping, pushing the trolley around the supermarket aisles, mindlessly tossing items in with just one thought going around in her head. 'I think I might pop back to the park. It's such a lovely day.'

She smiled happily as she handed her money over to the salesgirl, laughed at the toddler who stood behind her in the queue kicking her in the heel, and then commented on what a glorious day it was to the carpark attendant. All the while she kept thinking about ordering a focaccia. Perfect with a coffee. Just the thought of it made her feel so very good.

It was as she parked the car opposite Rushcutters Bay Park that she allowed herself a burst of honesty. She was hoping to see him, the mad count, that unconventional, irrepressible, entertaining man. Really, that was the truth. There was no way around it. With that realisation came a moment of indecision, as that little voice, niggling away at the back of her mind, strained to be heard. Was that really such a good idea? Should she be doing this? The thought of James hovered just on the periphery. She sat for a moment in the car.

She looked out at an ordinary Saturday morning. The cars flashed past her, all strangers, disinterested, separate, going about their business. What do they all do? she wondered. She thought of Amanda, all bare legs and blonde hair draped over James. She thought of him going into the office that morning. She thought of the empty apartment. She didn't consciously decide anything, she just allowed her resentment, anger and suspicion to surface.

Then, quite deliberately, she dismissed those thoughts from her mind.

She told herself it was a perfectly beautiful day and she should be out in it. There were other stirrings further below the surface, but she shied away from looking too closely at those. She stayed determinedly unaware of the workings of her own psyche. It was a technique she had perfected many years ago when she wanted to do something she knew would make her father disapprove.

She opened the car door, her mind made up. And with that her thoughts turned directly and unapologetically to meeting that mysterious, amusing stranger. She hoped he would be finishing his Saturday morning boat maintenance around about now and would pass by her tree on his way home.

Leo, also, had been wondering, hoping, wishing that he might find her by the tree. There was absolutely no reason why she should be there. It was illogical to assume that because she had been there once before, she would be there again, Leo rationalised. But the feeling persisted all through the morning.

When he finally spotted her, on his way across the park, he was delighted and relieved but not really surprised. Of course she would be there. It was fate, he told himself. He bought a coffee at the kiosk and took it over, watching her all the way, waiting for her to look up.

Nina didn't need to look up. She had been keeping a surreptitious eye out for Leo for the past half-hour. Though her head was carefully turned away from the yacht club and she gave every indication she was absorbed in the newspaper on her lap, she had angled herself in such a way that she had spotted Leo the minute he stepped onto the path. Then she had kept her head steadfastly turned away.

Nina's look of sudden surprise, and Leo's cry of 'what a coincidence' were both unconvincing. They immediately knew the other was lying, which lent a sense of mischief and flirtation to the already charged atmosphere. Nina moved over and Leo settled with his coffee into the roots of the tree. They picked up exactly where they had left off. It was as if the time between had dissolved completely.

'When was the last time you climbed a tree?' asked Leo.

Nina remembered exactly. 'On my brother Larry's twenty-first birthday.'

Leo raised one eyebrow.

'We were both living in Vancouver, studying at

the university there, and we decided to go home for the weekend of his birthday to surprise our parents. Larry took a bottle of French champagne. You've got to understand that my parents don't drink, never have. So Larry and I drank the bottle ourselves over lunch and got quite silly. It was something like minus five outside and it had finally stopped snowing. So we dared each other to climb the old oak tree in the garden. We used to spend hours up there when we were kids. Our names are carved into the trunk, just out of view of the ground where our father might see them.

'The two of us got up there and I will never forget my mother and father standing below telling us to come down. It was the funniest thing.

'You have to know my father. All our lives he had been telling us to go outside and climb a tree. We were never allowed to just sit inside by the fire and do something quiet. He always wanted us outside, being active. So here we are, up this tree, both half drunk and our parents are standing beneath telling us to get down out of the tree this minute. "Enough of your shenanigans," my father kept saying. I can picture him now.

'We were both laughing so hard we nearly fell out. Normally we wouldn't dream of disobeying our father. But I don't know what got into us that day. The more they told us to behave, the naughtier we got.'

Nina smiled happily at the memory. She was twenty then and had lived away from home for two years. Yet it was only at that moment that she had felt like an adult, in control of her own life. Seeing her father, her tyrant father, as a comical figure so small beneath her and with the Dutch courage of too much champagne, the moment had marked the beginning of her realising her independence.

Leo smiled with her, trying to imagine Nina's family. The childhood she described was so foreign from his own. They were relaxed in each other's company and their conversation was peppered with nods of understanding and frequent eruptions of laughter.

Around them the world went about its business. People strolled, pushed prams, threw frisbees, jogged, shared picnics, snoozed in the sun, read newspapers and cut across the park on their way to somewhere else. Because of the position of their tree Nina and Leo had the impression they were at the hub of all this activity. Yet, surrounded as they were, they felt quite separate and everything else was just a colourful backdrop. So absorbed were they in each other that at first they didn't notice when the light started to fade as dark clouds moved unexpectedly across the sky. Although only mid-afternoon, the park started to empty.

Leo, attuned to the harbour's ever-changing moods, noticed with a start that the boats were bobbing up and down furiously in the marina. The boats further out on the harbour were lit by the sun, their white sails glowing eerily against the contrasting grey light that was encompassing the park. As the first raindrops landed, heavy and pendulous, the last of the people in the park bolted in all directions.

It was sudden and surprising. Leo leapt to his feet. Nina was a second behind him. She looked about her at the deserted park, then with astonishment at Leo who was climbing the tree.

'What are you doing?' she asked.

Leo shimmied up the trunk to the first branch, just above her head, and grinned down at her. 'Come on up,' he said.

He leaned down offering his hand. Nina hesitated. There must be a thousand reasons why this was not a good idea, but right then she couldn't think of one. Feeling reckless and a bit giddy, she kicked off her sandals and took Leo's hand. Using her other hand for balance, she allowed Leo to take most of her weight and walked her bare feet up the trunk. She was amazed at how strong he was.

The first branch was almost two metres off the ground and once there she could lift herself up to the next branch and then make her way to the fork in the centre. Half-a-dozen branches shot off in all directions, creating a large natural cradle that was covered in leaves and soft moss. Nina felt perfectly safe with her bottom nestled into the cushioned surface and her legs dangling over the edge. Two massive branches, each twenty metres long, ran in opposite directions, parallel to the ground. Leo moved part way along one of these, testing with his weight how far out he could go.

Above them a thick canopy of leaves blocked most of the rain. The occasional droplet found its way through, bouncing off leaves at different angles, getting smaller and smaller until it was just spray that struck their warm bare skin. Around them the rain increased its power, hitting patches where the grass had worn away, sending little sods of soil flying.

While the sun shower rained over the park and bay, further away the sky was still vivid blue and the sun shining. A rainbow appeared above the Cruising Yacht Club. Nina pointed it out to Leo but he had trouble seeing it from where he was sitting. He sidled back along the branch towards her. She made room for him in the comfortable moss-covered cradle. The rainbow was a beautiful sight. Perfect streaks of transparent colour, delicately arched and disappearing behind the apartment blocks on the hill.

They sat perched together, legs hanging over the edge, admiring its flawless beauty. The patter of the rain muffled the noise from the streets around. The park grounds were deserted and awash. Warm and sultry air sat densely around them. Nina was aware of Leo's physical proximity. She felt the heat in every part of her body that was touching his. Both were covered in a sheen of perspiration. Where the bare skin of their thighs rested against each other lightly, they were wet with sweat.

Nina was aware of a delicious throbbing starting deep in her body. She instinctively tightened her thighs together. It created a space between their skin and cooler air wafted past. Leo moved his leg over, to reclaim the space. Nina was instantly and powerfully aroused. It hit her like a bolt of energy. She turned to face him.

Leo leaned forward and with agonising slowness took her lower lip between his teeth. He licked at it with his tongue, then ever-so-gently nibbled it.

Nina closed her eyes and groaned. She wanted him. It was the only emotion she was aware of. It filled her entire body, obliterating everything else from her mind. Her right hand crept around his neck and grasped his warm, sweaty nape, pulling his head into her, his mouth against hers.

Leo returned her passion, probing her mouth with his tongue. Nina leaned against the trunk, feeling it solid and hard behind her back, holding her securely in place. She gave herself over to the sensations that engulfed her. Leo kissed her slowly and deeply. His mouth tasted of fresh coffee, hot and sweet. He licked the rain from her chin, letting his tongue trail down her neck, across her collarbone to the swell of her breasts.

He undid the top button of her shirt and then another, exposing her breasts to the gently falling rain. It was as if every muscle, every cell had melted into warm, liquid honey. As Leo's tongue made contact with her nipple she felt it as an electric charge that shot along the nerves throughout her body. She squirmed and moaned with delight.

Nina had little space to move about. She wanted to be underneath Leo, to feel his weight upon her, to pull him inside her. It was an unbearable ache. The different sensations of pleasure rolled over her, each one stronger in its intensity, building the tension in her body. She was half-mad with lust. Take me, her mind screamed. Leo rolled his tongue slowly and languidly around her nipple, moving his head with agonising slowness down her body, licking and nibbling as he went. With one hand on each branch, and her back hard against the trunk, Nina braced herself as Leo pulled down her shorts.

Nina's hips rose off the seat to meet him, her thighs tensing as her body sought more of that tortuous, darting tongue. It caused such sweet exquisite agony.

Leo sat up and in an instant Nina moved herself onto him, straddling his lap. They fumbled together, their hunger wild and urgent, wanting, needing to meld together. Nina groaned loudly as she felt herself stretched and filled. Their bodies discovered a natural rhythm, a primal dance as old as time. Nina felt her body swell and pulsate. Her pleasure reached a crescendo. No longer aware of what she was doing, she sank her teeth into Leo's shoulder.

Her climax was fierce and violent, leaving her trembling. As she slowly became aware of her surroundings again she was aware of Leo laughing delightedly in her ear. His eyes were closed and he wore an expression of such carefree bliss. She watched fascinated at the joy and wonder that played across his face. Slowly he opened his eyes.

They looked at each other for such a long time, sharing a new knowledge and understanding. Nina had never felt so intimately connected to anyone in her life. Some deep, indefinable need she had carried with her had just been met. It defied articulation but cried out for acknowledgment. She felt humbled and grateful. They stayed entwined, the rain continuing to fall about them, gently swaying and nuzzling into each other's neck.

CHAPTER 91

Wednesday, 6 February 1991

James felt panic, total blind panic. He tried to end the conversation normally, with a cheery good-bye to his father. He thought he had achieved it. Frederick sounded perfectly relaxed and unsuspecting as he rang off.

James had spent days agonising over what he would say and how he would say it, before he made the call. He needed to know if Wilde Wines could pay out Lloyd's. He wanted to know if there was some cash that they could call on. He couldn't ask his father outright but after days of planning different strategies, James believed he had found one that was half plausible. So he picked up the phone and dialled the winery.

James intimated there was a big government program being planned to push Australian wines in

London. Lots of money would be spent on marketing and expensive advertising campaigns. It was not to be anything like the embarrassingly parochial campaign of the early eighties when the government promoted Australian wine under labels like Wallaby White and Roo Red, he assured his father. This campaign was to be sophisticated and slick, putting Australian wines on par with the American wines that were now flooding the British market.

James thought it would be a good opportunity for Wilde Wines to try a toe in the water overseas. But it might require some capital expenditure from Wilde Wines. So, he said, trying to sound businesslike to his patient father, would there be any cash available in the business that they could get at easily if they suddenly needed it? Just if something did come up? Was there any money in the kitty for emergencies or opportunities?

Frederick had appeared interested in the idea. It was something James should definitely keep close to, in case there was some potential for the business. But unfortunately there was no money in the kitty right now. Mark had just spent a few hundred thousand on an osmosis filtration unit and it would take some time for them to pay it off. He had explained that it was all a question of timing and right now Wilde Wines had enough debt. He had chuckled at James's impatience but praised his enthusiasm.

'Good on you, lad,' he said warmly.

James had heard his own voice, trying to sound

cheerful and not reveal the devastation he was feeling. He had switched into automatic mode, saying what was expected. Take care. Have a good week. Love to Mum. His mind was concentrating on making his voice sound normal and steadying his hand, which was shaking uncontrollably as it gripped the telephone receiver.

James burst into Felix's office.

'I'm fucked,' he said. The tic below his eye was working furiously. 'Fucked, fucked, fucked.'

He paced around the room trying to find the words to explain. Felix had a fair idea what was coming but he waited for his friend to tell him.

'There is no kitty. They have just bought some fandangled new osmosis filtration thing that Mark didn't need last year but apparently had to have now.'

Felix slowly shook his head. James didn't have to ask what that meant. He knew. In the pit of his acid-churning stomach, he knew. The sweat broke out on his forehead.

'There is no money to pay out Lloyd's. Felix, does that mean what I think it does? Tell me I'm wrong.' His voice dropped to a whisper. 'Tell me it's not what I think.'

Felix started smoothing his hair. His voice became even quieter. James had to lean forward to hear what he was saying. He felt icy fingers of dread along his skin.

'I'm sorry, James. Lloyd's want their money. And in cash. They don't want a third share in a winery, no matter how much promise it shows. Whatever your share is worth they want it in cash. If you don't have it, they will force you to sell the business to get it. And they are legally able to do that.'

James heard Felix's voice coming to him from what seemed to be a long distance. Confirmation of the ramifications hit him in the chest as a physical blow. He had trouble getting the breath into his lungs. There didn't seem to be enough of it in the room. He leaned forward, his head between his knees, looking for relief. If he could just get some air. The blood rushed through his ears loudly and painfully. He could feel his heart straining in his chest. Panic threatened to overwhelm him.

James breathed slowly and deeply, concentrating on each breath. He wasn't having a heart attack, he told himself. He almost felt disappointment. He accepted that he was in Felix's office, facing a disaster and he just had to deal with it.

'What are you saying?' he asked finally, his voice hoarse. James hoped Felix wouldn't say it, make it real.

'James, your family is going to lose the vineyard.'

In the centre of Leo's living room was a console. It was the nerve centre of his penthouse apartment and from here he could feast on a 360 degree view of Sydney, as well as dictate his world. He turned the living room lights up, the air conditioning off and selected a CD, one of eight already loaded into the Bang & Olufsen player discreetly tucked into a wall unit. *Carmina Burana* rang out, triumphant and vivacious. Leo pottered around the huge apartment, absorbing the power and grandeur of the music.

He unzipped his sailing bag and pulled everything out, tossing dirty polo shirts and socks towards the laundry as he hummed, breaking into Latin for the sections he knew and translating them in his head into English. He set aside a round brass clock, shaped like a porthole, that he had removed from the boat. It had stopped working and he planned to pull it apart later on.

. . . via lata gradior more iuventutis (I travel the broad path as is the way of youth) . . .

The music built to a crescendo of powerful pagan sensuality which he allowed to rise within him.

. . . implicor et vitiis immemor virtutis (I give myself to vice, unmindful of virtue) . . .

He picked up his old sailing jumper. Like most sailors, Leo was superstitious and wouldn't sail out of the marina without this necessary favourite. It was grey, stretched out of shape and had been hand-knitted in cable-stitch by his mother for his father over twenty years ago. Leo forced himself to put it out for the cleaning lady, Mrs Rossetti, to hand-wash every six months or so.

The smell of perfume wafted to his nostrils as he lifted it. It was *her* perfume. He had lent her his jumper briefly in the tree, when he feared she might be cold. He loved seeing her in it. Then she had taken it off and sprinted up the path, out of sight. Leo buried his nose in the wool.

. . . voluptatis avidus magis quam salutis (I am eager for the pleasures of the flesh more than for salvation) . . .

It gave such a faint, delicious hint of that woman. It was an intoxicating scent that had filled his head when he nuzzled between her breasts. It was tantalising to remember it, to try to recapture it. The memory, like the traces of her perfume, was potent but ethereal. The more he tried to grasp it, the further out of his reach it retreated.

He carefully set the jumper aside. Mrs Rossetti wouldn't be getting it this week.

Thursday, 7 February 1991

Leo was early for the scheduled lunch with his accountant. He had found a taxi easily, the traffic had been unusually light, even the traffic lights had continually turned green as they approached. Leo laughed out loud. The whole universe was conspiring in his favour it seemed. So the old saying was true, all the world loved a lover.

He sat patiently at the table, bantering with the waiter Bepi as he juggled dishes and diners around the room. Leo's mood was infectious and Bepi's own bad humour, brought on by too little sleep and too many customers, dissipated. Leo found himself grinning.

'You're sure in a good mood today,' Bepi said. 'Did you win lotto or something?'

Leo laughed. 'Something like that.'

Leo thought of those large brown eyes that

could be so sad and vulnerable one minute and full of mischief the next. He remembered her teeth biting into his shoulder and the sensations that had shuddered through his body. He wondered what *she* was doing right at that moment. He hoped she was thinking of him. For the past few days, since they had come down out of the tree and gone off in their different directions, she had been constantly in his mind, hovering there whether she was the subject of his thoughts or not.

He had never before felt this way about a woman. Usually they fell for him while he kept his heart safely tucked away. Married women, he had found, were a lot less complicated. They knew the rules of the game even better. They didn't demand all his time and energy and the endings were less messy. But that was before he met *her,* she of the lilting voice and laughing eyes. Leo wanted to give her all his time and energy. He wanted to climb back up that tree and stay there.

He explored his emotions. Joy. Euphoria. He planned to feel this way forever. He looked around him and was overcome with pity for everyone else in the room because they couldn't share this bliss.

He sat back in the chair and allowed Bepi to light his cigarette and pour him a glass of chianti. He didn't mind being kept waiting. He would be happy to daydream the rest of the afternoon away. And if he hadn't had classes he would have.

Leo was so absorbed with his thoughts he didn't even notice the pretty blonde woman at the neighbouring table as she played suggestively with the stem of her wine glass, casting him flirty looks from under long thick eyelashes. Bepi noticed and hoped his favourite customer was all right. He really didn't seem to be himself today.

Finally Felix arrived, flustered and frowning.

'Sorry I'm late.'

Leo, not the least bit fussed, tried to put him at ease. 'Relax, I've only just arrived myself.'

Felix was a long way from being relaxed. As he took off his suit jacket Leo noticed large saddlebags of sweat spreading from each underarm across his back. When he was seated he kept running his fingers through his short hair.

Leo poured him a glass of wine. 'This will make you feel better.'

It didn't. Felix felt sick to the core. Seeing Leo so jovial didn't help. Felix was fairly certain he could wipe that smile off his face without too much effort. He had become used to doing that in the past few weeks. Some clients needed more explanation than others. Some had been angry with Felix, others bewildered, one couple wanted to fight Lloyd's all the way. Felix felt personally responsible for them all. The toll of such a burden was beginning to tell.

Leo prattled on about sailing, excited about some race he had won. Felix had trouble concentrating on what he was saying. He didn't care much for sailing himself. Too much water. Leo enquired after business and Felix at last saw his opening. He brought a file out from his briefcase and placed it on the table.

'How long have I been managing your affairs?' he began.

'Eight years. Since I was twenty. Two years after my parents died.'

Felix nodded.

'You've been a great client, Leo. You've always taken my advice and I hope that over the years I've given you good advice.'

'Hey, Felix, I'm happy. Always have been. You sound so serious. What's this all about?'

Felix opened the file and took out some papers. Leo noticed they carried the letterhead Lloyd's of London. Leo remembered leaving a meeting about Lloyd's just . . . when was it . . . three weeks ago? That's right. And what a good thing he had, he thought with a smile. That was when he had met her. Quite simply the sexiest woman alive.

Lost in his private reverie Leo missed some of what Felix was saying. He pulled his mind back. '. . . I don't know what the individual exposure will be. But I have to be honest with you, Leo, it doesn't look good.'

So one of his investments had gone belly up. Is that what was upsetting Felix? Leo was a wealthy man but he paid scant attention to the details, leaving that in Felix's capable hands. And Leo had no reason to doubt he was doing a good job.

Leo lived a conservative life, spending most of his time attending lectures, studying in the university library or pottering about on his boat. In the two years following his parents' death when he was eighteen he had been overwhelmed by financial matters that needed to be attended to, so he had turned to that financial whiz from his school days, Felix Butterworth. In their fifth year of secondary school Leo had paid Felix to do a couple of economics assignments and had been delighted to score high distinctions. When he needed real life financial advice, Felix was the obvious choice. He had told Felix how much he needed to live on and received a generous income to cover it. A few years later when he wanted to buy an apartment, he had bought the nicest one he could find that was within walking distance of the Cruising Yacht Club and Felix had arranged payment. Leo was confident that everything else was being invested and reinvested, which suited him just fine. He was free to get on with what really interested him.

Leo didn't know how much he was worth and it never occurred to him to ask. He had been a Lloyd's name for six years, as his father had been before him. His complacency about his wealth was the result of being born into it. Leo's parents, who were in their forties when he was born, hadn't been flashy people and money was seldom discussed in the family home. They were academics, interested in the pursuit of knowledge and the world of ideas.

Leo, as he had been taught, accepted wealth as his due and then never gave it another thought. He knew his money was spread across many different businesses from shopping centres to hotels to ultra-conservative stocks and bonds.

Now it seemed one of the investments had

gone bad. He wasn't about to lose sleep over it. But he would humour Felix, who really did take such things far too seriously. To be fair, thought Leo, that was what he paid him for.

'How much do I have invested with Lloyd's?' asked Leo.

'It's not that simple,' replied Felix. 'There's just no way of telling at this stage.'

'Bottom line, Felix. What's the worst-case scenario?'

'I don't know. I just don't know. I think you may have to sell off some other investments. And it's not the best time to sell, with what is happening in Asia. But your investments are so varied I think you can weather it. It just depends how much they want from you and at what price I can get them to settle. I won't know that for another few weeks, maybe months.'

Nothing Felix said had caused Leo any alarm. But his fierce expression and obvious agitation did. His skin colour wasn't good and his eyes were bloodshot. Leo thought that Felix needed to lighten up. Find a girl. Fall in love. Leo thought he owed it to his friend to tell him, to try and share his own new-found joy.

'Felix, there is more to life than money. I know it's not exactly an original line but I can't think how else to put it. Money is just money. It's the other things, the things that are harder to define, that make the difference between being truly happy and just existing.' Leo warmed to his theme. He was aware of a profound change occurring in his own life and he struggled to express it in words. 'Perhaps you can only really appreciate that when life shows it to you individually. Happiness is like a precious gift. You know it when you are given it. You can't chase it. You just look up one day and realise you have it. It's when you stand outside yourself, when you lose yourself.'

Felix was looking at him with complete bewilderment and some impatience. Leo sighed at the expression on his face. He realised that to his business-minded accountant who was trying to give him some bad news, he was sounding half mad. Leo chuckled to himself. He didn't mind how he sounded.

'Do whatever you have to do. Just leave me my boat and a roof over my head. Can you promise me that?'

Leo was joking, and laughed as he called for the bill. He was too distracted to notice that Felix didn't respond.

Saturday, 9 February 1991

Nina settled herself by the tree, the newspaper spread across her lap. She didn't bother with any pretence of reading it. The count was all she could think about. She kept rolling his name, Count Mauro de March, around on her tongue. It sounded so voluptuous. She knew he would be expecting her and it was highly likely that whatever he was doing right at that moment, he would be thinking about her. Nina kept flexing her feet, pointing the toe then her heel, then the other foot. She tapped her fingers on the newspaper, enjoying the sound it made. She collated what she knew about him. He did a terrible Italian accent, he liked coffee and he possibly was the greatest storyteller that ever lived. He also had the most appealing smile, a quirky sense of humour, and the nicest neck she had ever nuzzled into.

When James had gone off to work that Saturday morning she had felt nothing but relief. Nina insisted he take the car.

'I won't be needing it,' she had called to him from the shower.

And now she was waiting for her lover. Wicked, lustful woman that she was. Nina felt light-headed with excitement. She kept her eyes fixed firmly on the path from the Cruising Yacht Club, knowing he would be walking towards her some time soon.

Leo seemed distracted all morning, which surprised his crewmate Nick. He kept picking up his binoculars, scanning the park, then putting them down and returning to the job at hand.

'Are you in a hurry?' said Nick.

'Who me?' asked Leo innocently. 'In a hurry to leave you? What could be more important than working on my boat with my best buddy? My favourite part of the week.'

Nick frowned. Leo had been behaving quite oddly all morning. Grinning and unable to sit still, he had leapt around the tiny boat as if charged with energy. Nick decided to stay on and help with the sails, an awkward job for one person. Then, just as Nick settled in to help him retie the spinnaker, suddenly Leo was bounding off, leaving him on his own to sort out the pile of sail and ropes.

'Have a good week, mate,' called Leo as he took off at a fast trot up the ramp, sailing bag slung over his shoulder.

Nick watched him go. 'Well, well, well. That has to be about a woman', he thought to himself. Nick wasn't put out. Leo usually looked after all the boat maintenance and Nick knew how much work that entailed. He appreciated his regular Friday night crew position on this beautiful boat.

'Have fun, mate,' he said to Leo's retreating back.

Leo didn't hear him. His eyes, his ears, his mind were all focussed ahead of him. It was as if he was already with her and yet he ached that he was not. It was such a delightful paradox. He walked quickly.

Nina saw him almost before he appeared. Or that was how it felt. She knew he was coming, sensed it somewhere deep inside, felt a tremor of anticipation, and then he was there, moving rapidly up the path. A short, stocky figure in baggy shorts, baseball cap turned backwards on his head and sailing bag slung over his shoulder.

Nina felt her excitement rise with every step he took towards her. By the time he was standing in front of her she was flexing her toes so hard it was starting to strain the muscles. She barely noticed. He stood in front of her, grinning his lopsided grin. She grinned back.

Leo felt suddenly shy and unsure how to proceed. He wanted her so badly it hurt. He had thought of little else all week. But he didn't want to offend her by being too direct. He had no doubt they would end up in bed, he just wasn't sure of the steps preceding it.

Nina just wanted him to touch her. She ached to feel him.

'You live in one of these apartments, don't you?' she asked. She said it sweetly, with a small coy smile, but her gaze was direct and there was a knowingness in her eyes.

Leo put his hand out to help her to her feet. At his touch Nina felt muscles inside her contract. His hand was firm, dry and warm. Hers was cool and the skin soft. Nina held onto him while she brushed the dirt and leaves from her skirt, moving her hips languidly as she tidied herself.

She let go of his hand and they walked across the edge of the park, a determinedly casual pair of people. Nothing to suggest they were a couple, or intimate in any way.

Every step was delicious agony. They wanted to run, to be alone to savour each other. They walked side by side, occasionally brushing bare arms. The air seemed to buzz with expectation. Anticipation. She wanted him. He wanted her. Their desire vibrated through them and between them as they walked. Nina smiled as they passed the woman and her pet rabbit soaking up the sun. The woman recognised Nina and gave a little wave.

They strolled in a leisurely way down the path

beside the tennis courts, past the two golden retrievers tied to the council sign warning patrons not to bring alcohol or dogs into the park, and across the road to an ultra-modern high-rise.

Leo led her into the foyer of his apartment block and into the lift. He pressed the button for the top floor then stepped back, beside her. They stared at their reflections in the highly polished steel lift doors.

'Shiny doors,' commented Nina.

'Glad you like them. I cleaned them myself, just in case you dropped by,' replied Leo.

As she followed him across the threshold she was aware of the merest twinge of guilt. It was an intellectual awareness, without emotion, and for a fraction of a second she hesitated. Then Leo took her hand, gently squeezing it. Desire was instant. It obliterated all thought. She felt it rising inside her. Unstoppable.

Later as they lay together he propped himself up on one arm to watch her face. He studied her closely, singling out each feature, analysing it, then moving on. Nina responded to his intense scrutiny. She arched one eyebrow, pouted, narrowed her eyes, then opened them wide with surprise. Leo was transfixed.

'Who are you, my lovely?' he said softly. 'I don't even know your name.'

'My name is Ni –' Nina was sorry as soon as she opened her mouth, stopping herself in mid sentence. She felt so relaxed, lying beside him with their legs entwined, she had responded without thinking. But this wasn't part of the game.

Leo thought he understood. He watched her face close over. He wanted her back. 'Knee, now that's a nice name,' he responded lightly.

Nina smiled. 'You can call me Miss Knee,' she said formally. 'It goes better with Count Mauro, don't you think?'

'Miss Knee it is.'

Nina's tension eased and she looked up into Leo's eyes. He traced the line along her cheekbone.

'And was Miss Knee also Miss Canada?'

Nina laughed. 'Actually no, though I nearly won the Miss Eyebrow title when I was thirteen. If it hadn't been for nasty little Judy Jenkins, I would have won.'

'Miss Eyebrow? Am I to believe this nasty Judy Jenkins was considered to have nicer eyebrows than my Miss Knee?'

Nina giggled. 'No, no, no. Eyebrow is the name of the town I grew up in.'

Leo rolled his eyes. 'Of course it is. Miss Knee from Eyebrow.'

'No, truly.' Nina sat up. Sharing her past with this man was part of the game. It reminded her of who she was away from the Wildes. It was what she missed.

'I promise you. I grew up in a town called Eyebrow. It is in Saskatchewan and there is an eye-shaped lake, called Eye Lake. Above that is a row of huge poplar trees that have been there for at least a hundred years. They say that's the eyelashes. The hills around it are the eyebrow and that's where the town is. My parents still live there.'

Leo grinned with delight. 'Stop it, you are making that up.'

Nina knew how it sounded but persevered. 'I'm not. It's true. I promise you. You need a pretty detailed map of Canada to see it but it is there. It's a small town. They say if you blink you'll miss it.'

Leo winced at the pun. 'That's pretty tragic.'

'Oh, we have lots of tragic puns. You want to know where it is? Not far from Elbow.' Nina laughed at the look on Leo's face. 'It's true. There is a town called Elbow not so far from Eyebrow, which is not so far from Moose Jaw.'

Leo shook his head.

'And to think people laugh at some Australian names.'

'Like what? Go on, give me your best shot. What strange names do towns have in Australia?'

Leo thought for a moment. 'Book Book, Willi Willi, Emu Bottom Plains, Spiders Web, Struck Oil.'

It was Nina's turn to look disbelieving. 'Go on, what else?'

'My all time favourite, Pakenham Upper.'

'Pakenham Upper?' repeated Nina.

'Yep. That's a town in Victoria. I've never been there but I have driven past the turn-off. There is a sign, bold as day, that says Pakenham Upper.'

'And people live there?'

'I believe so.'

Nina shook her head. 'You Australians are mad. Moose Jaw suddenly sounds perfectly reasonable. And Eyebrow positively refined.'

Leo traced his finger along her brow. 'What's it like growing up in a country town so small that if you blink you miss it?'

'We have a saying. A little town is where, when you get the wrong telephone number, you can talk for fifteen minutes anyway. That's kind of nice. Frustrating but nice. When I am at home there, somehow I am never in that much of a hurry that I can't spare fifteen minutes for a chat.'

'Sounds idyllic.'

'Mmmmmm. Maybe. The highlight of the year is the lawnmower races at the Eyebrow Fair. That is unless you count climbing the Saskatchewan Wheat Pool Elevator. It gives you the best view of the town and the countryside for miles.'

Leo leaned across and traced her brow with his nose. 'Enough of the geography.' He moved his lips down till they met hers.

CHAPTER 10

Tuesday, 12 February 1991

Nina looked through the photos for the fourth time, slowly studying each one. There were a dozen different shots, all showing her mother and father going about their daily business. Dorothea Lambert in the garden, by the stove, standing next to her father on the front porch, another with her father by the gate. Jake Lambert appeared in only two, which didn't surprise Nina. He would have been much harder to convince to pose. Nina was impressed Larry had managed to get any photographs of him at all.

Jake Lambert stood by his wife, diffident and uncomfortable, smiling shyly at the camera. Nina laughed out loud. She would have liked to have been there to see how Larry managed it. 'Come on, Dad, for Nina.' She could hear him cajoling, begging, praising, trying every trick in the book. Larry was a charmer. It may take him some time but eventually he got his way. After two shots Nina could imagine her father throwing his hands in the air and heading off to his shed. He'd had enough. By then all the charm in the world wouldn't have budged him.

Dorothea stood proudly in her little garden, wearing a faded floral dress and a blue wool cardigan. No, thought Nina with affection, it was a frock. What her mother was wearing should definitely be called a frock. She had half-a-dozen of them, tight-waisted, with full skirts and large floral prints. Nina had never seen her wear trousers. She was stuck in a time warp, circa 1950. Dorothea was smiling shyly, her hand, caught in mid-air, reaching up to neaten a stray wisp that had escaped from her bun.

They were such familiar images; their very ordinariness made them all the more precious.

Larry had enclosed a letter with the photos. It was full of family news and ended by reminding Nina that they were all expecting her home for her birthday in May. Nina looked forward to that. How she missed them all. A trip home was just what she needed.

When James came home she showed him the photos. He looked through them all while Nina read out the letter. '"All Shima's puppies have gone and she is back to her old self, chasing the birds, terrorising the chickens and generally misbehaving . . ."' Nina felt a pang. 'She's too old to still be behaving like a puppy,' she said in an aside to James, then continued reading the letter aloud. '. . . "But you can see that for yourself in May. Mum is very excited about your birthday and I'm not allowed to say anything more about that so I won't (except that I think our Dad the carpenter, ha, ha, is working on something very special for you. Should be a treat for you to take back on the plane . . .!). Anyway, Nina, we all miss you lots and look forward to seeing you soon. Love to James. Larry."'

Nina folded the letter carefully and returned it to the envelope.

'I hate to think what Dad is making out in his shed,' said Nina. 'It will be some piece of furniture for us. It's bound to be hideous. But, whatever it is, when you see it you have to look excited and say something suitable like "Just what we always needed". Okay? Promise me that? No matter how dreadful it is you have to promise me you will love it.' Nina was enthusiastic and bubbly. Her face was radiant. She looked at James. He wasn't smiling. He wasn't sharing her jovial mood at all. 'What is it?'

James sighed. He couldn't lie to her. Not outright. He might be able to justify to himself keeping some things from her because he didn't want to upset her, but he couldn't lie to her.

'Oh, Nina. I'm sorry. I don't think we can afford to go back to Canada in May.'

He watched the smile fade and then her face harden. It took just a matter of seconds. The happiness, the sense of fun and playfulness that had been there ever since she had opened the letter, was wiped away in an instant. She looked angry.

'May I remind you of a promise we made to my parents just eight months ago?' she said slowly and clearly, enunciating each word. 'Once a year, we said. Once a year we would go home.'

James remembered. He had promised Nina's mother he would bring her home every year, rain, hail or shine. He had taken Dorothea's hands in his as he said it, reassuring her that although he was a stranger who was taking her daughter to the other side of the world, she didn't have to worry. He would look after her and bring her home regularly. He believed in families. Indeed his own family would make Nina very welcome. And when they had children it was important that they grew up knowing as much about Canada and their Canadian family as they could. Dorothea should relax. She would see almost as much of her daughter as if she were still living and studying in Vancouver. And when Nina wasn't visiting she would be on the telephone, whenever she wanted. And James had meant every word. He had even known how he would pay for it all.

No matter what other financial commitments came up, he vowed that from the moment he married Nina, those Lloyd's cheques that came in each year would pay for whatever Nina needed to stay in touch with her family.

Nina glared at her husband. Then she picked up Tiger and walked into the bedroom, slamming the door behind her. James had banned Tiger from their bedroom and Nina had happily agreed. Tonight she made it clear the dog was welcome but James was not.

Nina sat on the bed with Tiger in her arms and cried. She wondered again if she had made a mistake. Maybe she had been hasty. She hated to admit her father might have been right. She thought of the money in her sock drawer. It wasn't quite enough for a ticket to Vancouver. The flight prices were advertised every other day in the newspaper so she knew she was a few hundred short. But they were always return fares that were quoted. Nina wondered what a one-way ticket might cost. It was her last thought before she fell asleep.

Wednesday, 13 February 1991

Felix pushed a pile of recent newspaper cuttings across his desk to James, stories from Britain that had been faxed to him overnight.

'Nightmare on Lime Street,' screamed one tabloid headline.

'Signing my name cost me years of my life,' said a more conservative broadsheet.

There were dozens of them, from the finance pages, news pages and feature sections of each of London's ten daily newspapers.

'Thirty-four names have committed suicide directly as a result of losing everything to Lloyd's,' Felix read aloud.

He slid it across to James to continue reading.

> Bailiffs in Britain will start knocking on the doors of some of the grandest homes in the land, threatening to ruin families that in some cases have been wealthy for generations.
>
> If they refuse to pay, bailiffs have instructions to start putting stickers on valuable objects that they intend to seize and sell.
>
> Paintings, carpets, furniture – all will be up for grabs, with Lloyd's hoping its debtors are sitting on some choice pieces that will easily help clear the debts. It could turn out to be a bonanza for auction houses and the antiques trade.

'Can they do that?' asked James in horror. 'Come in and just take your belongings?'

Felix nodded. 'I'm afraid so.'

James had a vision of Tuckfield in his striped regimental tie and Lloyd's cufflinks standing next to his pasty-faced sidekick on his father's doorstep, holding a pen and clipboard. He could see his father's shock turn to outrage as they started putting stickers on the furniture, his valuable collection of Grange reds, even the Jacob Leesing vine growing outside, his parents' most prized possession. He pictured himself wearing just boxer shorts and socks, hurling those precious gold cufflinks after them as they got into their black funeral cars.

He picked up another cutting, banishing the image from his mind.

> In Parliament conservative MPs accused Lloyd's

> underwriters of protecting their own interests while dumping Australians into 'victim' syndicates.
>
> One analysis shows that twice as many Australian names were in high loss syndicates as British members. These allegations are supported by research by a group of loss-making members of Lloyd's in Britain, called the Devonshire Action Group.
>
> Their survey shows Australian members of Lloyd's syndicates were among the biggest losers.
>
> The analysis confirmed the widely held view that Lloyd's is a club for London insiders, particularly in view of the finding that only 9 per cent of working syndicate members – the London insiders – were in loss.
>
> 'The further away you were, the more likely you were to be dumped on one of the bad syndicates – and if you did not speak English you were ripe for the taking,' one researcher said.

'Felix, is that true? Were we dumped into bad syndicates?'

'I don't know. Lloyd's denies it. Their agents deny it.'

'But do you think they did?' insisted James.

Felix was a conservative man. He liked to deal with numbers, tangibles. He seldom operated on gut instinct. It had been so many years since he had heeded any such inner voices that they had long ago fallen silent. When faced with a choice between a conspiracy theory or basic human fallibility, he would always veer towards human error. But this didn't smell right. The problems with asbestosis had been known for a long time. How did so many foreigners – and not just Australians but also Americans, New Zealanders and South Africans – end up in the hardest hit syndicates while the British names continued to make money? Mere coincidence? He thought the conspirators might just have it right this time.

'Yeah, I'd have to say I'm suspicious.'

To James it was the final humiliation. The final spit in the face. The establishment he had been so proud to join had sold him a pup, played him for a sucker. James felt angry. It was a burning ball of irritation in the pit of his stomach.

'Wouldn't that be fraud . . . or insider trading . . . or something?' he asked.

'Yes, but it would be a tough one to prove.'

Felix opened the financial section of that morning's newspaper. He scanned the lead story on the front page and about halfway down started reading aloud.

> According to Melbourne businessman and yachtie Ian Robertson, to be a 'name' meant you should be able to put your hands on readily available cash to pay for the immediate underwriting losses. 'The people who are hurting now, are those who can't,' he said yesterday.

Robertson said that Australian 'names' who claimed they were deliberately placed in loss-making syndicates were wrong.

'That's just sour grapes,' he said. 'Insurance is a very, very risky game.

'If you get into the wrong syndicate, it's just like backing the wrong horse. You lose. Just like a punter. But it's sour grapes to say you were deliberately put into one.'

People who joined in, say, 1988 are horrendously behind the eight ball.

'And mostly they were farmers who, because their cash flow was starting to hurt, thought a way to get out was to put their farm up as collateral for Lloyd's membership. Now, they have no cash to pay for Lloyd's losses and so they're being forced to sell their farms.'

James thought of Mark's school friend William Nichols, the red-haired boy with the long legs who could outswim anyone and who had lost his family's sheep farm. James wondered how he had broken the news to the rest of his family. Sorry, guys, I lost Dad's farm.

At least Nichols didn't have to tell his father. He was already dead. As it was, this news probably would kill James's own father. How would it be to live with that on his conscience? Imagine his poor mother. Or, Frederick would kill James. That was a possibility.

James wondered who he could turn to for help. Who would know the best way to present such news? A psychiatrist? There might be a technique for this sort of thing. The best words and tone to use. A policeman? They had to break tragic news to people all the time. Sorry, sir, your daughter jumped under a speeding train. What about Nina? That was what marriage was supposed to be all about, for better or worse. He pictured the scene. Nina, darling, I've lost Dad's vineyard. How do you think I should tell him? James imagined Nina's face dawning with the realisation that she had married the world's biggest loser. He didn't think he could bear that.

He looked at his friend, bent over a newspaper story. He had a red marker in his hand and was judiciously underlining sections he thought were relevant.

'Felix?'

His friend looked up.

'How do I explain this to my father? What do I say?'

For just a moment Felix stopped thinking of the numbers. He had known the Wilde family since he and James had started senior school together. He had spent holidays at the vineyard. He had taken part in his share of Sunday night family dinners. And on more than a few occasions he had borne the wrath of Frederick. When they were just fifteen and Frederick discovered an empty bottle of a prized museum wine in his cellar, he had dragged the two boys out of bed and made them walk the three kilometres to Broke in the full summer sun to buy him fresh tobacco.

Felix had never suffered so much from a hangover before or since.

He knew how hard Frederick and Patty had worked to build up their business and how much they loved it, every millimetre of it. He knew better than anybody what James was facing. He sought to find the words.

'I don't know, mate,' he said softly. 'I am so sorry.'

Saturday, 16 February 1991

They lay together on the floor of Leo's lounge room, a gentle harbour breeze wafting over their naked skin, drying the sweat and cooling their heated bodies. Nina ran her toe along the arch of Leo's foot.

'You are the most desirable woman I have ever known,' he declared.

Nina believed him. She felt completely sensuous. This man aroused feelings in her of wantonness that she had never felt before.

'Who are you, Miss Knee? Where did you spring from?'

Nina continued caressing Leo's foot, pushing her foot between his toes, then pulling it out and pushing it back in. It was lewd, unsubtle and highly erotic.

'I am your most wicked desire. I am your love slave, here to do obscene things to you . . .' Nina smiled suggestively and slid her body slowly across Leo's. The apartment faced north and the dappled sunlight moved across the carpet, over the rug and their writhing bodies and then up the wall as the afternoon turned into early evening.

Leo knew almost nothing about this woman. She was enigmatic and mysterious. When they were together he felt that he had all of her, she was wholly present. It was only after she was gone that he realised he had nothing.

She talked happily of her past but completely avoided the present. He knew she was married. The ring on her left hand told him that. And he guessed she was unhappy. But those details seemed irrelevant to what was between them. When they were together they were both who they wanted to be. Leo gave more of himself than he ever had before. And Nina gave him her very essence, while remaining impossibly elusive.

He was intrigued, tantalised. And completely smitten. The more she held back, the more he wanted her. He asked her to call him Leo. He didn't want to be Count Mauro any more. He wanted to hear her say his name, his real name. He delighted in the sound of her lilting Canadian voice speaking his name.

He had wanted to ask for her phone number but as he skirted towards it, he had sensed her pulling back. It was enough for today. She was calling him Leo. He lay on his back on the carpet staring at the ceiling for a long time after she left. She was so mercurial, he didn't want to force anything. He knew instinctively that he had to be patient or risk losing her forever. He didn't doubt her feelings for him. He believed they connected on every level. When they were together he felt light and playful. With Nina he was constantly laughing and filled with energy.

He would have to be content waiting until their date next Saturday.

Today he discovered her name was Nina, she was 28 years old and her birthday was 20 May. He had seen it on the inside of her small silver watch as he removed it and laid it aside on the carpet. Happy 21st Nina, love Larry. 20/5/62.

Nina. I want you, Miss Nina.

Tiger nearly bowled Nina over when she finally returned home just after six. She'd raced down the driveway feeling guilty. She hadn't meant to be out this long. She was surprised and relieved that James hadn't come home yet. She heard his key in the lock just as she stepped into the shower. Seconds later his head appeared over the shower curtain.

'Hi. Sorry I'm so late.'

He looked exhausted. His face was grey and he had bags under his eyes. Nina didn't notice.

'That's okay, honey,' she replied, unable to meet his eye as she soaped her body. 'Boy, it was a hot one today wasn't it? Just freshening up. I'll be out in a second. Why don't you open a bottle of something cold?'

James walked back into the lounge room. He had been worried that Nina would be angry with him for all the time he was spending at the office.

Miranda wasn't speaking to Felix at all, completely pissed off at what she called his total neglect of her over the past few weeks. James was relieved that Nina was giving him space. He had told her he had a lot of work things to attend to and she understood. No childish attention-seeking tantrums from his Nina. Not her style. He was such a lucky man. He wondered if she would still feel this way after tomorrow night. D-day. Time to throw himself on his sword.

For now he wanted to make the most of it. A quiet dinner in front of the TV with his loving wife.

CHAPTER 11

Sunday, 17 February 1991

They drove in silence up the freeway to the Hunter Valley. James was consumed by what was to come, what he was going to say. He thought of fleeing the country. Just taking off, never to return. Like Christopher Skase. Spend the rest of his days living it up on a Spanish island. Unfortunately he didn't have any money to live it up anywhere and he couldn't imagine doing that to his mother, never being able to come home.

Then there was the face-the-music approach. Take what he deserved and rebuild his own self respect. There'd be some tough years where everyone would hate him but eventually he would come out the other side. Sounded workable in theory, but how would he actually cope when he was in the eye of the storm?

Well, he would know soon enough. In a few hours that is exactly where he would be. He would be announcing to his family that they were all screwed. He had screwed them. Not deliberately. He wasn't that smart. He was an idiot. A fool. But the result was the same. They were screwed.

He was concerned that Nina had no idea what was to come. He had tried half-heartedly to broach the subject with her but had not been able to. She would look up from whatever she had been doing, her expression dreamy and far away, and somehow the words would not come out. But in a perverse kind of way James was happy that she did not know. That it would be as much of a shock for her as for the rest of the family. It was a way of focussing the disaster. Giving it a climax. Making it as hard for himself as he possibly could.

He supposed he could have prepared Nina, then tried to get each member of the family alone and told them individually, tried to explain himself, one-on-one. But that didn't seem practical. Instead he was going to drop the bombshell and then stand there, a ready target for the combined force of all their outrage and anger. He deserved it. It would be cleansing. He just hoped he was up to it.

Nina, sitting beside her husband as they motored down the freeway, was miles away from him. She was wearing that absent expression that James had noticed but misunderstood. She was thinking of Leo. The smell of his skin. The feel of his hands. The urgency and lust she had felt. She was astounded by its intensity, shocked by her own wanton behaviour. She knew she shouldn't be thinking these thoughts, sitting next to her husband, but she couldn't help herself. She felt wicked and lecherous and bad. Not the good little Nina that the rest of the world expected. But bad. It was glorious.

She thought of their farewell yesterday. She was reliving every lingering moment, when she and Leo had been trying to say goodbye, and feeling the bittersweet pain that set in as soon as she had left him. She marvelled at how she could find pleasure in such pain. Missing him hurt, but with a kind of poignancy. She was happy knowing he was in the world, in her life, and confident knowing that he would be thinking of her too. It made it seem like they were still together even when they were not.

She was thinking also about that spot below his ear, where she liked to nuzzle. She was remembering his hands, not large, but strong, with long tapering fingers and neatly trimmed fingernails. Just the thought of those hands, roaming over her body, sent a wave of longing through her. Those hands that knew her so intimately, knew her secrets, responded to her body's sighs.

Patty cooked her famous lamb roast with everybody's favourite baked vegetables. She always remembered and served each person plenty of whatever it was she knew they liked. For Frederick it was potatoes, Mark preferred pumpkin, Amanda – beetroot, James – carrots. Nina had once admired the baked turnip, more as something to say than because of any great love for the vegetable, but it had been duly noted and, in keeping with Wilde family tradition, Patty gave her a heaped serving of baked turnip at every opportunity. There was rich, pan-juice gravy, homemade mint sauce and a few bottles of choice red wine from the cellar.

James had hinted to his mother that he had some news to share so he hoped they could get dinner out of the way early. Patty had worried what it could be. She hoped James and Nina hadn't decided to leave Australia and move back to Canada, though she kept her fears to herself. She didn't like to think how Frederick would respond to that after James had only just returned to the family fold and business.

Patty kept looking anxiously at James, hoping for some clue as to what might be going on. 'Isn't it lovely that we can be together again for a meal?' she said for the third time. 'I feel very spoiled to have all my family around me again so soon.'

James smiled wanly. Amanda admonished her sons loudly as they bickered and played with their food. It was a tense meal, though no-one really knew why. They were all relieved when it was over and James suggested they move into the sitting room. He stood in front of the huge open fireplace as he waited for the family to make themselves comfortable on the couches and armchairs around the room. Amanda sat her two boys in front of a Wiggles video in another room, then settled herself by Mark's side. Her face was icy.

Nina was surprised by the sudden formality

James was obviously keen to impose. She was further bewildered by Patty's insistence that she sit near James, in the armchair where Patty usually sat. Then her mother-in-law perched on a low ottoman by Frederick's feet. What was James up to? Nina noticed James wasn't meeting anyone's gaze. He stood still, shoulders slightly slumped, hands behind his back, swaying slightly on his feet. Nina noticed the tic beneath his left eye. She felt suddenly and inexplicably apprehensive.

'Go on, boy, we're all here. What's your news?' said Frederick.

James winced. He realised that in getting them all together he might have overdone the theatrics. All his bravado deserted him. He couldn't bring himself to look up and into the faces of his family. His mouth felt like cotton wool. His hands stayed tightly clasped behind his back, gripping each other to quell their shaking.

'I have some rather bad news, I'm afraid,' he began. 'I'm sorry for getting you all here thinking I may have some good news to announce. I don't. But it was important that you all be present to hear what I have to say.'

The mood in the room changed from expectant to wary. Everyone subtly shifted their positions, suddenly not so comfortable in their seats. James noticed and decided it was best if he ploughed right in, before he lost heart.

'I've lost my share of Wilde Wines. I listed it as an asset on an investment some years ago and I'm afraid I have lost it. All of it.'

There, he had said it. As plainly and bluntly as he could. It was out in the open. But there was no thunderclap, no bolt of lightning to accompany his words and James felt no relief. His announcement was met with blank faces. James's heart was racing, pumping the adrenalin around his body. He was ready for fight or flight but his audience was way behind him.

'What are you saying, boy?' asked Frederick Wilde. The old man's tone was gruff but not unkind. To him it seemed his youngest son had his knickers in a knot over something that made no sense. Frederick was prepared to be patient, get to the bottom of whatever was bothering the lad, then sort it out. He was looking forward to uncorking that eight-year-old cabernet from Coonawarra that he had been given and which was now sitting on the sideboard.

James realised no-one in the room was following him. He had thought spilling it all out would bring on the storm, but he was still only on the outside edge, working his way in. He sighed and started on one of the many speeches he had rehearsed in the past week. He nearly lost his nerve a few times, but he had started this and he had no choice now but to keep going.

'When I went to London at the end of 1987 with Felix, I became a "name" for Lloyd's of London Insurance. To do that I had to show that in the unlikely event of being called upon, I had assets of at least $250,000. So I gave them a copy of my letter of deed of Wilde's Wines . . .'

At the mention of Lloyd's of London, Mark and Frederick each felt a tremor of unease. Frederick remembered snippets of a conversation some years ago. He couldn't remember the details, just that he had told James no. Mark thought of his friend William Nichols, who had lost the sheep farm left to him by his family.

'. . . I joined a couple of syndicates, underwrote them, and, although I was assured this would never happen, it has. Due to a series of unprecedented disasters in America, my syndicates have been called upon to pay out a lot of money – millions.'

James's voice wavered and he paused.

'How much do you personally owe?' asked Mark.

James swallowed. Straight for the jugular. Thanks, brother. James lifted his face and looked about him for the first time. He felt the fixed attention of his family like piercing arrows, trained on him and shooting relentlessly. He found a spot on the wall behind them all and kept his eyes focussed on that.

'I showed that I had assets of $250,000 but due to the clause of unlimited liability, I am required to pay everything I have. Every single cent that can conceivably be called mine. Down to my cufflinks.'

Mark looked at his younger brother. His face and his voice were incredulous. 'You signed an investment contract giving unlimited liability? Are you mad?'

James felt he was almost at the centre of the storm. Nearly there. He felt like he was outside his body, watching and appraising. 'Here it comes,' he thought.

He said aloud: 'Mark, it was an incredibly stupid thing to do. I realise that now. Mad, no. Very, very stupid? Yes. Oh yes. Believe me when I say I have never felt so stupid or angry with myself in my life.'

Frederick Wilde spoke. His tone was cold, controlled and direct. 'You invested your share in Lloyd's and now you have lost it. Is that what you're saying, boy?'

He rose in his armchair, his arms taking his weight as he found his legs were suddenly unsteady. But his mind was sharp and completely focussed. He understood in an instant James's phone call the previous week about cash in the kitty. He also understood the ramifications of what James was saying.

'Have you lost my winery?' His eyes bulged and his voice rose from a growl to a roar. 'HAVE YOU LOST MY WINERY?'

Frederick's words surged across the quiet room, ominous and threatening, like a rolling wave of thunder. He glared at his son, his mouth open, a gob of spittle hanging from his bottom lip, while his words reverberated inside the head of each person present. It sent a chill up Nina's spine. Frederick Wilde at the moment of realisation that all he had worked for all his life, all he had built up, was under threat, was a formidable sight. Nina had always sensed he was a man of passion and fire, holding back his energy, keeping it on a tight rein. She felt she was watching the real man emerge, his emotions exploding before her eyes.

James fell back against the mantelpiece as the force of his father's anger and rage hit him. It was a like a solid blow in his abdomen, into his very core. He felt nauseous, as if he really had taken a punch.

Mark also leapt to his feet in shock, though he was unaware he was doing so. He stood facing James, his face a mirror of his father's. Amanda, overcome by the tension in the room, burst into tears, gasping with deep, silent sobs.

James's whole body was tense but his mind stayed strangely calm. He thought he had finally reached the epicentre of the storm. But he was wrong. Sitting quietly on the footstool, unnoticed by everyone else, was James's mother. She had said nothing, given no obvious indication of how she was feeling. While everyone's attention was focussed on Frederick, Patty slid noiselessly to the ground.

CHAPTER 12

Monday, 18 February 1991

James sat on the edge of the bed, his hands hanging limply over the ends of his knees. Nina sat watching him from the swivel chair at his desk. They were in his old bedroom and except for the recent addition of a new double bed, it was exactly as it had been when he lived at home. The bookshelves were filled with school textbooks. *Trigonometry for Year 10. Web of Life. The Oxford Companion to Macbeth.* Photos were pinned to the wall with Blu Tack. Groups of boys in rugby uniform. In one posed photo Nina recognised James and a very young Felix with uncharacteristically long hair reaching almost to his shoulders.

The old house sighed around them.

It made Nina's heart turn over to see James so beaten. She sat beside him on the bed and wrapped her arms around him. His hands stayed limp on his legs, but he let his head fall on her shoulder. Then his body started to shake. He sobbed, without tears. Nina held him, stroking his back, gently scratching that spot beneath his shoulder blades that always seemed to be itchy.

It would be dawn in an hour or so. An end to this awful night. The pitiful sight of Patty Wilde lying very still and pale on the floor was seared onto Nina's brain. It made everything else seem trite. Conversation was clumsy. So they sat together in silence, their exhausted minds still trying to make sense of what had happened.

Nina kept going over and over that moment when Patty had slid to the floor. In her life she had had little experience with illness or death and she wasn't sure what she was seeing. Frederick had cried out Patty's name but she hadn't moved. And then everyone else had. They had rushed to her. Frederick was bending over her, calling her name in a panicked voice. Mark was taking her wrist to feel a pulse. James was on the phone calling an ambulance. It was like a surge of energy with everyone suddenly moving at once. There was a sense of unreality about it all.

The ambulance seemed to take forever to arrive. And when it did two young men came quickly into the room, moving everybody aside with their quiet authority. They took her pulse, lifted back her eye-lids and asked a few questions of the family. As they started to roll Patty onto the stretcher, she began to come round, moaning and talking incoherently.

One of the two ambulance drivers positioned

his face in her line of vision and spoke slowly and loudly. 'Can you tell us your name?'

Patty's eyes swivelled around in her head as she continued to make meaningless sounds. She didn't seem able to hold her focus still or respond to what was going on around her.

'It's going to be okay, Mrs Wilde, we're just going to roll you onto this stretcher and take you in the ambulance to the hospital.'

Patty didn't seem distressed. She kept mumbling but appeared completely unaware of what was going on around her.

The men had carried the stretcher out to the ambulance and driven up the driveway with the red light flashing but no siren. Frederick travelled in the back of the ambulance with Patty. They drove to Singleton Hospital, then Patty was flown by emergency helicopter to the John Hunter Hospital in Newcastle.

Amanda had taken the boys home while James, Nina and Mark had followed the ambulance, then driven the 35 minutes to Newcastle. James took the wheel with Mark sitting tersely in the front seat and Nina in the back. Very little was said by any of them. There hadn't been anything to say. They were all numb.

Dr Barnes, the new young resident doctor, was asleep at his home nearby when the call came in. He arrived at John Hunter Hospital at the same time as Patty. After examining her he came out to talk to the family. He told them he thought she had suffered a stroke.

'What was she like beforehand?' he asked. 'In the hours preceding the collapse?'

They all thought back to dinner. It seemed such a long time ago. Patty had been so happy to have all her family around her.

'Did she show any signs of blurred speech or complain of a headache or tingling in her fingers? Did she complain of feeling unwell? Anything like that?'

They all shook their heads.

'She was pretty happy,' said Mark. 'But then we had some rather . . . er . . . bad news.' He searched for the right words. 'It was some bad family news. It came as a bit of a shock.'

He said it evenly, looking straight at the doctor and not at James. No-one looked at James. They didn't have to. James felt the knife twist in his stomach.

The doctor pursed his lips thoughtfully. 'Why I am asking about any other physical symptoms is that it could tell me whether she suffered the stroke earlier and this was a secondary attack or a worsening of the original symptoms.'

The family looked at each other, remembering their own version of the dinner. They had all been consumed with their own thoughts and realised how unaware they had been of Patty.

'I didn't notice anything,' said Frederick. 'Did any of you?'

The three shook their heads.

'She seemed bright and relaxed,' said Nina. 'As far as I could tell.'

James and Mark both agreed.

'She cooked dinner, seemed happy. She didn't give any indication there was anything wrong,' said Mark.

The doctor seemed satisfied. 'Well, that's a good sign. You got her here pretty quickly. The long-term damage could be minimal. We'll know soon enough.' He suggested they go home and come back in the morning. Frederick preferred to stay, planting himself in a chair pulled up to Patty's bedside. The night nurses hadn't minded, bringing him a cup of tea, pillows and a blanket, without Frederick really being aware they were there.

When James, Nina and Mark said goodbye to Patty, she had looked pale and small against the white hospital linen with an intravenous drip taped to her arm. James had stood awkwardly by his father, wanting to express some of the tumultuous feelings in his heart, but Frederick had been almost oblivious to his presence. Nina took James by the hand and gently led him away. They dropped Mark at his home in Broke and pulled into the driveway of Wilde Wines Estate just after 3 am.

It felt like they had been gone for days.

When finally they lay together under the hand-crocheted bedspread in James's old bedroom they didn't sleep. Nina spooned her body around James's, stroking his arms and his hair. He didn't respond. He was almost catatonic, his breath coming in shallow bursts. He lay in the bed, absorbing her warmth, but with one thought reverberating around his frozen brain. 'Oh my God, I've killed my mother.'

The words spun around in time with the rhythm of Nina's caresses.

It wasn't long till light started to creep through the curtains and the new day dawned.

The family met Dr Barnes and his boss Dr Wilson, the consultant neuro-registrar, in the reception area of the hospital. Dr Wilson was a no-nonsense kind of man in his early fifties. He had an efficient manner that seemed to forestall any emotion. He was here to give the facts as he saw them and that was it. He looked around at each of them, Mark and Amanda, James and Nina and, standing slightly apart and looking like he had slept in his clothes, Frederick.

Dr Wilson addressed himself directly to Frederick, looking him straight in the eye. Frederick took to him immediately.

'Your wife has suffered a stroke,' he said without preamble. 'A blood clot has blocked the blood flow somewhere in her brain. We will know the exact region after a CAT scan. A stroke is like an assault on the brain. The attack is over, has passed, but we can't tell what damage has been done until the associated swelling of the brain has gone down. The first 24 to 48 hours are crucial but it will be six to eight weeks before we know exactly how much residual damage there will be.'

The family absorbed this information. It sounded to them like confusing jargon and didn't really tell them what they needed to know.

Mark voiced their thoughts. 'Is she going to be okay?'

Dr Wilson tried to explain complicated medical information as simply and easily as he could but it was always hard for people to understand, particularly when they were upset and non-medically trained, like the five people looking at him.

He was a patient man. He tried again.

'A stroke can cause instant death or pass by leaving no residual damage. If you put that on a scale, you would have to say that Mrs Wilde is at the good end. She is conscious. Her blood pressure is stable. All her vital signs are good. She is however a little disoriented with some slurring of her speech. This may or may not improve with time. We will be looking for some improvement of that over the next 48 hours, though it will take six to eight weeks for the swelling to reduce completely and only then will we really know the full extent of damage. A CAT scan will tell us more. She is scheduled to have that later today.'

Dr Wilson paused. He thought it was best if the family asked the questions. Providing lots of medical detail usually just confused and further distressed them. In his experience they would ask as and when they needed to know.

'Can we see her?' asked James.

'Of course. But she needs lots of rest so please keep it to a minimum. Don't stay too long and please try not to get her excited.' Dr Wilson sensed his role was finished for the minute and excused himself.

As soon as he had gone Dr Barnes assumed charge and repeated his boss's instructions. 'Please don't tire her or get her overexcited,' he said, adjusting his glasses on the bridge of his nose out of nervous habit. It was his way of reasserting his authority.

The family ignored him. Amanda and Nina took a seat in the waiting room while the men went in. The two women sat in plastic stackable chairs staring at each other.

'What was James thinking . . .?' started Amanda.

Nina cut her off. 'Don't! Now is not the time,' she said coldly.

'No,' agreed Amanda and burst into tears. She looked completely bereft, like a little girl. Nina really didn't like her but found it impossible to ignore someone so clearly in anguish. Almost in spite of herself she leaned over to comfort her.

'I couldn't bear it if she . . . Patty . . . if she . . .' sobbed Amanda. She couldn't finish the thought. It was too horrific to put into words. She clung to Nina, tears splashing down her face and onto Nina's bare legs. Nina watched them slide down her calf.

She was surprised by the other woman's concern for her mother-in-law. This was a side to Amanda she had not seen before. Nina found a clean tissue in her handbag and passed it to her.

'She looked so still lying there on the floor,' sobbed Amanda.

Nina's own eyes filled with tears.

*

Patty was dozing as the men filed silently into her room. Frederick returned to his spot in the armchair pulled up beside Patty's head and his sons stood around the bed. No-one spoke. Patty's skin looked grey against the white sheets. Frederick took her hand, stroking her wrist and she stirred, her eyes flickering open. She looked up at Frederick and smiled.

'How are you, my darling?' Frederick spoke softly and tenderly to his wife.

When Patty tried to speak unintelligible sounds came out and she looked surprised.

Frederick put his fingers to her lips. 'Ssssh, my darling. You need to sleep.'

Patty seemed to think about this, her eyes blinking. She looked confused and worried, then her face relaxed. She looked slowly around the bed, smiling with recognition at each son.

James gave a little wave. 'Hi Mum,' he said.

Patty reached her hand out to him and he took it. Then she closed her eyes again, clearly exhausted by the effort.

They stood there watching her and looking at each other. No-one seemed to want to make a move to leave.

'Go home, Dad,' said Mark. 'Have a shower. I'll stay.'

Frederick's face crumpled. James didn't think he had ever seen him look so old. He put his arm under his elbow.

'Mark's right. Come on, Dad. We'll take you home.'

Frederick didn't put up a fight. He felt numb. He allowed James to lead him out of the room.

The world outside the hospital seemed surreal. To everybody else it was Monday morning and there was business to be done, lives to be organised. James, Frederick and Nina moved through the bustling community feeling a world apart. They spoke little on the drive home. James kept checking his father in the rear vision mirror, wondering what he was thinking and whether there was something he could say. Frederick just looked out the window. Once inside the house he turned to his son.

'We need to talk.' He stared at James for a moment, then, with a sigh, lowered his eyes. 'But not right now.' He looked drained. The fire and passion of the previous evening was gone. Frederick Wilde didn't have a spark of life in him. He walked slowly up the stairs, as if every step pained him.

Nina and James sat together in the kitchen.

'Do you want to tell me about this Lloyd's business?' asked Nina.

James shook his head. 'No.'

'Is there anything I can do?'

'No.'

They sat silently for a moment.

James reached for Nina's hand. 'Just don't leave me,' he whispered, grasping her fingers. His face showed his panic.

Nina felt the tears slide down her cheeks. They

were part pity, part empathy and part jolting recognition.

She felt her life recently had been like a hologram, or one of those tricky three-dimensional images she remembered from fun fair postcards as a child. If she tilted the image it showed a completely different picture – the eye that was open would wink if she shifted it ever so slightly. As a child she had marvelled that another picture was there, hidden, like some kind of parallel universe.

The moment that James reached out for her, so humble and vulnerable, needing her in the midst of the calamity, and clearly scared he would lose her, the picture Nina had of her life shifted. In that moment she saw everything differently. James, herself, their marriage.

At that moment the bond between Nina and Leo snapped, although she was unaware of it at the time. She was all consumed with worry for James. She sat herself sideways on his lap, wrapped her arms around his slumped shoulders and gently rocked him.

'I'm not going anywhere, my love.' As her tears fell into his hair she continued to rock him, telling him she loved him. 'We're in this together. For better or worse. I don't care where we live or what we do as long as I'm with you.'

Nina telephoned her office to say she wouldn't be in for the rest of the week. She was tempted to tell them that she would never be back and what they could do with their lousy job but held herself in check. She and James may need that income. Lots of things were suddenly very uncertain.

James telephoned Felix to say he would be out of town for a while too. He explained that his mother had suffered a sudden stroke. Felix was shocked – Patty seemed such a healthy, fit woman. As James talked, Felix found himself worrying about his own mother and deciding it was far too long since he had spoken with her.

'That's terrible news, James. Please give my best to your mother and father.'

Felix wondered if James had spoken to Frederick yet about the vineyard. He assumed he would not have had a chance. Patty's stroke would have pushed any such conversations aside.

'James, I'm sure this isn't the time to talk to you about Lloyd's but you should at least know that I think I may have a solution for you. I may have found a way to stop Lloyd's selling the winery out from under you.'

'I'm listening, Felix . . .'

For weeks Felix had been working on negotiating a final settlement with the Lloyd's lawyers for himself and each of his clients. He considered the sum was reasonable under the circumstances. If each client accepted the final figure, that would be the end of it for them. They could pay the sum and move on. If they chose not to, preferring to fight it out in the British courts, their unlimited liability clause would leave them susceptible to claims by Lloyd's for many more years to come.

To sort out the best deal for each of his clients, Felix had spent many late nights poring over their individual portfolios. Immersed in piles of paperwork, he had come up with some clever ideas. The best of them involved Wilde Wines.

'I may be able to form a consortium of investors or I may have a client in a position to buy out your debt. I just need a few days.'

James felt the faint stirrings of hope. 'Are you serious?'

'Yes. I have a few clients that it may appeal to. Wineries are seen as glamorous and exciting and sophisticated. A lot more interesting than pig-farming or building cement factories, let me tell you. I have a couple of people who may be interested, which could mean setting up a new business structure for the winery, or perhaps it would suit an individual investor. I need to look into it further.'

Felix had a couple of questions for James. They were specific and private but James didn't mind revealing such things to his friend. He lowered his voice to respond, unsure where in the house Frederick may be.

'Okay, James, leave it with me. Wilde Wines is in good shape and there just may be a way to keep it away from Lloyd's. I need to make some calls, see some people and then I'll come back to you.'

'Oh, Felix, we could do with some good news up here right now.'

'Have you told your father about Lloyd's?' asked Felix.

James looked through the kitchen window, across the vineyards. He spoke very quietly. 'I told them all. Last night. I told them, then Mum . . .' James stopped, remembering the sight of his mother lying in a heap by his father's feet.

'Oh God, James. I'm so sorry. You poor bastard.'

'Yeah. It couldn't be worse. Please do what you can.'

Felix was determined. He cancelled all his appointments for the day, then took a pile of files from his briefcase and his filing cabinet and lay them on his desk. He loosened his tie, and lined up his calculator, a couple of freshly sharpened pencils and a foolscap pad. Then he set about methodically working through the files.

The rest of the day he stayed hunched over his desk. He checked through his latest batch of correspondence from Lloyd's. He made lots of phone calls, speaking to a couple of colleagues, the agents for Lloyd's who he was getting to know quite well, their lawyers, his own lawyers, a judge of the Industrial Commission who was a member of his club and finally a wine journalist he once dated to chat about the current state of the Australian wine industry, and one label in particular.

Felix wanted to help the Wilde family but he was a completely honourable man. He wouldn't do anything illegal nor would he help them at the expense of another client. Before he would even put the proposal forward he needed to assure himself that Wilde Wines would be a smart and profitable investment.

Finally, at 4.14 pm, he was satisfied.

Over the next few days life settled into a strange kind of routine for the Wilde family. Someone was always by Patty's side while the rest of the family came and went from the vineyard, trying to go about their usual duties, all the while under a dreadful unspoken cloud. It was up to Frederick to broach the conversation with James and, until he did, the others were helpless.

Nina drove back to the Elizabeth Bay apartment and collected clean clothes for herself and James. It took her two hours to reach the apartment. She stayed twenty minutes, piling things into a suitcase, then drove the two hours back again. She was at the hospital in time to collect James just as Frederick came to take over with Patty.

Frederick had managed to avoid being alone with his younger son, though they were living under the same roof. Every ounce of everybody's attention was directed towards Patty.

On the afternoon of the first day after her stroke, Patty's speech had started to become recognisable, if a little slurred, and she was responding well to all the tasks the staff gave her – squeezing a ball, answering their simple questions about who she was and what year it was, and having her pulse and blood pressure taken every hour. By the next day she was explaining to the doctor about the woolly feeling in her head. Her blood pressure showed every sign of dropping. She was able to express herself, and articulate her emotions. All good signs, Dr Wilson assured the family on his next visit to the hospital a few days later.

She still had trouble articulating certain sounds. Dr Wilson said that may or may not improve. Only time would tell. And she appeared to have no recollection of the events leading up to her collapse. She was surprised to see James and Nina. She had no idea they were in the Hunter Valley.

'How lovely of you to come all the way to see me. What a shame I am in here or I could cook you my roast lamb. I know how you miss that, James. And baked turnip for you, Nina. I remember.'

She smiled at them both, pleased with herself. James looked away.

'Next time, Patty. When you're feeling better,' said Nina.

On the morning of the third day everyone fell into a schedule. James was due to sit with Patty. Mark and Frederick were having the new osmosis filtration unit installed. Nina would drop off James and then do the shopping.

James waved goodbye to Nina and walked down the corridor, smiling his greetings to the nurses on duty. He was expecting Patty to be asleep so he was surprised to find the bed empty and Amanda sitting in the armchair.

'Where is she?'

'Having a CAT scan,' replied Amanda, flicking through a magazine.

'What are you doing here?'

'I'm her daughter-in-law, a member of the family. I care about what happens to her.'

There was an edge to Amanda's voice that James did not like. He wondered if he could find where his mother was having tests and go to her there.

'She'll be back soon. Sit down, I won't bite,' said Amanda.

She sounded perfectly friendly, even giving a little smile. James didn't believe it for a minute. He did not want to be alone with Amanda and tried to keep as far away from her as possible. But he had been cornered. James was supposed to be here. She wasn't. He sat on a plastic stackable chair that had been brought in from the reception area. Amanda continued to read the magazine. James could think of nothing to say. Her presence made the room seem stuffy.

She turned another page and, looking up at James, said sweetly, 'You are an arsehole.'

She turned back to her magazine.

James sighed. He didn't want to have this conversation. 'Don't, Amanda,' he replied. 'Just don't.' James was emotionally exhausted. It was the worst possible reply.

Amanda snapped shut her magazine. 'You were an arsehole then and you are an arsehole now. I can't understand what I ever saw in you.'

The veneer of civility was gone. Their loathing of each other was instantly at the fore.

'What exactly are you angry about, Amanda?

Huh? A fling we had when we were both pissed? Or are you angry that you may not get the Wilde money after all? Which is it? Your bruised ego or your greed?'

Amanda looked as if she had been slapped. Her eyes glittered dangerously. 'How dare you!' She spat out the words. 'First you walk out on me –'

James cut her off in mid-sentence. 'I did not walk out on you. We had a drunken fling. I'm not exactly proud of it but I'm not ashamed either. We were both consenting adults. Now let it be.'

'Easy for you to say. You treated me like a tart. Had your way then took off, without so much as a goodbye. I deserved better than that.' Amanda paused for breath.

All was silent in the little hospital room.

When James finally spoke he sounded weary, resigned. 'I am sorry if I hurt you. I didn't mean to. You do deserve better than that.'

Amanda was having none of it. The more reasonable James sounded the more irate she became. 'Mark is worth a thousand of you and it has taken me this long to realise it. I used to want an apology, some kind of explanation. You behaved like a pig. Now I want nothing more to do with you. You have ruined this family. It's all your fault.'

The small white-walled room started to close in on James. The antiseptic hospital smells filled his nostrils and added to the feeling of claustrophobia. James had to get out of there.

He stumbled out into the hospital carpark, his mind filled with loathing for his sister-in-law. She brought back such unhappy memories. He preferred to forget his years working for his father on the vineyard. It had seemed to him then that everything he had done in his life he had failed at. He had returned from the Olympics a few years earlier feeling like a failure and tried to stay out of sight of the media and his team mates, as far from the skiing world as he could flee, living quietly at the vineyard. But the farm had seemed impossibly small and irrelevant after he'd had a taste of overseas travel. His friends had moved on in their careers and he felt like he had nothing. Frederick had given him a job on cellar door sales. He hated the drunken holidaymakers that came through. He hated the small-town focus of the family. He hated everything about the winery. Then his father had stamped on the only opportunity he felt he had to achieve something and regain some self-respect, becoming a Lloyd's name. He had decided it was time to go. He didn't fit in here.

James hadn't told his family of his plans to leave. He hadn't known himself. It was an idea he had been toying with for a few days then, that final Saturday, the others had taken off to promote their wines at a jazz festival at Pokolbin, leaving James with Amanda to look after cellar door sales. It had been so hot, the flies had fried on the windowsill. The coolest place on the property was the tasting barn, the huge vaulted sandstone building with stone floors. The relentless heat could addle a man's brain. James had heard somewhere that human beings couldn't cope at temperatures above 48 degrees Celsius. Their thinking became muddled. That's how he felt.

Amanda and James had no way of knowing whether it would be a busy day or not. In this heat probably not. But they put the 'open' sign out on the road in case.

They were soon bored. It was too hot to go out and there was nothing to do inside the tasting barn but drink and banter. James had been glad Amanda was there. He had always considered her to be good fun. She made James laugh, through a combination of flirty innuendo and ribald humour. Men found her attractive and she knew it, revelled in it. James had been happy to spend the afternoon in her company.

They decided to test each other with blind tastings. James couldn't remember whose idea that was. Probably Amanda's. She had a formidable reputation for having one of the keenest palates in the Hunter. Amanda made James sit on the customer's side, then she lined up six wine tasting glasses in front of him. She had brought out four bottles of white from the fridge. They were their current stock used for tastings.

'Too easy,' James said when he saw them.

'Oh, you think so, huh,' she said, disappearing into the back room.

She returned with two unopened bottles from the neighbouring vineyard. Same varieties, same years.

She lined up the six bottles for James to study the labels. Two Wilde semillons from different years, and a semillon from the winery next-door, an unwooded Wilde chardonnay and the same from next-door, and a Wilde verdelho, the current vintage.

'Are you ready?'

James studied the labels. Satisfied, he gave the thumbs up sign. Amanda untied the red silk scarf from around her neck and moved behind him to blindfold him. The scarf smelled of her perfume, sweet and light. He was immediately suspicious. Ninety per cent of tasting involved the sense of smell.

'Nice try, Amanda. I'm onto you. Trying to give me a handicap with the perfumed scarf. It won't work, you know.'

Amanda sniggered. 'Just concentrate on your palate, buddy boy.'

James sat in the darkness and waited. He listened to a bottle being opened and the wine being poured. He felt Amanda's hands place the glass in his hands. He swirled the liquid about the glass, releasing its aroma, and inhaled deeply.

Quite pungent. An overlay of tropical fruit. The Wilde verdelho. He took a sip and swirled the liquid about his mouth. Honeyed. Silky. Definitely the verdelho. It was cool and refreshing. He downed the rest of the glass.

'Wildes' Verdelho 1986. Next.'

Amanda took his hand and placed it around another glass. Round, clean, light. A touch of grapefruit. The current vintage semillon by Wilde Wines.

Amanda had tied the blindfold securely and no light seeped through to James's world. He found himself straining to follow her movements, listening to the bottles being uncorked, the wine poured and anticipating her touch. They moved down the row, James savouring generous amounts of each of the six wines before finishing the glass. Amanda made notes of each selection.

Next, it was Amanda's turn. James untied the blindfold and moved behind her, tying the scarf securely. She made her selections as James recorded them on a pad.

They finished the whites, emptying each glass into their mouths and then moved onto the reds. By the fourth glass, James was laughing and dribbling so much Amanda had to help him find his mouth, placing the glass against his lips and pouring. They both started to giggle uncontrollably. Wine dripped down James's chin. Groping around for a cloth he struck Amanda in the chest and knocked the wine out of her hand, spilling its contents all over his shirt.

Laughing and half falling off the chair, Amanda pulled the shirt over his head, flinging it across the counter. James finished the row of reds. His motor coordination started to falter and he fumbled clumsily as he attempted to retie the blindfold behind her head.

Amanda waited in darkness for James to pour the first red. He was giggling so much he kept missing the glass. Then, ignoring her hands, he put the glass straight to her lips. Amanda was renowned for her love of a good red. She swilled the wine around in her mouth, enjoying every texture and sensation. She groaned with appreciation.

'You started with the 1986 Shiraz, my favourite.' She rolled her tongue slowly over her lips, savouring every last drop.

It was the most incredibly erotic thing James thought he had ever seen. Soon Amanda complained of being hot and peeled off her skimpy T-shirt, tossing it aside. She sat in just her shorts and lacey white bra.

'Where are you, I can't see you,' she called out.

James poked her in the ribs and jumped aside as she tried to grab his hand. Sweat gave her tanned skin a sheen. She was laughing so much she dribbled the next glass down her cleavage. James couldn't take his eyes off her breasts as the red wine dribbled across the white lace, spreading like a stain and falling into the deep cleft. It seemed incredibly lewd to James to be able to sit and stare all he wanted at Amanda's breasts. He watched them move as she breathed, jiggling in time with her giggling.

James found this notion highly amusing – jiggling from the giggling. Amanda wanted to know why he was laughing. As she spoke they jiggled more. James was laughing so hard he couldn't speak. Amanda reached out to him in the darkness and her hand brushed his bare chest. It was wet with wine and sweat. At her touch James abruptly stopped laughing.

Amanda started to move both her hands over him, feeling him like a blind man would. Her fingers caressed his bare waist. James held his breath. He enjoyed the sensations, closing his eyes and focussing on the feel of her cool fingers running over his hot, naked torso. Amanda climbed onto James's lap and finding his mouth, started to kiss him.

They fell over each other lustily. Sweaty, wine soaked, hot and panting. James tore off what was left of his own and Amanda's clothes then hoisted her onto the counter. Amanda pushed her feet against an upturned barrel and they thrust against each other. Hard and urgent.

It was all over in a matter of minutes.

They dressed clumsily, still laughing.

James went into the back room and put his head under the tap, splashing cold water over his neck and face. Amanda came in and stood behind him, running her hands over his buttocks, spooning herself around his bent body. They swayed like that for a moment but the heat of the back room quickly became oppressive.

James started to sober up and went inside the house and up to his room to fetch a clean T-shirt. He had forgotten what he was looking for when he got there and lay for a moment on the bed. He didn't mean to leave Amanda with the mess to clean up but he fell asleep for some hours and when he woke up everything was in darkness. Amanda was nowhere to be seen.

The next day James went to see Felix in town and tell him he couldn't become a Lloyd's name. A week later he was on a plane with him to London. Three months after that he received a letter in

Whistler from his mother, telling him Mark was getting married, to that nice girl Amanda who he might remember. She worked on door sales.

James didn't bother going home for the wedding but sent a telegram wishing the happy couple a successful future.

He hadn't seen Amanda again until four years later, when he stood in the family lounge room introducing his bride Nina to his brother and sister-in-law.

CHAPTER 13

Thursday, 21 February 1991

Leo noticed a mark on his shoulder. It was an ugly blue bruise with a tinge of yellow around the edge. It didn't look so new. Leo wondered when he had hurt himself. His body was a mass of scars and bumps from sailing mishaps. He thought of his last race. He couldn't remember falling over or being hit by anything. Then it came to him. Nina biting him, playfully at first, then, no longer aware what she was doing, she had sunk her teeth in and hung on. Leo smiled to think of it. They had a date this Saturday. He wanted it to be special. He looked about his bachelor penthouse. It didn't look right. He needed to go shopping.

★

Felix was already chatting with Frederick on the verandah when Nina and James returned from the hospital.

James had been expecting him but still he was nervous at the sight of his friend standing beside his father. He knew he was in for a long and uncomfortable discussion about what had happened with Lloyd's. There were some issues that would only be discussed away from Felix, personal issues including why James had gone against his father's express wishes and gambled with the family's financial future. That was a conversation James knew they would have privately.

As far as Frederick was concerned, Felix was here to talk about Lloyd's, not become involved in Wilde family business. Nina placed a bottle of wine and three glasses on the outdoor table, then with a little smile of reassurance to James, discreetly withdrew.

'Tell me about Lloyd's.' Frederick directed the remark to Felix.

Felix cleared his throat and began. First, he explained about the unprecedented losses, the syndicates that were being called in and where James fitted into the scenario. When Felix got to the part about James agreeing to unlimited liability, Frederick shot his son a withering glance, but said nothing. Frederick sat very still, allowing Felix to paint the full picture without interruption. James also remained quiet, watching and listening and finding it impossible to know what his father was thinking. Felix outlined the settlement they had been offered by Lloyd's lawyers, whereby they could quarantine their loss. If they could pay that sum, that would be the end of it. If not, they would come after the winery.

Frederick closed his eyes for a moment and scratched his head. 'It is that bad then,' he said quietly. He looked out across his vineyard, the rows and rows of neatly planted vines that stretched as far as the eye could see in the east and across to the waterwheel in the west.

'When Patty and I first saw this place it was an old dairy farm. We knew it would be a lot of work but we were young and determined. We used to stand over where the Jacob Leesing vine is planted and plan where we would put everything. We wanted the house to overlook the vines so we could watch them grow. One thousand acres. That's 400 hectares planted with world-class grape-producing vines.' He stopped and sighed, his eyes watery. He suddenly looked very old. 'I know every single grain of this soil, every leaf on these vines. What you are telling me is . . . it's . . . I . . .' His voice trailed off.

James felt the saddest he had ever felt in his life. There was nothing he could say.

'We're finished,' said Frederick Wilde at last. 'What do I tell her? What do I tell Patty?'

James put his hand out to his father and touched him gingerly on the knee. 'Dad, I . . .'

Frederick recoiled. 'Don't say a word. Nothing.' His voice was harsh and James winced as if struck.

Felix spoke again. 'I think you may have two other alternatives.'

Frederick continued to stare out at the vineyards. 'Go on.'

'You could refuse to pay. You could join the groups that are fighting Lloyd's. There is a chance they may win. I don't know. I have my doubts. But even if you lost, it could take years before they were in a position to make you pay. That may give you breathing space to come up with the money to pay James's debt, without it hurting the business.'

'Mmmmm . . .' said Frederick.

'Or there is another possibility.' Felix hesitated. 'I may have a client who is interested in investing in Wilde Wines. He has a few spare million. He could pay out Lloyd's, plus any other loans you may have – and I assume you probably have a few. I'm sure you would also have ideas on how best to utilise an injection of cash, which could also be a possibility.

'In effect he would become a silent partner in your business. He has no interest in running a vineyard himself and not the faintest idea about how the business operates. He is an old schoolmate who has also been caught up in the Lloyd's fiasco and would be most sympathetic to your predicament. I think I can see a way to rearrange some of his finances and make investing in your vineyard work for him too. He has money to spend and I look out for business opportunities for him. Like many financial analysts, I happen to believe that the Australian wine industry is worth investing in.'

Frederick looked through narrowed eyes at Felix. He was surprised by the suggestion and more than a little bemused. 'Without seeing our books, this client of yours would like to invest millions in my business?'

Frederick didn't miss a trick. He was surprised that Felix seemed to know so much about his business. He shot another scornful glance at James. He shook his head, then turned back to Felix. 'My son, who is obviously as indiscreet as he is stupid, has informed you of all our business affairs and, knowing all that, this client of yours would like to take over the business and I could work for him. Is that it?'

'No, sir. We would put in place a company structure that protected his investment while maintaining your authority and autonomy. You would be partners but on paper only. His only job, if you like, would be to supply the finance. Of course, he would want a return on that finance but he does recognise that this would be a long-term investment with limited short-term returns.

'As I said, he has no interest in becoming involved in your business. He would want a representative, namely myself, who would be involved in all financial decisions. If you needed to buy new equipment, try new varieties, whatever, that would of course be up to you. If you wanted to pursue a course that involved major outlay of capital, say marketing overseas, new production facilities or extra land, then I would need to be involved on his behalf.'

Frederick looked like a man at war with himself.

His brow was furrowed. His eyes darted around the verandah, not taking anything in. He was thinking quickly, weighing up his options. Finally he sighed. 'Keep talking, boy.'

Felix stayed on for dinner. It was a subdued meal, but for the first time since Patty had taken ill Frederick dined with them in the kitchen rather than in his office. He spoke only to Felix, remembering as an afterthought to thank Nina for preparing dinner. He avoided James completely. As soon as dinner was over he drove back to the hospital.

James and Felix sat out on the verandah. The tension of the past few hours, plus the alcohol, left James feeling light-headed. His relief was enormous. Frederick hadn't committed himself to anything but both Felix and James knew he was interested. For the first time in weeks James allowed himself a glimmer of hope.

'God, Felix, I hope this works out. I can't believe you managed to set this up.'

'No big deal. It's what I do. I manage rich people's money. People who need venture capital to start up a company come to me and if, after looking into their business, I think it sounds promising, I put them in touch with a client who has money to invest. Such investments obviously carry a great deal of risk but the returns are also much greater. Your business, though you may not realise it, is actually a very good opportunity for the right investor.'

'You are a man of many talents, Felix.'

Nina appeared with two mugs of coffee. 'You look much happier, both of you. I take it that the meeting with Frederick went well.'

James wrapped his arms around Nina's waist. 'How could he help but be relaxed after that superb meal.'

He tickled her waist and Nina laughed with surprise. James hadn't been this amiable for so long.

'Felix has a client who may be interested in buying out all our debt.'

'Really? That's wonderful. Well done, Felix.'

Nina felt instinctively that everything was going to be all right. Patty would recover. Felix would find a way to save the winery. And she and James would work it out.

She leaned down and kissed James on the forehead. 'Everything is going to be okay then,' she said softly.

He smiled into her eyes. 'Yeah.'

Nina extricated herself from James and disappeared into the kitchen for the milk.

The earth seemed still but was filled with the sounds of the night. Cicadas and crickets beat out their shrill song. James drank in the familiar sounds. He felt the calmness spread down through his limbs.

'Whose dumb idea was it to become a Lloyd's name anyway?' he said.

'Beats me,' said Felix. 'Must have been that Count Mauro de March.'

At mention of the name, both James and Felix burst out laughing.

Nina, standing on the other side of the flyscreen door, froze.

The two men chuckled to each other.

'It's a long time since I have heard that name.'

'The evil Count Mauro de March,' said Felix. He sounded out the name, rolling it around in a pseudo-Italian accent, which for Nina was shockingly familiar.

She felt sick to her stomach. Her hand on the door dropped away and she was suddenly very faint. She crouched down behind the door, out of view, till the feeling passed. He knows. He must know. How the hell does he know? What could he know?

Nina was suddenly back in a steamy taxi on a wet Friday night hearing that name for the first time. What had Leo said? He was Count Mauro de March, heir to an Italian coffee empire. He had been joking. So how did James and Felix know about Count Mauro de March? This made no sense.

The optimism Nina had felt vanished in an instant. Instead she felt a terrible foreboding. Had she thought she would get away with what she had done? She would pay. You always had to pay. It was the natural order of things.

'Were you ever the count?' asked James.

'Yeah, a couple of times. It never worked for me. What about you?'

'I tried it but no, it never worked for me either,' laughed James.

'It worked for Flat Freddy, you know,' said Felix.

'Yeah?'

'Yeah. He and his mates were at a pub in Adelaide after the Grand Prix. He reckoned he was an Italian racing car driver.'

'Yeah?'

'Well, that's the story. Flat Freddy kept ordering lots of campari for some local signorina and bingo, she thought she was going home to see mama.'

Nina listened to the ribald laughter that ensued. What the hell were they talking about? She walked hesitantly onto the verandah.

James changed the subject as soon as she appeared and they talked of other things. He seemed as warm towards her as before but Nina was sure she hadn't imagined the sudden switch in the conversation at her appearance. The feeling of foreboding persisted. It cast a pall over the rest of the evening for Nina. She found it impossible to join in with the laughter and jokes. Eventually her face ached from the effort of pretending to be jolly when she didn't feel it. She felt as if her world was about to come tumbling down. Her treachery and deceit were about to be uncovered and her fly-blown heart laid bare in all its putridity for the rest of the world to see. She felt shamed. She wondered if, unbeknown to her, the exposure had already begun.

Frederick came home. He looked happier than he had in days.

'She's looking good,' he said with a grin. 'She's getting back to her old self. She told me off for not bringing you in to visit her, Felix. And asked after your parents. Perhaps tomorrow, after we've looked at the books, you may like to pop your head in before you head back to town.'

'I'd like that, sir, if Mrs Wilde is up to it.'

'Good. Well, I'll turn in. That was a good dinner you cooked, Nina. Thank you. Patty was pleased to know you were looking after me.'

Frederick inclined his head towards James, without looking him in the eye, then turned to go back inside.

'Goodnight, sir,' said James quietly.

'Yes, well, goodnight all,' said Frederick, throwing his words over his shoulder.

James looked crestfallen.

'Give it time,' said Felix when Frederick was out of earshot.

'Yeah, sure,' said James. 'It's not like I crashed the family car. It's a bit worse than that.'

Frederick's appearance dampened the boys' high spirits and they agreed to call it a night.

Once they were alone in their room Nina was edgy and unable to relax. While James prepared for bed she roamed around the room, looking at things on the shelf, peering at the faces of the schoolboys on the wall. One photo showed James sitting next to a boy who looked remarkably like Leo. He had that same lopsided grin and big baggy shorts. Nina was imagining him everywhere. She had to shake herself out of this.

'Who is Count Mauro de March?' she suddenly blurted.

James looked sheepish.

'Oh, you heard that? Whoops.' He hesitated.

Nina braced herself.

'It's the name we used to impress girls when we were at school. We made him up. The exotic rich European count who could be anyone you wanted him to be – a racing car driver, European royalty, French movie star. It was just harmless fun when we were trying to impress the girls to get them into bed.'

Nina's mind worked furiously. What *was* he talking about?

'It never worked for me,' said James.

Nina continued to stare blankly at him. Her mind, awash with incriminating pictures a minute ago, was having trouble making sense of what he was telling her.

'So who would use the name Count whatsisname?'

'Well, anyone could. We didn't designate who could use it before we went out. It just sort of happened.'

'Who's we?'

'The guys at school.'

'They all had access to this name?'

James laughed. 'Well, it wasn't like that. No-one had copyright on it or anything. I don't remember who originally came up with the name. I wonder if Felix would remember. But why do you ask?'

Nina knew her face was behaving oddly. She should be relaxed and flippant about this boyhood fun, matching James's lightness, but she was struggling with her expression. She couldn't make herself smile.

'What's wrong, Nina?'

'Nothing . . . I . . .'

James watched her.

'Darling, what is the matter? It was just a silly boys' drinking game. It was a joke. Why has this upset you so much?'

Nina shook her head. How could she explain the pain that pierced her heart. Sudden, inexplicable, blinding pain. Count Mauro de March was the name they used to get girls into bed. She felt humiliated and foolish.

She walked over and looked again at the photo on the wall. Half-a-dozen schoolboys sitting in a row laughing. There was Felix, James, a couple of others and then someone who looked like a young Leo. They all wore the uniform of a private Sydney boys' school. Nina felt as if the walls were closing in on her. Everything had become so complicated and messy and sordid. She wanted to set it right.

'James, we need to talk.'

James sat up. He took in Nina's tone, her manner. Everything about her screamed serious.

'What is it, darling?'

Nina continued to pace around the cramped room. She walked from the top of the bed to the foot, around the end to the door, and then back again. She looked at the pictures and banners on the wall and the books in the bookcase. She couldn't look at James.

This was so hard. So much had happened. 'For

the past month or so I've noticed you were distracted. You seemed preoccupied and I didn't know why,' she began.

James tried to see the recent past from Nina's perspective. He saw her loneliness and felt bad. 'Nina, I'm sorry. I know I have been a pig to live with. I know I virtually ignored you. I am so, so sorry. I just did not know what to do. This Lloyd's thing has been a nightmare.'

Nina nodded. 'I know. Well, at least I know that now. But that's the problem. I didn't know what was going on. I can't see inside your head. From the moment I met you we have talked, about everything. For you to face that disaster and shut me out is probably the most hurtful thing you have ever done.'

James pulled at a loose thread on the bed coverlet. 'I guess I was trying to protect you,' he said softly.

'Protect me?' Nina was incredulous. She stopped pacing and stared at her husband.

James nodded. 'I didn't want to . . . to worry you.' It sounded so weak, even to his own ears. He hadn't really considered it from this angle until now and he was realising that his action didn't hold up to closer scrutiny.

'You think I don't worry when my husband doesn't come home? And when he does he locks himself in the study all night? You think I don't worry when he suddenly won't talk to me? James, I have been beside myself with worry. And I have been very lonely. I missed my husband.'

James murmured something unintelligible. He looked contrite.

Nina sat on the bed. 'James, you can't keep anything from me again. Not like that. If there is something worrying you, you have to tell me. Otherwise a gap opens up between us. And that's . . . dangerous.'

James agreed. 'Yes, you are right.'

Nina stood up and started pacing again. She hadn't planned this conversation and wasn't sure how to proceed. She was surprised when James blurted: 'In that case I do have something else to tell you.'

Nina stopped and looked at him.

'Now I don't want you to get upset or angry. It happened a long time ago. But I should have told you as it might explain . . . well, as it might explain something about what is going on.'

'I'm listening.'

'Years ago, before I met you, I had a drunken fling with Amanda. Don't ask me why. We were pissed and I don't know, but next thing . . . well . . . we did.'

Nina looked at her husband. This was so unexpected. Amanda. James and Amanda? 'How long ago?'

'Before I came to Canada. Before I went to London with Felix in 1987. Years ago.'

'Just the once?'

'Yes, just the once.'

'Does Mark know?'

'I have no idea. I certainly never told him.

Amanda was working on door sales with me. I left soon after and the next time I saw her was when I came back with you. As you know I didn't keep in touch with my family much, except for sending Mum the odd postcard. I was surprised when Mum wrote and told me Amanda was going to marry Mark. But then I thought, why not? They have a lot in common. They are passionate about wine.'

'Wow,' said Nina.

Her legs felt tired. She sat in the chair at the desk and faced him. James wanted Nina to know everything. It was suddenly vitally important to him that they not have any secrets.

'Amanda hates me. She told me the other day that she feels I used her and then dumped her. That I behaved like a pig to her. What can I say? I was drunk. I thought she was too. I didn't see it as the beginning of anything. But it looks like maybe she did.'

'Is that why she is so awful?'

'To you? Probably. I'm sorry, Nina. I should have told you. I know it's been hard for you, starting a new life here in Australia, without any of your friends and family around. And having her as your sister-in-law probably hasn't made you feel so very welcome.'

'No, you're right there,' agreed Nina.

Nina thought of Amanda. She didn't like her but she was beginning to understand her. 'I don't suppose Amanda is used to being rejected,' she said. She sighed deeply. This conversation had not gone the way she had intended. She wondered how she could bring it back. *Well, I have something I want to get off my chest . . .*

James got out of bed and knelt at her feet. He put his arms around her legs and looked up at her. 'Nina, I adore you. I would never do anything to hurt you. The day I stood beside you and promised to love and honour you I meant every word. Amanda will get over it. It's just hurt pride. And if she doesn't, well that's her problem. It has nothing to do with us, not that it ever did have.

'And I apologise from the bottom of my heart for the pain I have caused you over the past few months. I missed you, too. I don't ever want a gap to grow between us again. When I have a problem, I'll tell you.

'Let's draw a line in the sand tonight. Here and now. Let's forget the past. Everything that has gone on is behind us. It is irrelevant. We start afresh right now.'

Nina stared at her husband. Did he know? He was kneeling there in front of her, his face open and honest and was offering her redemption, a clean start. The force of his love almost overwhelmed her. She knew she had a choice. It was speak up now or forever hold her peace.

She leaned forward and took his head in her hands. 'A clean start. Here and now, my love. I'm all yours.'

CHAPTER 14

Dr Jones's rooms
7 February 2001

The doctor was deliberately ambiguous. His words hung in the air.

'*Your* son doesn't have *any* bad Wilde genes.'

Nina remained deathly silent. It was as if even the blood in her veins had stilled. She dared not look up. *He knew. The doctor knew.* It was obvious in the way he spoke, the choice of words and his manner. His voice was soothing but his light blue eyes were hard, and cold, staring at her with uncompromising directness. She felt like he was looking right into her soul.

Nina started to tremble. *He's going to tell James that Luke is not his son. He's going to do it sitting here, right now. No, no, no. It will kill James. Please don't tell him. Why does he have to find out? Oh my God. How can I get James out of here?* Nina ceased to think rationally. She saw her life with James and Luke crumbling into a pile of rubble. A wave of panic engulfed her.

James and the doctor watched as a range of expressions flitted across her face. It was partly hidden from them as she stared intently at her hands, clasped together in her lap.

'Nina,' said James softly.

She seemed to have retreated inside her own head. The relief that he and their son were healthy must almost be too much for her, he thought. He felt such tenderness for his wife. She was so vulnerable and he felt himself to be personally responsible for her happiness. It wasn't rational and Nina would have been surprised if she realised how deeply he felt it, but it was part of what he saw as his role as husband and protector. He needed to be needed. To see her this upset physically hurt him. That he and his son were the cause of her pain made his sense of responsibility all the more intense. He didn't doubt that she loved him. It was what drove him out of the house each morning to work and sent him home just as soon as he could. Not for James nights drinking with his mates or golf weekends out of town. He just wanted to be with her, around her, in her space, loving and protecting her. After ten years of marriage, that desire had never waned.

Nina felt James's voice coming to her from a long way off. She could feel the warmth of his fingers inside her elbow. Comforting, solid, tangible.

Anchoring. James did that for her. He was solid. Whenever she thought she might fade away, he was there, grounding her.

Nina lifted her face to him. He didn't seem to find anything unusual in what the doctor said. In fact he was looking relieved. He had been told what he wanted to hear. He was healthy and his son was healthy. The facial tic had stopped. He looked like he had just been handed the world. But Nina was getting a different message. She tried to appear normal, giving James a little reassuring smile that she didn't feel. She had to get him out of there. Fast. Before this oaf of a doctor said anything further.

'It's great news – we really should go,' she said, rising to her feet.

James looked surprised by her sudden hurry but stood also, placing a reassuring hand on her arm.

'Thank you, doctor, for such wonderful news. We are very grateful.'

Nina almost started to relax. The meeting was over. They could go home and resume their life, their happy cosy little life, just the three of them.

The doctor watched them.

'We are very relieved that the tests proved so favourable,' repeated James.

The doctor's face was impassive. *That's what you think.* He was in no hurry. He was enjoying himself too much. He allowed himself a small smile. Beneath the desk, his foot tapped out a slow rhythmic beat. *Not . . . so . . . fast.*

Often he had sat here watching women like

Nina, smiling through their deceit. Women, the weaker sex. Huh! The lying sex, more like it. Their doting men supported them, raised the fruit of their infidelities, and all the time the men were being treated like fools or, worse still, a meal ticket. It was an old, old story and it offended the doctor every time it was presented to him.

The cheap plastic folder beneath his clasped hands bulged with information, secrets that could destroy the web of lies that this woman had clearly woven around her son's birth. James's obvious anguish sickened him. How heartless this woman was.

But Dr Jones had just changed the rules. This one wasn't going to get away with it. He was going to have some fun. He felt powerful, almost god-like. It was an intoxicating feeling. He waited till they were almost at the door.

'Oh, by the way . . .' he began.

Nina stiffened.

In front of her James, hand outstretched, stopped and turned back to him, his face polite and enquiring. 'Yes . . .?'

CHAPTER 15

Saturday, 23 February 1991

Leo kept his eyes fixed on the tree. He packed the spinnaker under the bed in the boat's little cabin and knotted the ropes into neat piles. He wasn't concentrating on what he was doing, just killing time while he waited and watched that tree. Every few minutes he picked up his binoculars and scanned the park. He wondered what he would do if someone else came along and sat there. After all, it was a nice day and that was a damn fine-looking tree. But no-one did.

Leo had a couple of bottles of French champagne chilling in the fridge at home. He had bought new crystal champagne flutes. An enormous bunch of white lilies sat in a vase decorated with a huge tartan bow on the hall stand. They were the first thing Nina would see when she walked in. He had been planning their afternoon together all week. He was filled with anticipation.

'Ah, Nina,' he sighed to himself.

They would meet by the tree. Then they would walk slowly, casually, separately, not touching, back to his place. Every step would be delightful, excruciating suspense. Then they would fall on each other. He had never felt this way before.

Leo had hoped Nina would already be waiting by the tree. Every second apart was delicious agony. He remembered their farewell the previous week. Such tender soulful kisses on the landing of his penthouse apartment while they waited for the lift.

'See you next week,' Nina had called out just before the lift doors closed.

And Leo had been counting the hours ever since.

They hadn't made a firm time or confirmed the arrangement. Leo wouldn't know how to contact Nina. But it wasn't necessary. The world revolved around them. Nina felt it as strongly as he did. Leo was sure of it. It was in the way she had smiled, tilting her head on one side and flashing her eyes. They had a date. Late Saturday morning, by the tree, was a commitment as solid as if they had put it in writing. Leo would just have to be patient, he told himself.

He locked the boat away and made his way across the grass, stopping to pick up a coffee and a newspaper. It was his turn to pretend to read while he watched the pathway for Nina. He settled into their spot, nestled among the roots of the fig tree. He watched a couple argue a few metres away. They were sitting on the back of a park bench, their feet on the seat. She was wearing short gold shorts and a skimpy black halter top with a man's jacket around her shoulders. In one hand she held a pair of gold sandals and in the other a bottle of water. He was wearing denim jeans and a tight white singlet that showed off muscly arms. Leo tuned in to what they were saying.

'If Ghandi had been an elected politician he couldn't have achieved what he did,' argued the girl, waving her arms about.

'I don't think you can make that generalisation,' said the guy. He sounded quite angry.

'No, no, no,' insisted the girl, stamping her foot on the seat. She seemed equally agitated. 'He would have been forced to function within a corrupt system.'

Leo listened to them, fascinated. They were both vehement, worked up, talking over each other, desperate to make their point as if their very life depended on it.

'You are full of crap,' said the girl, shoving him hard in the chest with her shoes.

The man tipped backwards, lost his balance and fell off the bench, landing with a thud on the grass.

The girl looked shocked for a minute, then started to laugh. Her laughter had a manic quality that Leo found unnerving. The man stood up, brushed himself down, then pulled her backwards off the bench and onto the ground. They rolled around, kissing noisily. People ignored them. A woman in her eighties power-walked past them, not even bothering to look down. Her arms and legs were pumping furiously. She was followed a few seconds later by an identical woman. Leo did a double take, then realised they must be twins. The second one appeared to be trying to catch up to the first.

The park was home to anyone and everyone. Leo went back to his newspaper and idly turned a page. It was impossible to concentrate. He looked into the canopy above him, where the forks of the tree created a natural, leaf-covered cradle. It was mostly hidden from the ground but Leo could see it. A slow secretive smile spread across his face.

Nina saw the car pull into the driveway.

'They're here,' she called out in every direction.

James came quickly down the stairs. Mark rushed in from the barn and up the verandah steps. Amanda, waiting in the sitting room, readied the boys.

'Now you must be very careful with Grandma. Just stay very quiet and don't rush her. Okay?'

The boys, dressed in matching denim overalls, with their hair combed back behind their ears, stood side by side at the front door, wincing as their mother preened them.

James helped Patty from the car while Mark and Frederick retrieved her bags from the boot. The car was filled with flowers. She was a popular woman among the people of the town. Nina helped Amanda carry armfuls into the house.

Nina was shocked by how much weight Patty had lost. She was like a bird. Nevertheless, Dr Wilson was very pleased with her progress and had sent her home. She had a lot of healing to do, he said, and the best place to do that was at home.

Amanda and Nina had spent a full day together dusting and disinfecting every room. Frederick had turned the downstairs drawing room into a temporary bedroom, moving elegant period furniture out and a new bed and mattress in. Yesterday had been a long day working together to prepare and get the house in order. They started early and sat around the kitchen table, exhausted, eating pizza at the end of the day. Their common purpose had brought a temporary truce to the troubled family.

James towered over his mother, bending his head to hear what she was saying. Somehow in the hospital it hadn't been so noticeable. But, standing next to her strapping tall sons, she looked angular and fragile.

'I have put lunch out on the verandah, Patty, if that suits you?' said Nina. She felt suddenly uncomfortable, taking charge in another woman's house.

Patty beamed at her. 'That would be lovely.'

Frederick helped her through the house and outside. Patty stood for a moment at the verandah post surveying the vineyard. Their faces wore the same expression as they looked out across the rows and rows of vines.

'The red still hasn't been picked, eh, Fred? I thought you were going to do that yesterday.'

'We were but the baume still isn't up quite high enough. We hope to do it at first light tomorrow.'

'Will the rain hold off?'

Frederick shrugged. 'Should do.'

They continued for a few moments mumbling together in a kind of shorthand that only they could follow, using incomplete sentences. Their sons listened without interrupting. They were used to these kinds of conversations between their parents. So many of Frederick and Patty's hopes and dreams over more than two decades were out in those paddocks. When their sons and their wives looked out they saw neat, orderly rows of vines, a huge stone barn and a clear blue sky. They couldn't begin to see what Frederick and Patty saw.

After Patty had reassured herself it was all still there, just as she remembered it, she looked back around the faces of her family. Already she had more colour in her cheeks and an alert expression in her eyes. She settled into her favourite wicker chair with the faded floral cushion.

'You can take me for a walk later, Fred. Right now I want to know how my family are. Have I missed anything?' she asked.

The first Leo was aware of any commotion was a loud sharp bark followed immediately by a woman screaming. People all across the park looked in the direction of the noise. Leo twisted his body around and followed their attention. A skinny woman in her twenties wearing only a very brief black bikini was flailing her arms about and chasing a small Jack Russell terrier around in a circle. It was an incongruous sight, even for Rushcutters Bay Park.

As Leo watched he realised the dog had something in its mouth, which it was thrashing about at the same time as it evaded the hysterical woman.

'My rabbit, my rabbit . . .' she yelled.

A young teenager, a boy of about fourteen, was racing around with her trying to catch the dog.

'Pepper! Come here. PEPPER!' he yelled, adding, 'Sorry, lady.'

Pepper avoided them both, thinking this was all part of a game. He would let them get close, then effortlessly evade them. He wasn't trying to get away. He was having far too much fun.

A crowd started to gather. Leo stood, watching the spectacle.

The boy got a lucky break, catching Pepper by his collar when he was distracted by the woman. Throwing his body half across the little dog, the boy pinned him to the ground. The woman, happy to have a stationary target, started hitting the dog while the boy tried to prise Pepper's jaws open, at the same time trying to protect him from her blows.

Pepper finally gave up his quarry and Leo watched as the boy handed the limp, lifeless body of the rabbit to the woman.

She stopped yelling and took it. The crowd quietened as it realised what had happened. But no-one made a move to leave. They waited, wanting to see what she would do. The boy waited too. It seemed everyone in the park was holding their breath, watching the bikini-clad woman.

'I'm so sorry, lady,' he said.

The woman gave no indication she was aware of anyone watching her. She ignored them all. Cradling the small lifeless bundle of fur, she picked up her handbag and her clothes, and with enormous dignity, walked slowly out of the park and into the street.

Leo returned to his tree. It was way past lunchtime and he was hungry. He lit a cigarette and looked anxiously up the path in the direction of Nina's apartment block. He hoped she wouldn't be much longer.

The Wilde family slipped into a comfortable camaraderie, presenting a happy and united front for Patty's sake. No-one needed to be told. They all knew what was expected of them, what would make Patty happy.

Frederick praised Nina's efforts in Patty's absence.

'They say nice things now but they complained at every meal that it wasn't how you would have done it,' said Nina.

It wasn't true but it was in keeping with the mood of the afternoon.

Throughout the day James never actually spoke directly to his brother, father or sister-in-law. But

Patty didn't notice that. She noticed only how loving her sons seemed to be with their wives. Nina kept stroking James's arm, almost as if she couldn't get enough of him. Of course, they were still newlyweds, thought Patty.

But what did surprise Patty was the new deference in the way Amanda spoke to Mark. Patty often had been uncomfortable with the sharp tone Amanda used with her husband. It showed a lack of respect, Patty thought. It had first become apparent around the time of their wedding and it had made Patty uneasy. Something hadn't been right though she couldn't put her finger on what it was. Amanda just didn't seem to appreciate Mark enough, thought Patty. Then the boys arrived, one after the other, and life became very busy for them with two young children to care for. Those boys were a handful. Mark seemed happy, as far as Patty could tell. But today, Patty noticed a marked difference in the way Amanda related to her husband. She seemed positively adoring of him. About time, thought Patty.

As for the two boys, apart from a scratch on Harrison's nose they looked fine, playing with each other among the vines. Lachlan had the hose and was chasing Harrison, who was too small to get out of the way.

Frederick, who continued to hover nearby, was treating Patty like a piece of rare, fragile porcelain, terrified she might suddenly break and while she complained to him to let her be, secretly she liked it. She was touched by his worry and devotion.

Patty settled back into her chair and sipped her tea, happy that the vineyard had been well cared for and content to be the focus of all the family's attention. All was well with her little world.

Nina was finding the afternoon a bit of a strain. Her whole body was tuned into James. She could feel his tension. She was aware what it was costing him to take part in this happy family charade when he felt so miserable and guilty. She continued to stroke his arm, trying to impart reassurance and support.

There was a nagging feeling at the back of her mind, like something she had forgotten to do. A little niggling thought that kept poking and pricking the deepest recesses of her brain. It was a mixture of guilt, longing, shame and resolve – a cacophony of emotions that she wouldn't allow to come to the surface. She knew what it was and she wasn't going to let it in. The more it threatened, the more she focussed on her concern for her husband.

Leo watched the shadows move across the grass. His stomach grumbled painfully and he felt a chill. The sun had disappeared behind a clutch of buildings. It was still some hours till dusk but the heat of the day had passed and people started to pack up their picnics, rugs, frisbees, books and playthings to head home.

Leo was fearful. What could have happened? Was Nina hurt? How would he ever know? He could turn on the news tonight and see the debris of a smashed-up car, not knowing it was Nina that had been injured. That thought seemed unutterably tragic. Nina lying hurt in a hospital somewhere and he unable to go to her. Leo shivered.

He knew which apartment block she lived in. He remembered that day a few weeks ago, watching her run down the driveway, already sodden, trying to escape the rain. She had been a small, darting figure carrying lots of shopping bags. But he didn't know which apartment she lived in. She knew where he lived, but not the phone number. How would she get a message to him? Suddenly it all seemed so very flimsy. Evanescent. Fading before his eyes.

But he refused to give in to those feelings. What was between them was anything but flimsy. It was young and fledgling but it was a potent force. Something irrevocable had passed between them. He knew it. And yet he was aware of a heavy melancholy settling in his heart. Something *was* different. He felt sad and he didn't know why. Ah, lovely Nina. Where are you?

When the last light faded he set off home. He tried to sort some boating equipment but his mind wouldn't settle. What did he know of her, this wispy sprite, Miss Knee?

Nina had referred to her father as Jake Lambert, star of the Barbershop Chorus. So her last name was Lambert. And he knew Nina was her first name. It could be short for something. He couldn't think what. Janina? She wore a wedding ring so he knew she was married. But he had no way of knowing if she had a married surname.

He knew it was hopeless but he found himself scanning the death notices in the newspapers anyway. Then, with his heart in his mouth, he phoned the hospitals. No-one called Nina anything had been brought in over the past week, nor were there any unidentified females that fitted her description.

It was late but he walked up to Kings Cross Police Station, lining up with some drunks, a man who was bleeding from the forehead and a skinny abusive girl with the pasty complexion and unmistakable scowl of a heroin addict. A sympathetic policewoman listened to him, her expression altering only a little when he earnestly explained that this Nina must be missing because she had missed their fourth date. He thought he knew what the sergeant was thinking but she had looked up the name in the computer anyway. No-one called Nina Lambert had been mugged, raped, arrested or detained by police in the past week. Leo was both relieved and near despair. What had happened to her?

He walked home slowly. He didn't want this to be a game any more.

CHAPTER 16

Thursday, 28 February 1991

Leo hovered about the security entrance watching people come and go from the apartment block. These were Nina's neighbours, he thought, eyeing them with interest. They looked back at him suspiciously. They didn't seem to appreciate the presence of the young man in the baggy shorts and baseball cap, smiling cheerfully. People in exclusive inner-city apartment blocks didn't like strangers hanging around. It made them wary. Leo tried to look nonchalant and at ease, as if he was waiting for someone who would be along any minute.

He must have been partly convincing because a kind-faced sprightly woman in her seventies smiled a friendly greeting as she passed, and Leo plucked up the courage to ask if she knew Nina Lambert.

'Who? No, I don't think I know her. Sorry.'

Nina had gone, dissolved into the air like a wisp. He couldn't understand it. Where was she? It must have been something pretty bad to have kept her from him. Perhaps her mother had suddenly taken ill and she had had to race back to Canada? Or maybe something very trivial and ordinary had kept her away from the park last week. The flu? How would he know? How could she contact him? She would turn up this week with a perfectly reasonable excuse and Leo would feel foolish for having been so worried. Leo sighed and looked around him, hoping for some sign, something that was unmistakably Nina.

Letterboxes lined the foyer, each with a neatly stencilled name. Avery, McKean, Gerstle, Latham, Watson, Wilde. Dozens of names divided into neat rows of six. That must be how many apartments there were to each floor. Hardy. Muschamp. Lewin. Molloy. Porritt. Stubbs. It was a big building. Leo scanned them all. There was no Lambert.

He wondered what to do. He wanted to see Nina, to talk to her. He had been unable to concentrate on anything else all week. So he had come here. He was sure this was the apartment block she had disappeared into when she left the taxi that day they met and she turned his world upside down. Had she said anything that would indicate which floor she lived on? He tried to remember.

Nina, my pretty Nina, where are you?

Leo pulled from his pocket a white envelope. He placed it on top of the row of letterboxes. It looked brazen and obvious propped up for everyone to see as they walked in. He didn't like that. But his heart was too full. He couldn't wait. He would burst if he didn't express how he felt. It had come to him as a revelation, the sudden overwhelming realisation that he was in love – for the first time in his life, unless he counted ten-year-old Kimmie Butler from next-door, which he didn't. His feelings for Nina easily eclipsed those. Suddenly the songs he had sneered at made sense. He had so much he wanted to say to Nina. He felt foolish and happy and clever and vibrant, all at the same time. He didn't want to scare her but she had to know something of the intensity of his feelings. This wasn't a game for him and she had to know that.

He had jotted down some of his garbled thoughts in the blind faith he would find some way to get them to her. He left the letter there, telling himself it was in the lap of the gods, and they had been kind to him so far.

Nina spotted the envelope as soon as she pushed open the foyer doors. It looked out of place. She didn't get personal, handwritten notes to Nina Lambert. She was Nina Wilde. Mrs Wilde. James's wife. She felt a ripple of unease.

Her arms were full of bags of fresh vegetables from Patty's garden and Tiger was straining at his leash. She set her bags down and slipped the white envelope into her pocket. James was a few seconds behind her, bringing their cases from the boot of the car. She heard him panting as he came through the foyer door.

'I'll get the mail. You go on up,' said Nina. She couldn't look at him. She felt inexplicable panic. She didn't want James opening the letterbox. She had no way of knowing what else may be in there. This letter had something to do with Leo, she was sure of it. But he shouldn't know her name, Nina or Lambert. How did he find them out? What game was he playing? And had he come here? Surely not. She had been careful to compartmentalise her life. It was how she managed to deny the feelings of guilt that hovered below the surface of her consciousness. Nina considered James and their marriage as her day-to-day existence, while Leo was her fantasy, not entirely real. The thought that James and Leo could at some point collide was too horrific.

The happiness of the car trip with James, the feeling of being connected again, evaporated in an instant. Suddenly home didn't feel so safe any more. She felt it had been invaded.

Stop it – this was completely irrational, she told herself. It had been a long day and she was just tired. She forced herself to breathe slowly and deeply. There was a bundle of letters, mostly bills and junk mail. An apartment circular telling of body corporate rates that were due. Some fabulous special offers she had no interest in. She rifled quickly through it all. Everything seemed normal. Nothing untoward in there.

Nina took the lift up to their apartment on the sixth level.

Once inside she looked anxiously around. She couldn't have said what she was looking for, she just felt on edge. But everything was fine, exactly as she had left it. She should just relax, she told herself.

Nina unpacked the vegetables and fed Tiger, tensely aware of the white handwritten envelope in her pocket. James went into the study to phone Felix and Nina found herself alone. She stepped out onto the balcony and wedged herself behind the door. It meant she couldn't be seen from the room or any other balcony. It was unnecessary but Nina felt a strong need to be hidden when she opened the envelope.

The light was fading as the sun sank behind the city buildings, and the shadows lengthened across the water in front of her. The first of the evening's fruit bats flew across the sky. The air was still and the harbour calm. Some voices carried up from a lower balcony but they were a long way away. Nina felt alone. She let out a deep sigh, then tore open the envelope. A handful of dried blood-red rose petals spilled out onto the tiled balcony floor. She unfolded a sheaf of white writing paper.

Darling Nina,

I miss you, my lovely.

I feel like I was in the middle of the most interesting, all-absorbing conversation of my life when suddenly we were cut short in mid-sentence.

And yet there is an underlying feeling that has made it bearable. And that is joy. Joy at finding you. Joy at knowing you are in the world.

I have been in a mood that I can describe in no other way than being stunned. The sweetness and intensity of our time together is almost overwhelming.

I feel that we have the whole spectrum of potentials before us. At one end I feel an intense happiness at having discovered someone so special, loving, funny and sexy. At the other end is the urge to place myself irrevocably in your life. I know it is presumptuous, but I believe that you feel the same. I know it from the tenderness of your touch and the softness in your eyes.

It's rare to click with someone in the way we have clicked and I cannot treat that lightly. I know I am breaking all our rules. But I do it with lightness in my heart. I want to come out from behind my mask and stand naked before you.

Please meet me on my boat, *Bessie*, at 12 on Saturday. I have so much to say to you, so much I need to express. You have changed me, my darling Nina. I have missed you so much.

Until Saturday,
Your loving
Count Mauro de March

Nina felt the tears burn her cheeks and realised she was crying. Soundless tears that came from somewhere deep within her, spilling out of her eyes and down her face. What had she done? If she felt shamed before she opened the letter she felt doubly so now.

It was as if he had just moved on a notch ahead of her, confident she would follow. And while he was going forward at a rapid rate, she had been going backward. Where they had been as one, now they were poles apart in their expectations and desires. She couldn't love him. It wasn't allowed. She realised that with a sickening, heartbreaking certainty.

How does he know my name? He came to my home. Nina felt a ripple of panic shoot along the nerve endings under her skin. *He was here. He could come here again. Anytime he chooses.* The thought terrified her. '. . . the urge to place myself irrevocably in your life,' he had written. *NO, NO, NO. I have to get you out of my life!*

She felt vulnerable, spied on, threatened. She wished she could talk to James about this. What would he do? He would approach it logically. Had she given this man the impression they had a future? *Yes.* Had she encouraged him to such fervent feelings? *Yes again.* Would he understand that it could not go on? Would he just walk away meekly now that she had suddenly just changed her mind? *Oh my God. What if he doesn't?*

Nina wanted James and marriage and fidelity and trust and all those things she had promised. She wanted to be there for him while he faced this tough time with the family business and his guilt over his mother's stroke. He had once told her that he wanted to wake up next to her every morning for the rest of his life. That, she realised, was what she wanted too. How could she ever have doubted it? How could she have put it at risk?

What was I thinking? Nina dabbed at her eyes and took deep gulps of the night air.

She screwed the letter into a ball and placed it on the barbecue, then picked up some matches lying nearby and set it alight. The flames devoured it in a few seconds. It was a decisive action that felt good. She was banishing Leo, wiping him out of her future. It was what had to be done. How could she convey that to him? How could she get him out of her life without any hint to James of what had gone on?

And was that really what she wanted? *Yes, yes, yes.* Never to see him again . . . to walk away . . . to deny that part of her heart that cried out for him, his smile, his touch? *No, no, no.* The pain was excruciating.

Nina didn't sleep that night. While James snored softly she paced the balcony, watching the moon rise across the cloudless sky, climb above her head and eventually start to descend. She would ignore the letter. It was best if she never saw him again. It would be the cleanest for everybody. She made herself a mug of tea.

No. That was cruel. After what they had shared she owed him an explanation at the very least. A farewell. Give him a sense of closure. Wasn't that what the psychologists would say?

No. She slammed the mug onto the table. She didn't owe him anything. She couldn't trust herself to see him. Their connection was too powerful. She was married. She owed only James and she had betrayed him enough. To see Leo again would only compound her betrayal.

No. That was no good. It had gone too far. His letter showed that. She had to see him. One more time. To convince him to stay away. Make him understand it wasn't allowed to be.

Nina picked up the mug and resumed pacing. She stopped and looked out at the reflection of the moon on the still harbour.

He wanted to place himself irrevocably in her life. She felt scared. The tone in the letter didn't reflect the carefree playful fun they had shared. The game was over. He wanted more. What had she done?

Leo pottered about on the boat all morning. He degreased the winches, using kerosene and a toothbrush to get into the tricky corners. Then he applied liberal amounts of fresh new grease. He topped up the fuel container of the two-burner galley stove with methylated spirits and cleaned out last night's grains from the stove-top espresso maker.

The end of the cabin met in a V-point that had been converted into a large bed. It was where the crew took it in turns to get a bit of sleep on the rare occasions they sailed overnight.

He tucked the headsails into the stowage space underneath the bed and arranged the cushions on top. He frowned. It looked too much like a boudoir, so he picked up the cushions and rearranged them, flinging them around haphazardly. It looked far more casual and he was satisfied.

All the while *Carmina Burana* played loudly in the background. He had brought a few more CDs from home. He wasn't sure what Nina's tastes were so he grabbed a bit of everything

He moved onto the brass lamps on the walls, removing the tubs from their gimbal fittings, which allowed them to sway with the boat without spilling their contents, and filled them with kerosene. In each one he placed a new wick.

There were half-a-dozen small ones and one larger one at the cabin entrance to light the steps down into the cabin. He replaced each lamp, cleaning the glass tops and standing back to admire them. He would light them just before 12 o'clock. Even though some daylight reached into the cabin, they would create just the right mood. He checked his watch. She was still half-an-hour away. If she was coming. Of course she was coming, he told himself. And if she didn't then he would find her, somehow. He would go back to her apartment block. He would try the Canadian Embassy. He would phone the Eyebrow Post Office, if there was such a thing, and get an address for Jake Lambert, barbershop singer. 'I need to get in touch with your daughter.'

He would not give up. His excitement continued to build. He was desperate to see her.

James kissed Nina goodbye. It was a long and lingering kiss.

'I won't be late, darling,' he promised. 'Tonight it's just you and me. A romantic night in for the two of us. Perhaps you could slip into something slinky and we could send Tiger out for the night. There is a cute little puppy down the road who I am sure would enjoy his company.'

Nina laughed. She clung to James's neck, inhaling his scent, feeling the solidity of his shoulders and back.

'What are you going to do today?' he asked.

Nina's eyes slid off into the distance.

'Oh, I don't know,' she said vaguely. 'Go for a walk maybe. Take Tiger out to visit some of his lady friends in the park.'

Nina had made her decision some time over the past two days but she couldn't pinpoint exactly when. She had looked at her predicament from every angle and gradually come to the decision that it was best if she did go to see Leo. Just one last time. She had rehearsed what she would say. She would be cool and direct. She would keep it as simple as possible, telling him she loved her husband, while being as careful of Leo's feelings as she could. She would avoid all patronising cliches. She would not say 'I love you but I'm not in love with you' or 'It's not you, it's me.'

She would make him see that she was wrong to have ever started this, she realised that now. She had made her decision and she was immovable on it. He must never contact her again. It was over. Somehow she would say all of these things nicely. Naturally he would be disappointed, but he would be stoic and accepting. He would wish her well, she would wish him well and then she would leave. She would come home and resume her life with James.

It seemed straightforward enough and she held tightly to that thought. She had the unsettling feeling that she was not being realistic but she told herself it *had* to go this way. She had to set things right, for everybody's sake.

Nina and Tiger set off along the path through the park. The sky was overcast but the temperature mild. Still, the park was busy. Even without sun there were sunbathers in bikinis napping on towels. Two teams of teenage boys enjoyed a loud and energetic game of cricket. When she walked past *that* tree Nina deliberately looked away. To distract herself she thought instead of the rabbit lady and wondered where she was today.

As she followed the path along the low stone fence at the water's edge to the marina, she felt self-conscious. Was he watching her from one of those boats?

It was only a quarter to twelve when she reached the Cruising Yacht Club. She allowed Tiger to stop and sniff another dog on the footpath. It was a border collie puppy and more than twice Tiger's size. But Tiger was fearless. Nina smiled, despite her nerves. It released some tension.

With a deep breath she picked up Tiger and tucked him into her large, loose shoulder bag and entered the gate to the marina. She followed the yachties who were heading for their boats, carrying sailing bags and eskies. They all seemed purposeful, intent on their business, nodding to each other and exchanging the occasional brief greeting. A laughing group of men in suits and women in hats suddenly engulfed her. They seemed to be forming a procession behind a pram and she found herself being carried along with them.

A woman thrust a huge brightly wrapped box into her hands. 'I left my camera in the car. Can you give this to Kate?'

Nina looked at her blankly.

'You are part of Scarlett's christening lunch?' insisted the woman. She stared at Nina, obviously waiting for some sort of response.

Nina couldn't think what to say. She wondered what the woman was talking about. She was in too much of a state of anxiety to process sudden, unexpected information. 'Sorry?'

The woman clearly thought Nina was an idiot and snatched the box back in a huff. The group disappeared inside the doors to the function rooms, leaving Nina alone outside. She felt out of place, like a piece of flotsam being swept along in other people's currents. Nina desperately didn't want to draw attention to herself but she knew her very hesitancy made her stand out.

She was glad of her hat and sunglasses. She felt conspicuous and half-expected to hear someone call out her name. Some business associate of James's. Or Felix and Miranda, here for an impromptu harbourside lunch. She kept her head down and headed for the boats moored to a maze of floating pontoons. She strode purposefully ahead, pretending she knew where she was going.

The boats looked even more impressive up close, so much pristine white fibreglass and gleaming steel. They screamed of money and privilege. A middle-aged couple in shorts scrubbed the deck of their boat, nodding to her as she passed. She walked past dozens of boats. Their names were clearly painted on their sides. *Unicorn. Nerves Like Steel. Fishmonger. Lady 6. Jack of Hearts. Anaconda.* But no *Bessie.*

The pontoon swayed slightly beneath her feet while Tiger struggled in her bag. Lots of interesting sights and smells for him. He wanted to sniff around, but Nina held him tightly to her. At the end of the row Nina realised this was going to be harder than she had first thought. She was tempted to give up and go home but now she was here that seemed cowardly. She retraced her steps and approached the couple cleaning their boat.

'Oh yes, *Bessie,*' said the woman. 'Lovely timber sloop. You'll find her up there.' She gestured along another branch of the pontoon.

Nina thanked her and followed her directions. She felt incredibly nervous. She didn't want to be here and she didn't want to have to do this. But she knew she had to set things right. She was obsessed with the idea that James would somehow find out. It was incongruous that she should be so worried now when she had been blissfully cavalier about it before. It had been part of the excitement, all that risk and danger. As she looked at herself and her behaviour, she wasn't proud.

Let's get this over with, she thought, gritting her teeth.

Leo was standing on a boat about twenty metres away when she saw him. He was leaning against some vertical ropes just watching her, his head cocked to one side and beaming with that lopsided grin. He waved a pair of binoculars above his head in greeting. Nina had the impression he had been standing there, watching her for some time. She forced a smile and returned his wave.

Every step towards him was agony. Every instinct screamed flee, run. But she continued down the pontoon, placing one foot in front of the other. As she reached the boat she set Tiger down to give herself a chance to compose herself.

When she looked up there he was, just a few feet away from her. Baggy white shorts. Baseball cap. Open, friendly smile that encompassed everything in its path. Nina remembered him. Oh, how she remembered him. He radiated mischief and good humour. She felt herself falter.

He held out his hand for her to board. Nina hesitated. She had not intended to get on his boat. How unrealistic she had been. She could hardly say what she had to say from here, calling out to him on board. Just a few metres away a man sprayed a hose across the side of a neighbouring boat. He was looking at Nina with interest.

She took Leo's hand and stepped onto the wooden deck, looking down into the small gap of water. Tiger had never been on a boat – his tail wagged and he panted with excitement as Nina released him from her bag. But when the floor started to sway he barked at it, backing away in confusion till he reached the edge of the boat.

He looked so comical Nina had to laugh.

'Oh, how I've missed that sound,' said Leo.

He was still holding her hand. Nina pulled it gently away. He was smiling at her, his eyes expressing his joy. Nina couldn't bring herself to return his gaze. She dropped her bag onto the deck and looked around the boat, following the movements of Tiger who was poking his nose into bundles of coiled ropes. The boat was all polished wood and gleaming brass with one tall mast and a huge mainsail rolled up against it. Even knowing nothing about boats, Nina couldn't help but be impressed.

'Welcome aboard *Bessie*,' said Leo. 'An Admiral's Cup contender from 1976, lovingly restored by me, and now the terror of the CYC and all of Sydney Harbour. She may not be modern but she's fast.' He was clearly in his element.

Nina was concentrating on the shifting balance of her body weight as the boat swayed. It wasn't unpleasant, just disconcerting. She kept her feet apart, standing as firmly as she could, feeling her weight pass from one foot to the other, then back again. Leo, by contrast, was darting about, light on his feet, gesturing and talking very fast, never taking his eyes off Nina.

'She has one mast, one mainsail, one gib and, over there but not visible, a spinnaker. Down there is the cabin, sometimes called a saloon, where our champagne is chilling. It also has any amenities you might need while on board.'

Then before Nina realised what he was doing, he had picked up her shoulder bag from by her feet and tossed it down into the cabin.

'Rule one in sailing – no mess on top. Actually you shouldn't have any mess down below either, but I'm not such a stickler for that.'

Tiger watched the shoulder bag fly over his head and barked as it landed on a leather bench down below. He stood at the top of the wooden stairs, staring after it, looking at Nina, then staring back down into the cabin.

'You can go down. It's okay,' said Leo.

He dropped himself onto the stairs in one easy, graceful motion, scooping up Tiger on the way.

Nina moved carefully to the top of the steps and looked down. It was beautiful inside the cabin. The walls were covered in wooden panels with gleaming brass fittings. Small round portholes let in a little light and the oil lamps cast a soft warm glow across all the polished wood. Two long seats faced a small table.

'Come on down,' said Leo.

Nina put one foot gingerly on the top step. She wasn't sure she was brave enough to take the weight off it to step down. She felt incredibly clumsy and heavy. Leo, seeing her hesitancy, put his hand out and Nina took it. She clutched it and with her other hand clung to the doorway as she eased herself down the stairs. She felt better, more secure, when she reached the bottom. She sank onto the seat.

The kitchen reminded Nina of a dolls' house, everything smaller than normal and neatly compacted. Next to the small stove stood an ice-filled silver bucket with the unmistakable gold tops of champagne and wine.

Next to that was an espresso maker and an unopened packet of Lavazza coffee, placed so she would be sure to see it.

Nina winced.

The cabin ended with what looked to Nina like a double bed piled high with huge sumptuous cushions. The whole scene looked sinfully opulent and romantic.

No, Nina screamed inside.

She turned to Leo. He was looking at her with unabashed delight. He was so pleased to see her.

'I can't stay . . . I'm sorry . . .' she stammered.

Nina felt another wave of guilt. This hurt. It was so hard. How could she not have realised it would be like this. No matter what she did or how she did it, she was going to hurt someone. To say she was hurting as well was too glib.

She reverted to her planned speech. 'I came here today to tell you I can't see you any more. Leo, I'm sorry. I believe I have shared the most extraordinary time with you, but I was wrong to have started it in the first place.'

Her words sounded stiff and formal to her own ears. They had struck just the right note when she tried them out in the shower that morning, whispering them into the tiled corner while warm water cascaded down her back. Now they sounded all wrong. But she had nothing else in her repertoire, nothing to fall back on, so she kept going, her voice flat and toneless.

'I am married, which I guess you probably realised. And I have behaved very badly to my husband, who is a good and decent man and who I love very much. I cannot allow what was happening between us to develop any further. I must stop it. I'm sorry. Please forgive me for any hurt I may have caused you. I have been unbelievably selfish and I know now it is time for me to set things right.'

All the while she spoke he watched her. He looked at her eyes, which seemed so heavy and sad. Her slim shoulders were tense, the bones forming sharp peaks. Her hands were not the fluttering birds he so loved to watch as she waved them about to make a point. They stayed firmly by her side. She seemed flattened somehow in the way she was relating to him. It was like a screen had gone up. He heard her words but only dimly, perceiving them vaguely at some level in the back of his brain but not really digesting their meaning. He was reading the anguish in her body.

Something had happened to her to bring about

such a dramatic change. Who was this bastard husband? Had he found out about them and threatened her? Had he hurt her? It seemed to Leo that she was holding herself very tightly in check. She was nervous, hovering on the edge of hysteria. He meant her no harm so it didn't occur to him that the perceived threat may be coming from him.

'My darling girl. How can I help you? What can I do?' He put his arms out to embrace her, to pull her to him. It was instinctive but not what Nina was expecting. He wasn't listening to her. She recoiled, leaping up off the seat.

'No,' she said sharply, stumbling away from him. The cabin was small and there was nowhere for her to go. She bounced off the wall and back into Leo's arms. At his touch she flung herself away from him again, smashing her shoulder against the large oil lamp by the entrance and sending glass shards flying onto the cabin floor. The lamp tipped sideways, straining against its wall screws and spilling some of its fuel, then it swung upright again, somehow staying alight. Tiger, unnerved by the breaking glass and change in mood, started to bark and race around between their legs.

The sudden loud commotion on top of her already taut nerves panicked Nina and the cabin felt suddenly unbearably claustrophobic. The smell of kerosene from the spilled lamp filled the air. Leo was too close. She could smell his sweat and feel his physicality. He seemed to be everywhere, coming towards her, threatening to engulf her. She wanted to be away from him. She couldn't breathe. She wanted to be in fresh air. It was an urgent need that overrode everything else.

'No, no, no,' she cried out, grabbing her shoulder bag and starting up the stairs.

'I *have* to go,' she screamed.

She swayed and banged against the doorway. Tiger followed, shooting past her legs up to daylight.

It all seemed to happen in slow motion for Leo. As Tiger bolted past Nina he saw her start to stumble. He put his hands around Nina's waist to help her. She thought he was trying to hold her back and thrashed out wildly, flinging her shoulder bag out as much to ward him off as to steady herself. She connected again with the brass lamp. The screws, already loosened, were no match for the heavy contents of her bag and the burning lamp started to come away from the wall. Leo let go of Nina to catch it, bouncing the brass fuel pot in the air. It was hot and wet with kerosene and slipped out of his grasp, flying upwards and spilling fuel all over him. Leo watched in horror as the bright orange-and-blue flame from the lit wick followed the kerosene's course along his bare skin.

He called out to Nina to stop but she was on the top step. She heard him call out her name. The anguish and pain in his voice tore at her heart, but she didn't look back. She had to get out of there, off this boat. She shouldn't have come. She had made it worse. This was such a mess. It took every ounce of willpower and concentration to make her legs propel her steadily forward. Once she had both feet on the deck it was just a few steps, then a small leap across to the pontoon.

Tiger stood on the edge of the boat barking at the flames. Oblivious to what was unfolding below, Nina scooped him up and moved purposefully ahead. She heard her name again.

'Neeennnnaaaa!'

It was a long strangled cry of despair that would haunt Nina for years to come. She blocked her ears, kept her gaze averted and ran as fast as she could, wanting to put as much distance between herself and Leo as possible.

As the flames licked up his legs and across his trousers, igniting more of the spilt fluid and spreading to his hair, Leo's last sight of Nina was her retreating back, then he turned and threw himself onto the bed, rolling over and over to douse the flames.

CHAPTER 17

Saturday, 18 May 1991

James had been distracted and fidgety all afternoon. Nina wondered what was up. When she asked, James stared back at her blankly, denying anything was afoot. Nina shrugged and gave up. She didn't feel particularly playful. She felt sad. It was her birthday in a couple of days and she keenly felt the distance from her family. This would be the first year she hadn't spent it with them. Her mother had been disappointed when she telephoned to say she wouldn't be coming home as planned and had asked if everything was okay. Her tone had been concerned, which Nina appreciated, but still she felt defensive. Nina had said they were just having a few temporary financial difficulties. They hoped they would be able to come at Christmas. Then she had hung up the phone and her heart had been heavy ever since.

Nina had thought briefly of the money in her sock drawer but there wasn't enough for two air tickets and she wasn't about to go home without James.

'Why don't we pop up the street for dinner?' suggested James.

Nina was surprised. He liked to eat at home, particularly on their new tight budget.

'What about the Thai café? We could take Tiger.'

Nina found this even more surprising. 'You want to take Tiger?'

'Yes. Why not? We can eat outside and tie him up at the table. It's a warm night.'

'Okay.'

Tiger led them around the cul-de-sac, over-excited by the break in routine. He strained at his leash, sniffing out all the other dog smells. James picked a flower from the gardens of a neighbouring apartment block and handed it gallantly to Nina. It smelled beautiful and James looked so pleased with himself she felt her mood begin to lift.

They chatted as they walked, peeking into windows of ground-floor apartments, then looking quickly away if the occupants happened to be there. They admired some of the different architecture and derided others. Like most of inner Sydney, Elizabeth Bay featured apartment blocks from many different periods and styles. Some were beautiful and ornate, a legacy from the elegant thirties. Others looked like they had been modelled on eastern bloc ghettos, thrown together in the seventies. Many had been updated, creating hybrid styles. They all jostled for space.

James held Nina's hand as they ambled along the footpath. At the top of the hill James wanted to cross the road, which made no sense to Nina because the restaurant they were heading to wasn't on that side. Nina started to object but James was pulling Tiger's leash out of her hand and she was forced to follow. James picked up his pace. Having wandered along as if they had all the time in the world, he suddenly seemed in a hurry to get there.

'James, slow down,' said Nina. 'What's got into you?'

At first James didn't appear to hear her, continuing up the street, then he abruptly stopped.

'You're right. Let's wait here for a minute and catch our breath.'

Nina stared at her husband. 'What is going on with you? You're all over the place,' she said.

James gave her his bewildered look again and she laughed. It was so unconvincing. He was up to something and she knew it.

'I don't know what you are talking about,' he said, turning to look in the window.

They were standing in the doorway of an art supply shop. A 'closed' sign hung in the glass pane facing them. The window had been arranged with various-sized brushes and half-squeezed tubes of paints lying scattered on the ground around an easel. On the easel was a large canvas. Something about it was vaguely recognisable to Nina. She moved to the front of the shop, to see the canvas in full view.

The sight rendered her speechless. Her mouth fell open as she stared at the painted canvas. It was a scene so achingly familiar, and yet out of context in this shop window in Sydney. Nina felt as if in an instant the world had shifted on its axis and she was seeing everything askance.

The painting in front of her showed a couple standing in front of a two-storey weatherboard house, while behind them, stretching as far as the eye could see, were the harsh arid prairies of what was unmistakably Saskatchewan country.

Her voice, when finally she found it, was a squeak. 'That's . . . my . . . parents.'

James held himself in check. He was tempted to rush in and explain but he was enjoying her surprise too much. 'Why, so it is. It's Ma and Pa Lambert!'

Nina shook her head, incredulous.

The figures in the foreground were small but easily distinguishable as Dorothea and Jake Lambert. A gust of wind was blowing her mother's floral frock so that it billowed out beside her like a bell in mid-ring. Her father was wearing his fur-trimmed hat and overalls. The sense of space and desolation was breathtaking.

She noticed on the front of the easel, resting against the painting, a small white card. She read it and her eyes filled with tears.

'To my darling Nina, happy birthday. Your loving husband, James. XXX'

Nina looked at James, only half-understanding. 'It's for me?'

James nodded.

Nina was overcome with nostalgia, wonderment and gratitude. She could smell the dry earth, feel the chill of that late spring wind, almost see her mother smoothing the folds of her dress.

She flung her arms around James's neck, sobbing into his hair. 'How?'

James explained about the talented Canadian artist who owned the art supplies shop and had featured in the local newspaper. James had visited him, taking with him some of Nina's family photos and from those he had created this painting. It was not a copy of Nina's photos but his representation of life in that part of Canada, with the prairies, a couple of distant wheat silos, the expanse of sky and Nina's parents as the focal point.

Nina's face showed her complete astonishment. 'Can I take it home?'

'Well, yes, but there's a slight hitch,' said James.

His bravado was gone and he looked embarrassed and shy.

'Not yet. I told him it was your birthday but I wouldn't have the money to pay him till next month, so we agreed he would finish it in time for your birthday but it would sit here in the window for a month. It's been in the window all day. I was terrified you might see it before I had a chance to get the card to him.'

'Oh, darling. How *are* you going to pay for it?'

'Now don't be so rude. That's none of your business.'

Nina looked at her husband with new appreciation. 'You are the most amazing man,' she said softly.

From the verandah Leo watched a woman walk slowly across the lawn behind a toddler. She was patient, taking large occasional steps, keeping pace with the child who took dozens of little ones. The little girl was unsteady on her feet and every few steps she careered off in another direction, stumbling then righting herself. An elderly man smiled at the scene. He was sitting on a bench by a meticulously tended garden bed, roses swaying gently in the breeze. He was clearly enjoying the beautiful sunny winter's day and the sight of the happy child and its mother.

Leo hated it. Everything about it irritated him. He tried to manoeuvre his wheelchair so he didn't have to see the woman, her pretty curly-haired child or the contented old man. He rolled the chair back then forward, back then forward, till he was angled toward another corner of the garden. It was deserted and showed a bed of newly pruned rose bushes, scrawny and colourless. That suited his mood much better.

Leo wondered where the nurse was. Not the pretty, younger one. He didn't like her tending him, touching him. Leo wanted the older woman.

She didn't say anything, just coolly attended to his dressings then moved on. She was impersonal and professional. Just how Leo liked it. He didn't want to make small talk, chat about what a sodding beautiful day it was. It wasn't. It never would be again and he had neither the energy nor the inclination to pretend it would be. The new skin on his groin and cheeks was itchy and hot under the bandages. His buttocks ached where the new skin had been removed, leaving raw edges of flesh.

There were a few patients sitting on the verandah, some with visitors, but no-one approached Leo and the low murmurs of their conversations didn't disturb him. He was surrounded by an invisible wall of pain. People could sense it even if they couldn't see it and it made him uncomfortable to be around. His only regular visitors were his sailing mate Nick, every few weeks, and his accountant Felix.

Initially Felix had taken some urgent documents to Leo in the hospital to be signed – papers from Lloyd's agreeing to a settlement and the sale of some shares to cover the agreed payout, plus some new investments that Felix had been working on for his client. But when Felix had seen the state Leo was in, he found excuses to visit every couple of weeks. He said he had more papers to be signed or decisions to be rubber stamped. It increased his workload considerably. He had many clients and to devote this much time to one while still doing justice to the others was a strain. But Felix was worried about Leo.

Leo's body was healing but Felix wasn't so sure about his mind. His eyes were lifeless. He had lost his spark, his humour, his interest in anything going on about him. Felix persevered, talking and keeping him up to date with what was happening in the world, while Leo looked at him blankly, signed what he was asked to, then looked off unseeing into the middle distance.

Part of his mind was still frozen at that moment back on the boat when he had watched the kerosene run up his arm and felt the flames ignite on reaching the spilt fuel, then the sudden, searing heat across his groin. He heard himself calling out her name in one long, drawn out yelp of pain and shock. It was audible above the roar of adrenalin, pain and flames. She had heard him. He was sure of it. He had seen her half turn her head towards him, then she had turned away, quite deliberately. Tiger had stood at the top of the stairs barking at him as he writhed across the floor, calling after Nina. Leo's last vision, as the pain overtook him, was of Nina scooping up Tiger, leaping off the deck and running down the pontoon.

Leo remembered little of what happened next. Nick told him that because of the scorch marks on the bed he must have rolled around there for a while before bursting up the stairs, out of the cabin and flinging himself into the water.

According to the man on the next boat, Leo had sunk to the bottom of the marina and would have stayed there if he, the fearless good samaritan that he was, hadn't had the balls to throw himself straight in after him. He told the TV news and all the newspapers that he hauled an unconscious Leo back to the surface, singlehandedly got him onto the pontoon and performed mouth-to-mouth resuscitation before calling an ambulance on his mobile phone. With each retelling of his story, Leo's plight became more desperate and he became more heroic.

Nick had a bit of trouble imagining this balding 60-year-old Pitt Street yachtie accomplishing even half of that, but no-one else came forward to say otherwise so he grudgingly accepted this version and passed it on to Leo.

Leo didn't care. In the early hours of the morning when he sat up in bed unable to sleep, listening to the quiet sounds of the hospital, feeling muffled and claustrophobic inside the bandages, he wished he had been left at the bottom of the marina.

The past months had been hell.

When he woke up in hospital, his face was a mass of weeping bandages, his nose broken and his thighs and groin covered in gauze. Over the next few weeks they took fresh new skin from his waist, buttocks and back, leaving them tender and raw. The hair follicles on his face had been destroyed so while his eyebrows would never grow back, looking on the bright side, he would never have to shave either. The sweat glands in his groin were beyond repair so he may suffer some discomfort in the heat, but once the skin grafts healed he would be able to walk again. He was told he would never father a child. He may not be the same smooth-faced good-looking young man that had broken hearts all over the eastern suburbs of Sydney, but plastic surgery would fix up the worst of it.

It took weeks after he regained consciousness for him to fully absorb what had occurred. Because his memory of it was incomplete, it remained surreal, abstract, something that must have happened to someone else. But eventually he accepted what the doctors told him.

He tried to reconcile the Nina who had given herself to him with the Nina who had left him to burn in hell. He had waited for her to come to him in hospital. He had letters from schoolchildren who read of his plight in the newspaper and created get-well cards in their art class. The Cruising Yacht Club sent flowers. But nothing from Nina. Not a card or a phone call. Finally he had given up.

Study became his therapy. He chose research, spending many hours bent over a microscope and working out probabilities. It kept him away from people and that suited him just fine. He didn't like people so much any more.

But he never forgot Nina. He raged against her. He loved her. He hated her. He wanted to see her. He was a man in torment. It would take years for his body to heal and even longer for his heart. He was never again to be that carefree happy-go-lucky man who had danced in the rain with the stranger from the taxi. Eventually the sharp, brutal pain gave way to something more manageable, something he could live with. Whenever it rose in his mind, it was a dull ache, like the dying nerve in an old rotting tooth that only occasionally flares up. He had his work, his research and sailing to occupy his waking hours.

Saturday, 25 May 1991

Nina smoothed the deep red velvet dress over her hips. The bodice was low, revealing slender shoulders, while hugging her curves. If she stood side on to the mirror she fancied she could just see the faintest swelling at her waistline. It didn't worry her. She kind of liked it. She was fourteen weeks and the doctor had said it was likely she would start to show around now.

The dress was fabulous, worth every cent she had paid for it. At first she had despaired when James had told her that the evening would be formal. She had tried on everything in Miranda's wardrobe but the other woman was a much larger shape and nothing fitted. Then Nina had remembered her sock drawer.

She hated having that money there, secret from James. It felt disloyal. She didn't need an out clause and more importantly, she didn't want one. And so she had spent it. All of it. On a dress. Just one dress. It felt decadent but fitting. Tonight was an important night and she had to look the part – sophisticated, glamorous and classy. And in this dress she felt all of those things.

Nina knew James liked it. All night he kept

finding excuses to touch her – a hand on her lower back guiding her through the crowded ballroom to their table, a gentle pressure on her leg as he leaned across the table to speak to his mother. And for most of the evening Nina was aware of his arm, along the back of her chair, encircling her protectively. She felt sublimely happy.

Patty was in fine form, excited to be out with her family, and her mood was infectious.

'Whether we win anything or not, I am very happy to be here,' she announced as soon as they were all seated. She beamed around the table at each member of her family and their special guests, Felix and his fiancée Miranda.

Frederick raised his glass in agreement. 'I think we all second that. Here's to you, my dear. You gave us a nasty scare and we are all very glad to have you here.'

Patty smiled graciously.

The meal was interspersed with the announcement of awards. Trophies were handed out to the different wine companies and associated industries. The family cheered each winner, not expecting to win themselves.

'Give it a few years,' Mark promised. 'Then our reds will be up there winning everything, I promise you.'

So it was with some surprise that the Wilde family did hear their name announced on the podium.

'. . . and the award for Wine Campaign of the Year goes to Wilde Wines.'

They all sat in shocked silence.

Electronic screens above the stage showed the winning Wilde Wines campaign, a series of post-cards addressed to Mr Wilde, Mrs Wilde and Ms Wilde. Each carried the message, 'Wouldn't you rather serve your guests wine from your own estate? You're a Wilde. Be proud.'

The TV comedienne who was host for the night explained the campaign.

'These postcards were sent to the 14,000 people in Australia who happen to share that name. A simple idea. And an original one. Congratulations, Wilde Wines.'

Everyone at the Wilde table clapped and looked to Frederick, expecting him to go up and accept the award. He stayed seated.

'This is your award, James,' he said. 'Up you go.'

James was too stunned to move anywhere.

Frederick smiled gently. 'Go on, boy. It was your good idea and hard work that made it happen. Next year it will be Mark for those mighty reds. But tonight it's your campaign that is being recognised. Well done.'

Nina grinned and pushed James to his feet. 'Go on.'

James stumbled to the podium. He walked up the steps and across the stage. The head of the Australian Wine Federation and the TV comedienne handed him the wine glass mounted on a block of wood and stepped back.

James found himself alone at the podium looking out across an indistinct sea of faces. The lights above him were dazzling and hot. They made it hard for him to see beyond the front row of tables. He was shocked to be standing there. His father's words, 'well done', echoed in his head, giving him confidence. James felt humble and proud all at once. Nina held her breath as James cleared his throat, waiting while the applause subsided and taking the moment to get his thoughts in order.

'When I was a kid I was something of a brat,' he began. 'I used to complain to my father that our name was too common. Wilde.

'I didn't think it carried the panache of say a Rockefeller or a Baillieu. My father, a long suffering and patient man, used to listen and say nothing. I feel very humble when I say I have realised the strength in that name. Not just in marketing terms, which this award recognises, but in far more personal terms.

'To be born into the Wilde family with Frederick Wilde as my father was the smartest thing I ever did. My second smartest move was to hire him as my boss.

'I dedicate this award to my hero, my father.'

It was the most personal and emotional speech of the night. As James walked off the stage, the audience cheered. Many of them were families, used to mixing blood and business. For some it meant bitter public feuds. They appreciated James's humility. When he reached his own table Patty and Nina were both in tears. Even Amanda looked impressed.

'Well done, James,' she said.

He was moved by her sincerity.

Frederick looked embarrassed but proud. He ordered more champagne for everybody.

The successful evening and James's spontaneous speech marked the end of hostilities. Frederick never mentioned the name Lloyd's to James again. James assumed he must have explained to Patty what had happened but neither parent spoke of it.

Patty turned to Felix. 'It is nice to have you here to share this moment of triumph. You have become a part of this family now. It's a shame our new partner couldn't join us. He is part of it now too.'

Felix shook his head.

'I'm afraid that's not his style. He has other interests. This may sound harsh, and please don't take it the wrong way, but you are really nothing more than a page in his investment portfolio.'

Patty was about to ask more but Frederick interjected. 'And a good thing too,' he said. 'The less he has to do with the business the less he will be tempted to interfere.'

Patty laughed. 'Yes, I suppose you're right. What about we send him a photo of us all holding our winning plaque? Would he like that for his wall, do you think? Or to brighten up a page in his boring business portfolio? Perhaps a bottle of one of Mark's mighty reds to celebrate?'

Frederick snorted. 'I would prefer it if this family stopped trying to befriend this man,' he said. 'We have entered into a business arrangement with him and before you go sending happy family snaps, Patty, I would like to point that out. It is not in our interests to encourage him to take anything other than a distant view of what we do. I'm sorry if that sounds ungrateful or even uncaring, but there it is. That is how I wish it to be. Do I make myself clear?' Frederick used a tone that they all recognised. It meant he wanted no arguments.

But Patty was having none of it, not tonight. She laughed merrily at her husband. 'No-one would know what a lovely man you are from the way you go on at times,' she said, her tone gently teasing. 'Really Frederick, sometimes you are just too much . . .' She leaned over and stroked her husband playfully on the cheek. '. . . but we all love you anyway.'

Frederick's frown melted from his face.

When they got home James placed the mounted wine glass with the inscribed plaque on the mantelpiece beneath Nina's painting.

They stood together admiring it.

'What a night,' said James.

'Your speech was great,' agreed Nina. 'I was so proud of you.'

'I guess I'm forgiven.'

'I guess so. Your father was so touched by what you said.'

James pulled Nina to him. She helped him out of his suit jacket, then started to unbutton his shirt. When she got to his cuffs, she noticed for the first time that they were pinned together with safety pins.

'Where are your gold cufflinks?' she asked in surprise.

'It's all right. I – I – got rid of them.'

Nina looked confused. 'You got rid of them?'

She was about to ask why when she noticed the look on James's face. He looked caught out and a bit naughty. He grinned. In a sudden flash Nina understood.

She looked up at the enormous canvas that filled their lounge room wall, the painting that whispered to her of fresh, crisp afternoons, of winter air so cold her gums ached if she smiled outdoors. And the gentle-faced woman in the familiar floral frock with the tall silver-haired man by her side. The picture dominated the room and, it seemed to Nina, made the unmistakable statement that she, Nina Lambert Wilde, daughter of Jake and Dorothea, lived here.

She looked at James.

He shrugged and smiled. 'A fair exchange, Nina, don't you think?'

CHAPTER 18

8 February 2001
Dr Jones's rooms

The echo of the doctor's words reverberated in Nina's head. 'Oh, by the way . . .'

They had nearly made it through the door, out of his office and would have been on their way. They were so close. What was this man playing at? Wasn't there something in the doctor's oath about confidentiality, minding their own business? Surely it was nothing to do with him whether Luke was James's son or not? His role was purely medical, to check for a specific genetic weakness. He had done that. There was no genetic problem. His part was finished. Thank you. Goodbye.

But James, unsuspecting and ever polite, was turning back to face him.

'Yes . . .?'

There was nothing Nina could do. She felt the chill of the unnaturally cold room seep into her bones. She hunted frantically for something to say to divert James's attention. For one brief moment she considered pretending to faint but that would leave James alone with this doctor. Just moments ago he had been her saviour, telling her in medical language that she didn't understand that James was healthy. He would live. Now he represented an insidious threat to her family, her marriage, her entire future. She braced herself.

'How is business?' asked the doctor.

It was such an unexpected question that Nina wondered if she had heard him correctly. *How is business?*

James was equally surprised. 'Fine.'

He looked questioningly at the doctor.

The doctor smiled, his heart thumping, his foot frantically tapping under the desk. He was so enjoying himself.

'I have a bit of an interest in the wine industry myself,' he said.

James smiled politely. Another would-be wine expert.

'I have some money invested in a vineyard. It's an up-and-coming family winery and won this year's award for best shiraz, best chardonnay and, for the third time in the past ten years, the wine campaign of the year. And it just won a big overseas award, for one of the reds. I forget which one . . .'

James and Nina stood staring at him. Realisation

was beginning to dawn. The doctor could see it on both their faces.

'Perhaps you might know it?'

James looked delighted. 'Dr Jones? You're *that* Dr Jones?'

James remembered the day he, Mark and his father had signed the papers. Felix had said his client was an old mate from school, now a Sydney specialist, a Dr Jones. James hadn't remembered him from school and that had been the last time his name had been discussed. Felix had said his client had no desire to become involved in the business, which had suited Frederick.

Over the years he had become nothing more than the name at the bottom of the occasional document that had to be signed.

The doctor nodded, watching him carefully. *Yes, I'm that Dr Jones. So nice to make your acquaintance. But don't you recognise me? I guess not. Why would you Mr Hot Shot, Mr Sporting Star, Mr Olympic Hero? Why would you remember me? It's not like you noticed me when I was standing right in front of you. I didn't register on your radar then, so why should you remember me?*

James was looking surprised and delighted. 'Oh man, I want to shake your hand. You have no idea how you saved my life. You saved my whole family. If it wasn't for you . . .' James shuddered, remembering the whole awful summer of 1991 – the Lloyd's debacle, his mother's stroke. 'It was the worst three months of my life. It doesn't bear thinking about.'

James looked at the doctor with unabashed pleasure, like he was discovering a long-lost friend. 'Nina,' he said, grinning. 'This is Felix's client. Our investor. He is *that* Dr Jones.'

Nina nodded, looking fully at the doctor. His gaze was locked on James. There was something about the expression in his eyes that Nina found unnerving.

The doctor was enjoying James's delight but there was an edge to his manner that scared her. He was controlled, confident and yet . . .

She wasn't sure why her hands were suddenly clammy with sweat, when the room was so cool and dry.

The doctor was revelling in the moment. When his accountant, Felix Butterworth, had come to him and said he had a business proposition, a winery, owned by the little-known Wilde family, he had delighted in the irony. He had known the Wilde family. Or he had known one of them. James Wilde. The big school sports hero. There were two boys whose names were seared on his memory. James Wilde and the other champion of under-16 football, Malcolm Watson. It was always those two boys who chose the teams and they always left till last the skinny kid who couldn't catch a ball. They didn't care about his abject humiliation. Dr Jones, then a blushing fourteen-year-old in baggy shorts, would pray that this time he would be chosen. He never was. He was the last one left, dumped onto whichever team was unlucky enough in the draw to get him.

I was beneath you. I was one of the little people who existed to serve you. You're the guy who gets the fame, the glory and the girl. You were the winner. And I was the loser. But you didn't really win, did you? Your life is a sham, propped up by my silence. I own you. I'm the silent partner in your life.

'It is *such* a pleasure, Dr Jones,' said James.

The doctor accepted the compliment as his due, letting it warm him, enjoying the feeling of having James Wilde grateful to him.

'We were at school together, you know,' continued the doctor.

Nina started to stiffen. She had a nasty feeling about this man.

James stared harder at the doctor. 'I'm sorry, I don't remember.'

'No matter, no matter,' said the doctor. He turned to face Nina.

'It is so nice to meet you both. The Wildes of the famous Wilde Wines family. But Dr Jones sounds so formal when we have so much in common. We are partners.' He paused for the merest fraction of a second, then continued, 'Please call me Leo.'

Nina felt the world stop. It was as if the blood ceased to move around her body. The air stopped circulating in her lungs. Understanding and recognition came in a bright and blinding flash. She was aware only of Leo, he filled her vision, his gaze locked onto hers. It was unrelenting, boring into her, bitter, accusing, challenging, triumphant.

James was oblivious to the change of mood in

the room. He kept talking, wanting to share with the doctor some of the business success that his injection of money had afforded them over the years. He was unaware that both Nina and the doctor had stopped listening to him.

'. . . Thanks to your investment over the past ten years we have been able to not only clear our debts, but vastly improve our business. We are exporting to two overseas markets and looking at some fresh possibilities opening up in China . . .'

Nina stared at Leo with a mixture of shock and disbelief. James and everything in the room faded away. He looked so different. It wasn't just age. His whole face had changed. Only the blue eyes seemed faintly familiar, as they bored into her. But their expression was not of anyone she knew, or felt she had ever known. They held no joy or mischief. The doctor's eyes were dead and looking into them chilled her to the core.

Oh Leo, what happened to you?

She was completely motionless as the pain came, sharp and sudden, ripping along her nerveways. Its intensity shocked her. She hadn't expected it. She had sealed off those emotions a long time ago. Or so she had thought. But seeing him, realising this strange-mannered, balding man with the bitter smile was Leo, it all came rushing back in a torrent of passion, tenderness, longing and guilt.

Nina was no longer standing with her husband in the vast light-filled room of a blood specialist. At that moment she was sitting in a tree, barefoot and breathless. She could feel the hard wood of the branch under her thighs, through her cotton shorts. The air was wet, sultry and close. Large raindrops splashed onto the leaves, ricocheting into a hundred smaller droplets, down through the canopy to land on her bare skin. And Leo was gently, delicately nibbling her lower lip. Such exquisite sensations. She remembered feeling as if every muscle, every cell had melted into warm, liquid honey.

It was a poignant memory, a distant echo of overwhelming emotion, overlaid with other, stronger, conflicting emotions that came later and had torn her in every direction. She was suddenly aware that her legs had turned to jelly. Worried that they would not hold her weight, she moved back to the chair opposite Leo's desk. She sank into it gratefully. Her blood pressure plummeted and she felt faint.

'We will always be very grateful to you,' she said weakly. She spoke softly and meaningfully, her voice ending on a whisper.

In the same instant Nina was remembering, so was he. But it wasn't bittersweet memories of making love in the tree that were filling his mind. It was heat, scorching white heat. Flames licking up his thighs. Eyes burned dry. His throat raw from the smoke. He had called out to her. And she had scooped up Tiger and run away.

James's voice became a low hum, blending with the sound of the airconditioning. '. . . England now imports more Australian wine than French wine and our percentage of that gross has increased to . . .'

Seeing her now, Leo felt again an echo of that white seething anger. He had known for over a week that this meeting was coming. The medical questionnaire listing the most personal of details, and yet revealing nothing, had been processed at various points, passing through the office system to land in his in-tray. When he had read the name Nina Wilde, nee Lambert, mother of Luke Wilde, wife of James Wilde, he had been sitting at his desk and was struck dumb with the shock of seeing her name, after all these years. Nina, pretty Nina. The woman who had gently unwrapped his heart then killed it as surely as if she had set fire to it herself. She was married to James Wilde, that sporting stud from school, who had humiliated Leo all those years ago.

After Leo had composed himself he had rung Felix to check that he was right, the patient was the same James Wilde whose family owned Wilde Wines.

'Is his wife called Nina?' asked Leo, trying to quell the tremble in his voice.

'Yes, that's him. Don't you remember him from school?' Felix had replied. 'He was an Olympic skier.'

Leo remembered him very well, but he stayed silent. He felt he had come full circle. The papers sitting under his clasped hands were a time bomb, just waiting for him to set them off. He held the secrets of Nina and James's past in that cheap plastic folder. He had performed the tests. He had received the results. And when he discovered that

Luke didn't have the same genetic identifiers as James, he had pulled out an old diary and worked out the dates over the summer of 1991. It had meant reopening so many painful wounds.

Then he had his own genetic code read. He sat at this desk, his heart in his mouth, knowing, without even opening the envelope, what the results would be. He was Luke's father. Luke Wilde, ten years old, blood type O, with Antigen H present and a typically homozygous ii reaction. Leo knew his son's genetic blueprint. And yet he knew nothing about him. Did he like pizza? Did he inherit his interest in science? Did he look like anyone in Leo's family? Did he like boats? The Wilde file didn't even contain a photo.

Once the shock passed, the questions had burned inside him. How could she not tell him he had a son? It tore at Leo, stabbed into his heart. *How could she not tell him? After all she had done to him, all she had taken from him, how could she? How could she be so cruel?* Leo had screamed this question into the empty night, tortured and racked with pain. It was a molten ball in the pit of his stomach.

He had lived through the past week in a state of nervous anticipation, every moment filled with memories. He was thinking of her when he woke in the mornings. As his mind cleared away the last wispy images of sleep, she was there. Not always a visual image. Usually it was far more pervasive than that. It was a hint of her spirit, her energy, as if she had just left the room. He had been unable to rid himself of her and it had nearly driven him mad.

He had been able to think of nothing but this meeting. He felt that fate had just dealt him the ultimate vengeance hand. It was within his grasp to inflict maximum pain on these two people, the two people he hated most in the world.

He searched Nina's face. She was shocked to see him. She had sunk back into the winged armchair, her face shielded from James.

James, still standing, was continuing to share his excitement over the wonderful growth the winery had enjoyed over the past ten years.

Nina looked like she had melted into the fabric of the chair. Leo watched her. He was looking for something. Shame. Guilt. Apology. Some emotion that might reflect his own pain. The recognition and shock was evident in her little pixie face. Her hands were clasped tightly together as if to comfort herself. All colour had drained from her face. Leo felt a fissure open, a small crack in the hardened steel inside.

Nina's eyes pleaded silently across the desk. They were luminous and full of suffering. Leo was paralysed by their intensity. It was there. That something he was looking for was there in their depths. It reached out to him, communicated to him in a way that words never could. He felt the fissure inside him open a little wider.

She seemed so small and fragile sitting in the winged armchair. There was a quality about being in her presence that he had forgotten. The unique essence that made Nina so special. It swirled about her. It was in the way she held her head, the softness in her eyes, her gentleness, her tenderness. His bitterness was rendered impotent in the face of it. Pretty, bubbly, funny Nina. She wasn't laughing now, but still she carried that energy with her. He remembered it and he knew, with a poignant stab, that he could never willingly hurt her.

James talked himself to a standstill, suddenly aware that he had lost both Nina and the doctor. He sighed. He thought he had done it again – bored everybody with his talk of business. He tried to bring the conversation back on track, to include them.

'Well, doctor,' he said. 'We would love to have you as our guest next week. It is the end of harvest and we always have a bit of a celebration. There are wine tastings, food, a jazz band, rides for the children. You are welcome to bring your family.'

Leo continued to stare at Nina. 'I don't have a family,' he said.

He noted the flash of pain in her eyes. It didn't give him the satisfaction he expected. Instead he found he wanted to reach across the table and take her hands in his.

'Please come,' she said softly.

James continued talking, telling of the wonderful things Leo would find at the winery, how welcome Patty would make him. Leo heard all of it, dimly, as a couple of different scenarios played through his mind.

All the time he couldn't take his eyes off Nina.

Leo tried to picture Luke. He imagined a short faceless figure in baggy shorts with sandy hair and a baseball cap worn backwards. He was calling out 'Uncle Leo, Uncle Leo, come and look at this . . .' His childish voice bubbled with excitement, as if he had just found something through a microscope and he wanted to show it off. Leo saw James standing nearby looking at him with the same expression he wore now, a mixture of admiration and gratitude. He was thanking Leo and introducing him to an amorphous cheering crowd as the man 'who saved me'. It all seemed so wholesome and welcoming.

As the picture came more sharply into focus, Leo saw Nina. The expression in her eyes was just as it was now, soft and luminous, full of love and tenderness. But she was standing next to his imaginary James and it was he who was gently stroking the underside of her arm, the tender skin near her elbow, imparting his love and strength and claiming an established intimacy that made Leo's heart ache.

The image slowly dissolved. He smiled at Nina. It took some effort of will, but he managed. For the first time Nina saw a hint of the Leo she remembered. The smile held the faintest trace of his old, mischievous self. His hands relaxed on top of the medical files.

'Thank you. That's very kind of you. But I don't think so. I would prefer to stay where I am, in the background, as your silent partner.'

Nina's eyes were wistful.

Our silent partner. How fitting.

There was so much she wanted to say. And there

was so much Leo wanted to hear. They stared mutely at each other.

James, standing behind Nina, gave a little cough. Nina knew it was a communication meant for her. Unless there was some new topic for them to discuss, it was time for them to go. The appointment was finished.

Still she stared at Leo.

He felt himself grow warm under her gaze. Something sweet and precious, beyond words, passed between them. It took just a moment, then it was as if the light dimmed in Nina's eyes. Leo watched, entranced, as she gathered herself together, composed her face and rejoined her husband.

She and James walked together to the door.

Nina hesitated. She couldn't just leave like this. She had loved Leo in a way that had shocked and delighted her and she needed him to know that. But she knew also that she could never see him again. James was right behind her. She could feel his breath on the top of her back, where the zip finished, exposing her bare skin. She struggled with her conflicting emotions.

'You know,' she said, turning slowly back to face Leo, 'our son Lucas is very interested in science. He wants to be a doctor when he grows up. If he does, I hope he will be as kind and generous as you have been.'

Something hard and tight inside Leo finally gave way. The fissure cracked wide open and he felt it throughout his body.

Nina could see the change in the way Leo held

himself; his whole demeanour was transformed. The hard line of his jaw softened as he stopped clenching his teeth. He relaxed his shoulders and neck muscles.

They smiled gently at each other while James opened the door.

Leo watched her leave, knowing it was the last time he would ever see her.

When the door clicked shut, Leo picked up the plastic files beneath his hands, then swivelled his chair to face the magnificent view.

He sat very still, exploring the way he felt, savouring its taste and texture. He was lighter, freer. But also he was sad. Melancholic. It wasn't unpleasant, he decided.

As he watched, a huge luxury ocean liner entered the harbour, dwarfing the ferries and sailing boats it passed. Each of its four decks was crowded with holidaymakers waving banners and flags.

Perhaps he should give his old mate Nick a call, he thought. See if he needed extra crew for that fancy new boat of his. It was years since Leo had been out on the water. Suddenly he wanted to feel the gentle rhythm of a swaying timber deck beneath his feet and a stiff, salty breeze on his face.

Leo opened the Wilde files and removed the half dozen loose sheets. He carried them across the room and fed them through the document shredder, watching each one re-emerge as dozens of long white fingers, snaking into the bin.

Author's Note

Insurance giant Lloyd's of London is one of the financial world's most salubrious institutions, its name synonymous with wealth, privilege and security. It operates by way of syndicates which in the late eighties were made up of 32,000 individuals from around the world who underwrote Lloyd's various insurance activities, from insuring ships to a rock star's lips.

The entry requirements for syndicates were simple: you needed to be well connected enough to be invited and have assets of A$565,000 (£250,000), held as cash, shares, property or bonds. Each 'name' personally visited the impressive headquarters in London to be vetted by a high-level Lloyd's committee and have explained to them the cause of 'unlimited liability'.

For 24 years in a row the names had received returns of between 5 and 10 per cent annually on assets already utilised elsewhere and it became known as 'easy money' for those privileged enough to be invited to join. However, in the late eighties and early nineties an unprecedented series of disasters, including the sinking of the Piper Alpha oil rig, the Exxon Valdez spill, asbestos claims and numerous typhoons, meant that Lloyd's needed to find A$16 billion for payouts. An estimated 40 per cent of Australian names were called on to pay between $50,000 and $300,000 initially (and later some people up to $500,000) to cover Lloyd's liabilities.

Australia had about 600 Lloyd's names including federal politicians, business leaders, judges, Queen's Counsels and many gentleman farmers. In New Zealand 101 names were pursued for A$40 million. In Britain more than 60 Conservative Members of Parliament were Lloyd's names as well as business leaders and minor royalty.

Many did not understand what they had signed up for and suffered heavy losses. Some individuals were forced to liquidate assets and family businesses, or were declared bankrupt.

Under the terms of their contracts, names were unable to pursue legal action outside Britain and attempts for individual cases to be heard in Australian courts were unsuccessful. However, pursuing legal action in Britain was also problematic as an Act of Parliament provided Lloyd's with an extraordinary degree of immunity.

In 1995 a settlement was proposed to the membership to write off debts and restore the market. This was then reconstructed. Today the overwhelming majority of Lloyd's capital is supplied by companies with individual members in the minority.

MORE BESTSELLING FICTION FROM PAN MACMILLAN

Bunty Avieson
Apartment 255

They say I'm mad. I'm not. I'm just very, very smart.

Sarah and Ginny have been best friends since school. They both had their share of adolescent problems but now things are working out for Sarah. She's met Tom. He's handsome, a journalist and totally devoted to her. Her TV reporting career is taking off. She and Tom have moved into a stunning inner-city apartment.

But Ginny has not been so lucky. She wanted Tom, but she didn't get him. She wants the ease and grace with which Sarah lives her life. She wants . . . what Sarah has. She wants it all.

Ginny moves into an apartment overlooking Sarah and Tom's. She starts watching them. Then she does something more than just watch.

And so the torment begins . . .

Bunty Avieson has crafted a riveting tale of obsession and danger that proves we never really know who our friends are.